# bruised

## Markus Chambers

IMMERSIVE
BOOKS

**Content Warning**

This story includes elements that might not be suitable for some readers. Themes such as domestic abuse and rape are mentioned. There are other themes that some may find triggering. Readers who may be sensitive to these elements, please take note.

*To all the women who made it out, and for
all the ones who didn't.*

# Also By:
# Markus Chambers

Seven Days After

# Writing As:
# Esther P. Goodwin

The Body Among The Pines

# Part One:
# Mental
# Flexibility

Friday, April 14th, 2023

"You don't have to control your thoughts.
You just have to stop letting them control you."

- Dan Millman

# Chapter

# 1

I FRANTICALLY TIP-TOED around my Charleston apartment like a thief in the night to not awaken my neighbors, in search of the sticky note I'd written. I went from my bedroom to my living room and back again, ruffling through the loose papers on the walnut desk I'd purchased intending to use as a workspace but only ever ended up using as a hanger for my work clothes.

Hunching over the desk and pressing my palms to the wood, I sighed. "Where did I put it? The last place I remember is here... right here on the desk. It can't be anywhere else."

"Why don't you just tell me what it is you're looking for, Allison, so I can help," said Brett, leaning against the bedroom doorjamb. "We're already thirty minutes late."

"Shhh, you're being too loud. Whisper."

"Why?"

"It's four a.m. My neighbors are asleep."

Brett crossed his arms. "So?"

"The walls are thin. I've already been hit with two noise complaints. One more and I'm outta here."

"It's not my fault you come in at two in the morning every night."

Dropping to my knees before my nightstand, I eased open the drawer and sifted through some trinkets. "You'd understand if you were a nurse. Now have some courtesy, will you?"

"Fine," he said in a hushed tone. "Regardless, we need to go."

"I can't leave before I find it. You're acting like we've got to be at your parents by a certain time."

"I promised them we'd be there no later than noon."

I closed the drawer and stood. "Oh, give me a break. We've got plenty of time. Now stop being an asshole and start helping me look for it."

"Okay, okay, I'll help," he said, coming up behind me, wrapping his arms around my waist and cushioning his chin against my shoulder as if to calm me down. "Now what am I looking for?"

"My checklist. I wrote a few things on a sticky note and put it somewhere."

"You still use sticky notes? You've got a phone. What do you need one of those for?"

"For notes, duh."

Slipping from his grasp, I went to the kitchen, remembering the myriad of old stickies covering the fridge.

I prayed it was there, hidden behind another. Brett wandered into the living area and rummaged through the sea of photographs I'd left out on the coffee table like a forensics analyst carefully digging for evidence.

"Babe, you're smart," he said. "I don't see why you even leave yourself notes. It's not like you're going to forget anything."

"Tell that to my supervisor, because he sure thinks I do."

"Okay then. I'll just keep my mouth shut."

I felt a pang of guilt at his clipped tone. He was just trying to help, even though it didn't feel like it. If it wasn't for my paranoia, we wouldn't be in this predicament, arguing like siblings fighting over a happy meal toy in the backseat of Mommy's car. "I'm sorry, Brett," I said, wandering over to the decorative glass bowl on the kitchen counter where I kept my car keys, loose change, and other miscellaneous items. "I shouldn't have reacted that way. You know how I get."

"It's okay, I get it. You're nervous."

"Damn right, I am. This weekend needs to be perfect. I'd hate for your parents to think I'm a schmuck. That's why I need to find this note. I've gotta make sure I don't forget anything."

"You mean *this* note?"

*Oh no, he found it!* I spun on my heels to find his silhouette holding up a small square in the living area. He crossed into the kitchen, flicking the light switch as I poured everything back into the bowl.

"Where'd you find it?"

"Stuck to the back of one of the photos over there." He examined it, his hazel eyes glistening under the fluorescent beam overhead. "Says here it's our anniversary trip checklist?"

I slouched my shoulders in disappointment and sighed. "Yep, that's it."

"You don't sound so relieved."

"Of course I'm relieved, Brett, it's just... it's just—"

"You don't really want to go?" he suggested.

Refusing to answer, I snatched the sticky note from him and hurried back to my room to inspect my small suitcase and cosmetics bag, him trailing behind me like a lost puppy.

"We've been dating a year, Allison. I get you might not feel it's the right time, but that feeling will never come. Or maybe it will... when we invite them to our wedding."

*Wedding? Ugh, no. I'm not doing that a—* "It's just my last relationship was too much and I wanna take things slow. Is that a crime?"

He came up behind me and pressed his palm to the base of my back, sending a shiver up my spine. "We *are* taking things slow. They're just my parents."

I spun. "To you they are. To me they're strangers. I can't just up and run off with you to someplace I've never been."

"Huddleston is not a bad place, I promise you. You'll love it there. It's up in the mountains. It's quiet, relaxing, everything you'd want in a sweet escape. You're going to wish you'd come sooner once you see it. Now quit your fussing and get packing. I don't even know why..."

Sifting through my suitcase, I went over my

checklist. *Three pairs of underwear and bras? Check. Two casual outfits and one fancy? (In case his parents take us into town to a restaurant) Check. Medication?*—I unzipped my cosmetics bag and sifted through it. Inside was my toothbrush, toothpaste, makeup, leave-in conditioner, shampoo, and—*Ah, there they are. Ambien and Xanax. (One to put me out, the other to calm me down) Check. Sneakers and heels? Check. And last but not least, my cellphone? Check.*

"Allison, are you even listening to me?"

I zipped my suitcase closed. "No. Sorry."

He grabbed my arm, whipped me around. "Look, all you need to do is relax this weekend, okay? Nothing more."

I broke from his grasp. "You've been pressing me to meet your parents for months now, why?"

He opened his mouth, hesitating to answer as if harboring a secret of some kind.

I crossed my arms. "I'm waiting."

"You're the only girl I've dated that's taken this long to meet them."

*Of course. Avoiding the question. Typical. Maybe I should just break it off. That'd be easier. There's too much of a risk to get closer. I'm only with him for my needs. Oh, who am I kidding? That's not true. I like him. Like him a lot. He cares about me. I wanna move on, find somebody new; build a life I deserve. But I can't do that if I don't let him in. If I don't learn to trust. Maybe I should tell him about Ryan. Maybe I should—*

He took my suitcase and headed for the door. I followed after him, my cosmetics bag—I'd lazily draped over my shoulder—hanging on for dear life. "Wait for me."

I locked the front door as he continued down the long stretch of hallway toward the elevator, the rusty wheel of my suitcase whining.

"Pick it up!" I whispered loudly, pulling the key from the lock and rushing after him. "It's too loud."

"You do know my parents are going to expect an explanation for why you waited so long to meet them, right?" he asked, once we reached the elevator.

"I know they are. And I'm not gonna give them one."

"Why not?"

"I have my reasons."

"Allison, they're not going to mind. They're not your *typical* parents. You're just being paranoid of what they might think of you."

I shuddered. "Don't say that. You know I don't like that word."

"Well, that's what you're being right now."

I scoffed, rolled my eyes in disbelief, and tapped the elevator call button. "If I *was* being that, I'd have every right to be. But I'm not, okay?" I felt my cheek, the scarred lump —the aftermath of stitches—just under the skin, still very much there, and remembered how I'd been made a fool. *I'll be damned if I go through that again.*

He let out a slight chuckle. "Whatever you say, babe."

The elevator dinged, opened, and we entered. I pressed the button and the doors closed. Silence the whole ride down. The elevator shuffled to a thudding stop and the doors opened. The concrete cave was empty, its lights dim and eerie. The wind whistled incessantly through the openings like a stalker in the night, drawing the hairs on the back of my neck to rise. Damn this crippling anxiety. I clutched my bag tightly and stayed on Brett's heels, fearing someone might jump out and try to rob us.

The lights on his '06 Acura TL flickered as we approached, and then the trunk opened. I was inches from the passenger door when he said, "Here... hand me your bag," as he slung my suitcase into the trunk beside his.

I winced as my Louis Vuitton glanced off my suitcase's shiny hardened exterior, ricocheting into an oblong crevice. "Careful!"

He closed the trunk. "Funny. Get in."

# Chapter 2

"Wake up, Allison," Brett whispered, his warm breath tickling my ear like a feather. "We're here."

Kicking off the wool blanket I'd snuggled under after stealing it from the backseat, I rubbed my bleary eyes and gazed out the front window to find we had parked in front of a spacious two-car garage. Slightly to the right and very much behind, only a glimpse of the vast estate lay ahead, its dark gray siding gleaming under the bright sun.

"C'mon, let's unpack," he said, opening the door and getting out.

I unbuckled my seatbelt and followed. A whiff of the many scents in the fresh Virginia air met me as I closed the car door. *Mmm, is that lavender?*

Wandering off, I searched for the plant in the knee-high flower beds along the garage, but couldn't find any. Much of it consisted of other flowers: dandelions, lilacs, and cacti. I thought to wander further after noting the front of the house in hopes I'd find the lavender eventually but opted not to spoil the tour I'd most likely receive after we unloaded everything into the house.

I returned to the trunk as Brett said, "Here," and tossed my cosmetics bag.

It landed in my arms with a thump, almost slipping from my hands. Then I draped it over my shoulder as he retrieved my block of a suitcase. So much for packing light. He set it on the ground, pulled the handle up, and then went for his.

We crossed the driveway, heading left around the building toward the back onto a stone pathway that linked the detached garage to the main house. Further left stood a towering spread of Virginia pines that partially enveloped us. Their verdant leaves that rustled in the gentle breeze created a lush canopy overhead that filtered the sunlight into dappled patterns below. Their abundant foliage added to the property's grandeur and elegance, creating a harmonious blend of natural and architectural beauty that was to die for.

When we rounded the bend, the breathtaking vista of the mountainside and shimmering lake came into view within an opening along the trees, leading me to gape in astonishment. A burgundy boat dock stood in the foreground surrounded by some shrubs near the rocky shore and snaked a trail of planks back toward the house. Northern cardinals and Carolina wrens sang hymns in the distance as green herons and mallards flocked from one end of the lake to another, leaving a shallow rainfall in their wake.

"What is this place?" I asked.

"Smith Mountain Lake."

I took another whiff of the air surrounding us, feeling immersed in nature. Then I picked up the shrieks of joy from the kids playing in the lake and laughed.

"What is it?" he asked, climbing the steep deck stairs.

"Those kids down there... in the water. Don't you hear them?"

"I do. What about them?"

"Oh, I don't know. I guess seeing them down there is making me wanna go."

"You'll have plenty of time to swim later. Let's get these inside first."

I wanted to hand Brett my bags and race down to the water, but I knew the guilt of leaving him to handle our luggage would have gnawed at me incessantly like a ticking clock.

When I finally caught sight of the backside of the house, I gaped again. *I can't believe they live in a mansion. Three stories of pure elegance. And that wrap-around deck on each level... I'm speechless.*

There were also towering windows that stretched from the second floor to the top, showcasing the high ceiling. The sight was so alluring I couldn't help but gasp in wonder, prompting Brett to remark on my reaction.

"Wait until you see the inside."

When we reached the back door to the house, the living

room and part of the kitchen were visible. A chocolate leather sofa stood before a floor-to-ceiling fireplace, its L-shaped frame calling my name. Perhaps that was where I'd stay for the remainder of the weekend, cozied up under a blanket and looking out at the mountain range.

With his hands full, Brett tapped on the glass with his elbow.

"Why're you tapping, don't you have a key?"

"I do."

He tapped again. No one came.

"Why didn't we just come through the front door then if you had a key?"

He craned his neck back, his mouth taut and eyes glaring. "I just figured they'd be in the kitchen or on the sofa watching TV, all right?"

*Hmm, weird.* "Look, I'm not trying to be a pain but—"

"Too late, you already are," he said, releasing his bags and cupping his hands around his face before peering inside in search of his parents.

"Just check and see if it's unlocked," I shot back.

He tapped on the glass again, ignoring me. But despite his efforts, there was no response. Then he gripped the handle and turned. The door didn't budge. "I had a feeling this would happen."

"Had a feeling *what* would happen?" I repeated. "You did tell them we were coming, right?"

"No, I didn't," he said sarcastically. "I just figured we'd drop in and surprise them."

"That's not funny."

"I know it's not, Allison. I wasn't trying to be mean, but yes, I told them." Brett reached into his pocket, pulled out his car keys, and sifted through the bunch until he found the one he was looking for. "If I hadn't, they'd probably be on a cruise somewhere in the Pacific by now."

He opened the door. We headed inside, landing in the large family room.

"Mom? Dad?" he called out, his voice ringing through the grand halls.

Looking around, I noted the bamboo hardwood floors and the open concept that allowed for the second floor to overlook the living area and part of the kitchen. I dropped my bags by the sofa, came up behind him, wrapped my arms around his waist, and planted my chin on his upper back. "I sure as hell wouldn't mind spending every holiday here. Why didn't you tell me your parents were loaded?"

"Because they're not." He broke from my grasp, set his bags beside mine, and then wandered into the kitchen, calling, "Mom? Dad?"

Still no answer.

My anxiety set in as the silence persisted, believing his anger toward me had merit. Doubts about Brett's intentions for bringing me to this secluded peninsula crept into my mind. *I wonder what he really brought me here for. I know he said to meet his parents, but... they're not here. No one is. He couldn't have broken in, could he? He had the key.* I nervously itched my left arm like an addict waiting for their next fix as I walked around looking for any personable items—family photos, trinkets, stains on furniture—to prove someone actually lived here. *Perhaps he stole it. Yep, maybe he stole it from the lockbox on the front door because this place is on the market. That would explain why we hadn't gone through the front. We broke in.*

Suddenly, an image of the darkness within the barrel of a pistol flashed before my eyes. I shut them and pushed the thought away, telling myself that wouldn't be the case. *Brett isn't Ryan. He wouldn't try to kill me. He likes me too much. At least enough to want me to meet his parents. No, he wouldn't do such a thing. I'm past that now. Our relationship has been nothing but pleasant evenings spent together watching movies after dinner at fancy restaurants and deep philosophical conversations about life that would last for hours. There's no reason why he'd try to hurt me. Perhaps he brought me here for a romantic getaway only. Have us spend time in a secluded place so we could bond and fuck—escape the hustle and bustle of city life. But then why'd he lie about meeting his parents? Why not just tell me the truth?*

I took deep breaths, seeking to calm my frayed nerves as I came to rest in the grand foyer before the spiral staircase that seemed to run on to infinity, its snaking nature starting on the second floor, then disappearing into a dark pit. I'd found nothing that proved anyone lived here. Nothing but paintings on the walls and decorative bowls of fruit on the kitchen island and dining room table that resembled a spread put out by a realtor.

I pressed my hand to my chest and continued breathing heavily in search of grounding, my rapid heartbeat unwavering. Brett was nowhere to be found. He'd gone silent like a cricket in the night. Chirp, chirp, then nothing. Suddenly, a loud clack of a gear moving echoed throughout the house like a bell from a grandfather clock and the front door opened.

Two strangers entered.

# Chapter

# 3



THIS IS AWKWARD.

I stood alone in the grand foyer before two elderly people, my heart dancing in my chest like a tap dancer and my stomach queasy. I was brimming with fear from how they looked at me with sheer shock, mouths agape and brows furrowed as if wondering who the hell I was. I felt like an intruder caught red-handed with their most prized possessions. My attire, consisting of black sweatpants and a matching T-shirt, only added to the perception of me as a criminal. I only missed a ski mask to complete the image of a thief. But all was quickly put to rest when Brett emerged from the kitchen and took to my side.

"I was beginning to worry where you two had run off," he said, wrapping his arm around my lower back and pulling me in close to his chiseled frame. "I was about to round up a search party."

"Oh, we just went for a quick walk," said the man. "You know how your mother is; always wanting to be outside in nature."

*Mother? Oh, Christ, these are his parents. So much for first impressions. I hope my charming smile dispels any negative perceptions they have.*

"Yes, I do," Brett agreed, squeezing me even tighter. "But now that you're back, I have someone I'd like you guys to meet."

I smiled and waved apprehensively. "Hi, I'm Allison."

"What a lovely young woman you've brought home, Brett," said his mother as she approached just as he let go and wrapped me in a warm embrace.

She couldn't have been more than a hundred pounds soaking wet; frail like a person suffering from anorexia. She had slightly sunken eyes, light gray hair with streaks of blonde similar to racing stripes, and a very straight posture. Yet her petite frame belied her strength. Her embrace was a tight one, nearly cracking my spine. *Geez, his mother's strong.*

After our loving embrace ended, she motioned to her husband. "Well, I'm Lydia. And this is—"

"Jeffery," Brett's father finished, coming up beside her. "But you can call me Jeff. Welcome to our home."

"It's a pleasure to meet you two," I said, shaking his hand that enveloped mine entirely. He stood a foot taller than me, his posture stern much like his wife's. I had to crane my neck up just to make eye contact. The backs of his hands and arms were extremely hairy like a scruffy dog and seemed to run up his sleeves and out the neck hole where a small puff of hair seemed to connect with the gray at the base of his neck. One long hairstyle.

"The pleasure is all ours," he said.

Lydia slung her arm around my shoulder and led me toward the spiral staircase, her grip on me firm yet warm. "I was thrilled when Brett told me you were coming," she said. "But unfortunately, he didn't give me any insight into your interests or hobbies. So forgive me if what I planned for us doesn't satisfy."

"Oh no. Don't feel like you have to entertain me, Mrs. Eldridge. I'm a guest in your home. I believe whatever you have planned will suffice. I'm pretty much open to anything."

She gripped the handrail and headed downstairs, absently saying, "Dear, call me Lydia, please."

"I'm a little reluctant to do so, Mrs. Eldridge. Since childhood, I've been taught to address my elders by their surnames only, using the correct titles as such. Even when I was with—" *I shouldn't bring him up.*

"With whom, dear?"

"Nobody. It's just I've never addressed anyone's parents by their first names."

"Well, that tradition ends with us."

"Are you sure?"

She landed on the basement floor and turned to me with a look of sincerity. "I am."

I smiled back before we continued with the tour. Much like the main floor of the estate, the basement mimicked its decor with matching bamboo hardwood flooring and white painted walls that exhibited many colorful paintings. The only difference: it was a large playroom of sorts instead of sectioned areas like the kitchen and dining area. There were no support pillars, either. Just a long steel support beam in the ceiling that spanned the entire length of the room; a superb architectural design aspect worthy of praise.

"Follow me," she said, walking toward the hall at the far end of the room. "Let me show you where you'll be staying."

We crossed the vast living area, passing between a pool table that stood to the left by the window that showcased the stone patio beneath the deck and the large curved back sofa that stood opposite before a large flat-screen TV on the shiplap wall. Before that stood a circular coffee table. And beneath that lay a humungous plush rug, boasting a psychedelic design similar to a lava lamp with three different shades of blue.

As we approached a short hallway, I noted the enormous collection of books stacked on the in-wall shelves to the right, their spines gawking back at me. "I see you love books."

"I do," she answered. "Are you an avid reader?"

"I am. But nowhere near the amount you are."

"Well, perhaps you'll come across a book or two to add to your TBR during your stay."

I scratched the back of my head and let out a doubting chuckle. "We'll see. I've got quite a few on there already. If I keep adding to it, I'll never finish it."

Lydia laughed as we passed by it. A rectangular double-paned glass wall stood at the end of the hall, showcasing nature at its finest; a vast expanse of greenery in the backyard where a grazing deer stood, staring directly at us as if we were impeding on its breakfast. Such a sight created an inexplicable sense of peace and tranquility within my heart, leading the corners of my lips to purse up with gratitude.

"You like what you see?" she asked.

"What is there *not* to like? I've never seen a transparent wall in a house before. It's quite a unique touch."

"It sure is. You know when we first moved here, I set up a chair right there"—she pointed to a dark spot on the floor, indicating where she'd kept the chair for some time—"and would just... watch. There's something about observing wild animals in their natural habitat. You get to see everything; the way they communicate, what they eat, how they sleep, and the greatest of them all... how they reproduce. I look at it as a way to become one with nature; to truly understand God's gift to earth."

"I can see that. I'd probably do the same thing if I lived here. Get off work, come sit and watch. No need for TV at all."

Still lost in the serene image, Lydia opened the door to my left and said, "This is where you and Brett will be staying."

I entered and gaped in astonishment. A king-sized bed stood at the far end of the room, its headboard resting against another thick wall of glass that displayed an identical image to what I'd seen at the end of the hallway just outside the room. Being much wider in comparison, it showcased a larger view of the backyard and the mountain. A large sleek bureau with a mirror attached sat across from the bed. Venturing further into the room, lay the bathroom that housed a glassed-in shower enclosure and white marbled floors.

"This is a beautiful home you have here," I said, sitting on the edge of the bed and peering around the room in awe like a kid in a candy shop. "With the privacy of the trees and the lake access a few steps away... It's immaculate."

Turning toward the large window, I marveled at the beauty of the natural surroundings, feeling grateful that I could enjoy such a view in complete seclusion. It was truly one of those moments that makes life worth living.

"Oh, please. Honey, living here is only good for one thing."

She paused for a beat, perhaps to give me the chance to finish her sentence. But I hadn't a clue what she'd say. It could have been anything; sex, bonding, relaxation, or rehabilitation. I didn't know which.

"And that's to escape the headaches that come with living in the city," she finally finished.

"I know the feeling. Charleston can be so congested sometimes."

"It can't be worse than DC. The traffic in and out of that place is horrendous. And don't even get me started on construction. They always seem to be making alterations to the highways, the streets, buildings... ugh, it just irks me."

As we exited the bedroom, I noted the other door across from us—a stark contrast to the rest of the house; black and metal, completely different in appearance from the other doors that matched the color of the floors. "What's in that room?"

Lydia stopped and turned. "Huh? Oh, nothing. That's just a utility closet, where we keep all our cleaning supplies."

*Utility Closet? Why would they need to change the door for cleaning supplies?* "Okay," I muttered, brushing off whatever assumptions I'd made up about the door.

Lydia continued toward the sofa and sat.

"So it sounds like you lived in DC at one point." I sat across from her.

"Oh heavens, no. Fredericksburg, actually. It's about an hour south of there. Jeff and I commuted for work."

"What kind of work?"

Before she could answer, a loud rumbling sound coming from the staircase grabbed our attention. I turned to find my suitcase tumbling to a stop at the foot of the stairs. Brett was chasing after it like a cat to a mouse, his suitcase and duffle bag haphazardly hanging halfway off his shoulder, threatening to take him down. Without hesitation, I stood and hurried over.

"If I'd had anything delicate in there, it'd surely be broken," I joked, picking up my bag and extending the handle.

"Sorry, babe," he said, regret heavy in his tone. "But if I'd had some help, it probably wouldn't have happened."

I headed toward the bedroom as he followed. "I know, I

know, it's all my fault," I said sarcastically. "I'm to blame for your inability to carry a few bags."

"You didn't need to go that far."

I opened the door and scoffed. "I'm just giving you a taste of your own medicine. How do you like it?"

When we entered the room, I placed my bag on the bed as he set his on the floor beside it. I turned to leave and he grabbed my hand and pulled me into his warm embrace, answering with a shining glimmer in his eyes. "I'll let you know once you give me the full dose. But for now, I'll give you an A for effort."

*Man, does Brett get me hot. I can't resist someone who knows how to play the game. The way he grins, the way his hands caress my hips when we hug, the way we trade banter daily. God, do I love it. But I still need to take things slow. I can't risk getting caught up again.*

"It's not your fault, dear," Lydia said, coming into our room. "I shouldn't have tied you up with frivolous conversation. If anything, I'm to blame."

Brett released me and turned to her. "No, you're not to blame, Mom. Her and I just do this to spice things up, that's all."

Lydia lifted her chin and poked a smile, signaling that she understood what he meant. "Ah, I see. Well, I guess I'll leave you both to it then. I'm going to go get started on lunch."

She headed upstairs, leaving Brett and me alone in the room. He ran his hand through my luscious auburn hair, tucked it behind my left ear, and asked, "What were you and my mother discussing?"

"Oh, nothing. Just girl talk."

He shrugged. "Okay then, don't tell me. I'll go up and help her prepare."

Brett turned to leave, and I followed him out of the room and up the stairs. Though I wanted to explain to him what Lydia and I were discussing, I felt the need to skip on giving him the details since it mostly consisted of pleasantries and compliments. And though I was on the verge of uncovering what his parents did for a living, I knew there was plenty of time for conversation on the matter whether over dinner or lunch or even a simple activity Lydia had planned. With three days to spare, it was bound to come up again soon enough.

# Chapter
# 4

"Where are you headed?" Lydia asked, standing over a steaming pot of boiling water.

"Outside to take a stroll around the grounds," I answered, opening the deck door. "I wanna get a glimpse of what Virginia life is like since I've never been. From what I've seen so far, it seems like it isn't all that different from South Carolina. The simmering heat and greenery are pretty much the same, but I still wanna explore. I'll be back in time for lunch."

I walked out onto the back deck and paused, taking in the morning sun high above the mountaintop. Following a deep inhale, my heart warmed at the sight of gliding birds dipping down toward the lake like fighter jets, where their little feet clipped the water, and then climbed in elevation again.

The breeze whistled, drawing me to look to my right

where a line of trees stood. I descended the deck stairs and headed toward the woods, hugging the side of the house until I reached the end. As soon as I turned the bend, I was struck by a familiar sight. To my right stood Brett and I's bedroom. That certainly explained the familiarity.

I pressed my hand to the glass and peered in, trying my best to ignore the headboard that was pressed against the glass, however, I couldn't see much. Only my bags I'd left lying haphazardly on the bed and part of the bathroom. Suddenly, a chirping bird evacuated its nest, sending a twig to plummet to the ground beside my foot. I gasped. *What was that?*

I spun in shock, bumped a limb, and nicked my shirt, tearing a small hole in my left sleeve. I inspected the tear and expelled a sigh of aggravation. More ruffling came overhead, leading me to look up. A brown round refuge was tucked just beneath another limb, the faint chirps of hungry nestlings easing the unpleasant experience.

*I can't believe how close we are to the trees. That looks less than a foot. Way too close for comfort. What's gonna happen to those birds if bad weather comes? Better yet... what's gonna happen to Brett and I?* I pictured it; a raging storm with thirty-mile-an-hour winds, whipping the tree just above me like the inflatable tube man you see at car dealerships until a limb snapped and crashed through our window, bludgeoning us both to death in the middle of the night. *God, would that suck. But then again, it'd probably be a blessing in disguise. I'd rather die at peace in my sleep than scream in terror like those nestlings would.*

Considering it was late spring, the chances of such an event occurring this time of year were slim. But then again, Mother Nature always does what she wants. Turning away from the house, I continued exploring. I took a step and slid in sand. At my feet lay a small patch of dirt. *Is that the start of a trail?*

I pulled back a limb, revealing a faint and narrow trail. A few short blades of grass struggled to protrude from the dry soil, presumably because of the amount of shade the trees overhead cast. *I wonder where this leads.*

A slight chilled breeze came from the shadows and brushed passed me. I shuddered. *Maybe I shouldn't.* I turned back toward the house, biting my lip in contemplation. *Ah, what the hell... the chances of something going wrong in there are slim.* I turned back toward the dark abyss ahead, drew in a breath, and proceeded forward, disappearing into the thick brush.

*I can't believe I didn't notice this when Lydia showed me the bedroom. It was right here. I could have easily seen it. I need to be more aware of my surroundings. If I hadn't been so mesmerized by the decor and architecture, then maybe I would've noticed the subtle opening. Then I could've asked her about it. I guess I'll ask when I get back.*

I cautiously traversed the dark and grim trail, the thin line of brown dirt snaking off into infinity. Fresh grass and weeds had taken over much of the path, leaving behind a few rocks darting out along the route like kid's toys left about. One wrong step and you'd pierce your foot and curse under your breath. It was as if the trail had been long forgotten, hidden away by nature, left to be reclaimed by the sycamores, hickories, and white oaks of Virginia. With my gaze fixed firmly ahead so as not to crash into a tree, I took it slow and steady. Suddenly, my flip-flop caught on something and I tripped.

*Shhhhhhiiiiiiiiiittt!*

I fell flat on my front onto some overgrowth, my hands cushioning my fall. Rolling onto my back, I sat up and immediately spotted the culprit: a sturdy root jutting out from the earth a few inches away. It had been covered in the leaves of the previous autumn, which explained why I hadn't seen it. *Of course, just my luck. Thank God I didn't break a wrist. That would've certainly ruined our weekend. I can't imagine how long we'd spend in the ER. Maybe the entire day. A few hours for sure. God, that would've been so embarrassing. Brett's parents would've thought I was clumsy for sure.*

A throbbing pain in my foot drew my gaze away from the root I'd tripped over and I rubbed the fresh red scrape. What a shame. I thought I'd been cautious enough, but of course I hadn't. My unfortunate collision landed a sizable scratch on the top of my foot. Thankfully, my leather flip-flops were still intact. My short excursion around the property would have been cut short if they'd broken, let alone if I'd broken a bone or sprained my ankle. With no harm done, I took the misstep as a valuable lesson: *Pay more attention, will you?*

Using a nearby tree trunk as support, I braced my hand along the battered bark and regained my footing. My hands crept up the tree, brushed against something hard and jagged, and yanked away in fear, almost losing my footing and collapsing back onto the dirt. After a second, I took a closer look and found a carving in the bark of the tree. It was B + C enclosed in a circle. *Hmm, I wonder what those mean. Brett, maybe? But who's the C? Perhaps it's an old girlfriend or a friend.*

I ran my hand along the rest of the tree in search of any other carvings but didn't find any. Then I surveyed the neighboring trees in search of more. Still no other carvings. Running my hand along the arborglyph, I thought, *Interesting. I bet this is from Brett's childhood. I wonder if he remembers carving this.*

Suddenly, the click of a snapping branch caught my ear and I winced. A rapid flicker of light danced overhead. I searched for what might have made the sound. I scanned the darkness and saw nothing but black. No deer, no bear, no rabbit or squirrel; nothing. I drew in another breath and exhaled. *Must've been some birds, or maybe a squirrel. Whatever it was, it's gone now. Just relax. Don't get worked up.*

I brushed my sweatpants free of the dust and grime, then pushed onward, taking a mental note of what I saw so I could ask Brett about it later. After a few more minutes of walking, I reached the end of the trail. Assuming it looped back around to the house, I was taken aback when I stumbled onto the property of the neighboring home. I hadn't expected the house next door to be that close. I looked back over my shoulder to see how far I'd traveled, but only a green and black cloak of trees stood behind me. The Eldridge estate was nowhere in sight.

I continued onto the neighbor's property, wanting to explore. I knew trespassing was breaking the law, but my curiosity got the better of me. The home sat atop a small hill, its size and architectural essence similar to the Eldridge's home. White with black and gray accents. From the side, it looked perfectly symmetrical and grand with a unique glassed-in rear dome that showcased a large circular dining table with eight chairs. I retrieved my cell from my pocket and tapped the screen to check the time. It had been ten minutes since I left the house. I had a hunch that lunch was ready by now, so I turned to head back into the woods.

I was inches away from the tree line when a faint voice called out to me. "Hey, you!"

I froze as my stomach flipped upside down and my legs turned to jello. *Shit, I'm caught. Don't freak out, don't freak out, don't freak out.*

The voice called again and I looked toward the lake. There, down on a boat dock, sat a woman waving at me. *She must be the wife. Just smile and wave back, that's all you've gotta do.* I hesitantly waved back, which prompted her to motion for me to join her. *Great.*

Knowing Brett's parents were expecting me for lunch, I hesitated to heed her call. But then I assumed he'd call me once the food was ready. And so I shrugged and headed down toward the water.

When I finally reached the dock, the woman sitting on a bench greeted me. She wore white shorts that showcased her bony legs (that if I didn't know any better made me think she was a paraplegic), a pink tropical Hawaiian shirt with white accents, and a pair of large, opaque sunglasses to block out the blaring sun. Not to mention, she also had long, silky black hair and blotchy, wrinkly skin that was damn near red, as if her body had given up the years-long fight against the sun.

"What's your name?" the woman asked.

"Allison Sellers," I answered.

"Well, Allison, I'm Tammy White. It's a pleasure." She looked away at the water and the many anchored motor yachts without even an attempt to shake my hand. "It's quite a sight, isn't it?"

I followed, landing on what seemed to be the largest boat floating in the middle of the lake. The slight breeze that trailed off the water sent a shiver to my feet. The passing boats sent waves to follow, ripples upon ripples crashing against the shoreline, making a symphony with the gurgles and cries of joy from the nearby playing children.

"It sure is, Ms. White," I said, drawing in a breath of fresh air. Considering she wasn't wearing a wedding ring, I concluded she was single or perhaps, divorced or windowed.

"Please, call me Tammy. No one calls me Ms. White except for—" She caught her breath. There was a subtle reluctance in her tone as if she knew she had made a mistake in what she'd said. Who could she have been referring to? A friend? Brett? Another acquaintance of hers? Who knew?

"Other than, who?" I asked, expecting her to finish her sentence.

"Never mind, it's not important. But what is... is your being here."

I scratched the back of my head in regret, coming to terms with her mention of the elephant in the room. "Sorry for trespassing. I was just walking a trail next door and ended up over here. I couldn't resist. Your home is so beautiful."

Tammy quickly turned to face me as if surprised by where I'd come from. "Ah, I thought you came from the Eldridge's. Tell me, how do you know them? You family? Another neighbor? Ah, I know... you're the new girlfriend."

"*New girlfriend?* What's that supposed to mean?"

"Oh, nothing." She turned and looked back out at the glistening lake.

"That's bullshit and you know it. Now c'mon, tell me what you—"

"How long have you two been together?" she interrupted.

"I'm not telling you that. For all I know, you could be some weirdo freak who's—"

"Just answer the question, please."

I scoffed. "Sunday will mark one year. Why do you wanna know?"

Tammy nodded subtly as if she were impressed by the length of our relationship. Or perhaps, she was just trying to come up with a clever way to congratulate me but couldn't.

"That's impressive."

"What do you mean, '*impressive*?'" I asked irritably.

She grabbed a slice of pineapple from the glass Pyrex bowl beside her and ate it, having no care for manners as she chewed with her mouth open like a starving camel. Gnaw, gnaw, gnaw. I waited, expecting her to answer me but she never did. She grabbed another piece and ate it, and I awkwardly stood there in suspense. *Umm, hello? I'm still here.*

Finally, she turned to me, removed her sunglasses, and said, "Well, I hope you know what you're getting into."

I shifted my weight to one hip and crossed my arms, perturbed. "Excuse me?"

She took another slice of pineapple from the bowl and stuffed it in her mouth, her chewing beginning to agitate me even more now that she'd chosen to ignore me yet again.

"The family, I mean," she finally answered after swallowing. "They have secrets."

"Secrets?" I repeated in disbelief. "Secrets like what? You keep being vague and ominous for no reason. Just tell me already what you mean so I can be on my way."

"Let me put it this way. Have you ever asked Brett about his childhood?"

I tilted my head to the side as I thought about it for a second. "No. I don't think so. But that's not what you typically ask."

"Yes, it is. Wouldn't you want to know everything about your significant other? I know I sure as hell would. But then again, I guess it depends on the people in the relationship and how vulnerable they want to be with each other."

*Vulnerable?* That word stung worse than a bee on a hot summer's day. Being vulnerable was something I wasn't too fond of doing. Perhaps Tammy was right. Maybe being vulnerable depended on the type of people in the relationship, and how open they wanted to be with one another. I, for one, was not one of them. Not anymore.

I knew I certainly didn't intend to discuss my dark past with Brett. Even though we'd been together a year. And even though he knew a little bit about me, he didn't know everything. He couldn't. Even if we were to get married and stay together until our very last breaths, I wouldn't tell him. Because sometimes the truth is too much, too scary for even our loved ones to bear; poisonous like forbidden fruit.

"Well, I don't remember asking him," I continued, wanting to understand why she claimed the family had secrets. "But that's probably because it's never come up in conversation before. But what does that have to do with—"

"It's all a part of their twisted game," she interrupted again before grabbing another slice of pineapple from the bowl and tossing it in her mouth.

*Twisted game? What twisted game could she be referring to?*

Tammy had to have been drunk or stricken with heatstroke from being outside for too long because it seemed like she was rambling nothing but nonsense. I inhaled deeply to see if I could get a whiff of the lingering odor of alcohol on her breath, but I couldn't tell. It seemed like something was there—musty, leafy, fishy—but I couldn't quite put my nose on it. Perhaps the slight odor came from the lake. From the algae and fish that swam about.

"The Eldridge family seem like nice people," I said. "Granted, I only really know Brett, but still. That has to account for something, right?"

"You're right, they do seem like nice people. But you don't *really* know them. I promise you, you don't even know an ounce of Brett."

"It seems like you know them more than me. So tell me, what am I supposed to be afraid of?"

She expelled a half-assed laugh that mimicked a sputtering car running out of fuel. "Just think of it this way... question everything. Those questions might just save your life."

Tammy's claims were preposterous. There was no way in hell I didn't know the man I'd built a new life with over the past twelve months. Did he possess some promising traits that seemed a little farfetched, (chiseled jawline, tall stature, good manners)? Ones I felt would make great for our future children. Yes. But I also believed they stemmed from his parents, which I'd soon uncover throughout this weekend.

I pinched the bridge of my nose and thought of what to say to politely end this conversation once and for all. After a few seconds of silence, the words came pouring out of me like a marble fountain on the first day of spring. "Look, I'm no stranger to the beauty of not knowing every minute detail about your partner. It's the mystery that ignites the spark and fuels the desire to peel back the layers of their personality. And it doesn't happen overnight but through daily conversations spanning a lifetime.

"Without that mystery, you have nothing. So I'm getting to know Brett and his family—slowly. A lasting marriage isn't merely built on trust, unconditional love, and the pull of attraction. It's founded on the shared commitment to growth; an unspoken promise exchanged in vows, where two souls stride forward together. Getting to know one another falls into that category."

Tammy raised one eyebrow and boldly asked, "Who said anything about marriage?"

I froze. She was right. I'd gotten so heated in the moment that I brought up something that went beyond the conversation; completely took it to another level.

"I... I..."

"It's okay, dear. I won't hold it against you."

I checked the time on my phone. *I need to get back.*

I was no longer interested in hearing her babbling assumptions about the family I was just getting to know, nor wanting to explain the reason I'd brought up marriage. I couldn't allow her to ruin such a relaxing weekend, let alone sway my opinion of them. The Eldridge family's warm and inviting nature was homely, to say the least. I only expected it to get better.

Perhaps Tammy was crazy or envious of Brett's family. There could be many reasons as to why she'd make such outlandish claims; she never conceived and thus envied their son and the experiences that followed motherhood, such as shipping them off to college, meeting their partners, and witnessing their wedding; perhaps her marriage had crumbled in the past, and she envied Lydia and Jeff's relationship. That could have easily explained the missing ring print; it happened long ago. Maybe she simply didn't like them. Whichever the reason, it didn't make sense why she would stay living close by with this kind of animosity toward them.

With nothing else left to say I said, "I've got to get back. They're probably waiting for me."

She grabbed my wrist, squeezing it with a vice-like grip as I turned to walk away.

"Let go of me!" I exclaimed.

Her grip didn't falter. A searing pain shot up my arm. I turned to face Tammy, her grip unrelenting. We locked eyes. Her wide-eyed gaze was frightening as if she were a tiger, preparing to make me her next meal. Pounce!

"Look, all I'm saying is be careful, okay?" she urged, loosening her grip a little. "You're not the first girl he's brought home."

I yanked my arm away, freeing myself from her stranglehold. Then I marched across her yard and back through the woods, her voice trailing, "You're not the only one."

# Chapter
# 5

'YOU'RE NOT THE ONLY ONE.' *Where does she get off? I'm not gonna be able to get those words out of my head now. And it's all because of her. Who the hell does she think she is?*

We were all gathered in the dining hall off from the kitchen around a rectangular six-top table; a beautifully custom-carved piece of walnut that showcased the grains and discoloration of the hundred-something-year-old tree beneath a thick sheet of glass.

Lydia had made pulled chicken sandwiches topped with lettuce, tomato, onion, and a dollop of mayonnaise. Yum! The meat practically melted in my mouth. We all sat in silence as we ate. Only the gentle hums from our enjoyment of the meal filled the void. *I hope I can learn a thing or two from her this weekend. I need to alleviate the stress that crazy bitch caused.*

I swallowed what was in my mouth and started to

speak, but hesitated. I took another bite, thinking, *I need to build rapport with Lydia first before asking. Granted, she'd probably be delighted to show me her recipes. It would give us a chance to bond. But it just doesn't feel like the right time.*

I dipped my fries in ketchup and ate them. *Maybe I should mention Tammy. No, I shouldn't. What if they start asking questions? After all, if what she said was true, and the Eldridge family is hiding something, then doing so is only gonna alert them. No, I can't mention her. Not yet. Maybe not ever.*

I took another bite of my sandwich as I tried to forget the crazy neighbor. But when I ate more fries, the words Tammy had said circled my mind once more. *Of course... I can't just get her outta my mind. All I wanted was to relax down by the lake, catch some sun, and get to know the family. But now I can't stop thinking about what she said.*

After dwelling on it for another minute, I settled on an idea. The best course of action seemed to be addressing it to Brett in privacy—with someone whom I trusted and who wouldn't think I was clinically insane. *Okay... after lunch I'll bring her up. I'll invite him down to our room and I'll ask him if knows her. Yeah, that sounds like a decent plan. Yep, it sure does. Oh, who am I kidding? I'm spiraling.*

Though I believed Tammy was just speculating, the dark thoughts kept creeping, getting worse with every bite. *What secrets is this family hiding? Is there a corpse hidden somewhere on this property? Do they have a taste for human flesh? No, that's just crazy. They're not cannibals.* I peered down at my chicken sandwich, at the thick red sauce—that awfully resembled blood—the chicken had been coated in. *I don't taste any iron. Even if it was seasoned well, there'd still be a hint of iron, right? No, it's not blood. Maybe they are human traffickers. That would explain why they moved all the way out here.*

I wiped my mouth with my napkin, thinking back to how I'd never found out what Brett's parents did for a living. *I bet when he dropped my bag down the stairs, it was intentional. Maybe they have tiny microphones in every room, listening in to prevent each of them from explaining why they're really out here. But if that were the case, then where would the control room be? I've seen enough films to know all control rooms have a central location to monitor everything with ease. Wait?! The black door in the basement. Maybe it's in there, and Lydia simply lied about it, convincing me it was nothing but a utility closet for mops and brooms and bleach. Oh God, maybe they ARE hiding something.*

I grabbed my glass and sipped some water, trying to kick these crazy assumptions. *Don't let Tammy get in your head. She's just an angry old lady who's trying to ruin your mini vacation. The Eldridge family does NOT have microphones hidden across the home.*

I took another bite, disgusted with myself at how easy it was for Tammy to convince me the Eldridge family was evil. It was one thing to come to that assumption on my own but to be fed that heinous lie about what seemed to be a loving family was prejudice and erroneous.

I pushed the thought away and leaned toward something positive, like how I'd enjoy myself during my stay with calming activities such as getting a tan, drinking piña coladas, and swimming. But then the cryptic message on the tree I'd come across on my hike emerged shortly after: B + C. There it was again.

*Perhaps the C on the arborglyph is another woman, an ex that they'd murdered. Maybe B is for Brett, and C is for Candice, or Cynthia, or Cierra, or—*

A sharp pinch broke my focus. Amid my speculation, I'd bit my tongue and could now taste blood; the vulgar tang of iron, dancing in my mouth like a hardy pill I'd struggled to swallow. This wasn't the first time I'd hurt myself due to my tendency to jump to conclusions. Many years ago, Ryan had also hidden information from me, which in turn caused me to do the same thing—accuse and assume. The constant secrecy and hidden information had caused me to become paranoid and bite my nails until they bled.

I stared at my hands, cuticles still bearing the scars from that time, remnants of skin along the nail bed still peeled like old wallpaper. It was a harsh reminder of the impact he had on me. And though the nails had been covered with acrylics and glossed to perfection, I knew that once removed the crude images would come flooding back, each follicle brittle and fragile like a newborn.

Expelling my lingering frustration from my past relationship, I made up my mind about the Eldridge family. *They're hiding something, I just know it. I can't quite put my finger on what exactly, but they're hiding something. They just seem too perfect now that Tammy has brought it to my attention; too pleasant and welcoming. Their grinning smiles, calm demeanors, and level of maturity seem... seem... fabricated.*

*I've gotta put an end to this once and for all so I can finally start enjoying this weekend. I've gotta start asking questions.*

———

AFTER LUNCH, Brett followed me downstairs to our room. He was hesitant at first, claiming he wanted to go outside and enjoy the sunshine instead of being cooped up inside all day. But I eventually convinced him to join me, using sex as an incentive to shadow my real intentions.

"Your mother's cooking is amazing, Brett," I said, entering our room.

He sat on the edge of the bed as I dove onto it like a wide receiver going for a touchdown.

"I sure do miss it," he replied.

"Miss it, how?"

"I don't know. I guess when I moved away, I no longer had a woman in my life to cook meals for me."

"That was until I came into the picture, right?" I joked.

He shrugged. "I guess you could say that."

I rolled onto my back. "What's that supposed to mean? I thought you liked my cooking."

"Don't get me wrong. I love your cooking, Allison. But we only see each other like what... three times a week if we're lucky? The other days, I eat out. And I know you know firsthand just how quickly one can get sick of takeout."

Letting out a dry laugh, I sat up, scooted to the edge of the bed behind him, and began massaging his shoulders. "Yeah, you're right. Takeout can get tiring pretty quickly.

But that's why I rotate between two or three places. Just so it doesn't."

"Still, I'd appreciate a home-cooked meal more often."

"Sounds like you're implying I bring you food every night."

Brett stared at the blank wall across from the bed and answered, "Well, that's an option. To be honest, it wouldn't be all that difficult if we lived together."

I stopped twirling my thumbs along his shoulder blades in disbelief. *Did he just imply I move in with him? We've only been dating a year. Certainly, he doesn't wanna move that quickly, does he?*

"Allison?" he called, breaking my train of thought and the deafening silence that had consumed the room whole like a sound booth.

But I didn't respond. I sensed Brett's heart rate steadily increasing through his body as if the anticipation of my answer had become too overwhelming for him. I couldn't help but think he had brought me here for a different reason now. *I hope he doesn't plan to propose. God, I sure hope not. And in front of his parents, no less. Perhaps he wanted to bring me up here so his parents could meet me first, to see if I was a good enough prospect; a woman worth bringing into the family. They'll probably think I'm a bitch if I say no. What am I talking about? I AM gonna say no and it's gonna be so awkward afterward. I don't wanna get married again. At least, not so soon.*

I shuddered at the thought, my grip tightening around his shoulders until he said, "Ouch."

I snapped back to reality following his subtle cry of pain. "Sorry, babe. But you're real tight," I lied, playing it off as if I wasn't just lost in oblivion, thinking about what he'd inadvertently asked me. "I guess those six hours on the road really got to you."

He let out a sigh of pleasure as my hands drifted further south to his upper back. "It sure did. Now, back to what you were saying."

"No. I'm not gonna bring you food every night," I said sharply, and he winced as my fingernails dug into the base of his neck.

Despite how I felt about moving in with him, I tried to keep calm, resorting back to my gentle touch. I wanted to emanate pleasure and relaxation, not gloom and rage. Brett had enough of that at his job already, which was why he was so tense.

The stress of having to manage the everyday problems that would arise at an IT company kept him on edge most of the time; the scheduling, the customer service, and the constant malfunctioning of the computer equipment. It all gave him reoccurring headaches that I'd have to deal with regularly whenever we'd see each other. They overworked him, plain and simple. But they also paid him well, so he didn't complain much.

But I did.

I was all too aware of the toll his job took on him simply because both of our jobs were similar in nature with the amount of effort required to fulfill them. At times, it felt as though his coworkers saw more of him than I did, leading me to resent the company for exploiting his abilities.

Perhaps it was simply my insecurities that led me to those feelings. But I longed for more time with Brett. Was that such a bad thing? He had said it best. We only saw each other three times a week if we were lucky. Damn, those conflicting schedules. Being a nurse sure had its ups and downs, but I enjoyed it. Even if I failed to procure enough sleep most days.

So when the opportunity arose for us to spend three consecutive days together, I jumped at the chance. The prospect of a weekend at the lake, fishing, swimming, basking in the sun, and then returning to the comfort of his parents' home to shower and make love was a dream come true. Though I was still a little hesitant at first in meeting new people, I knew I had to if I were going to take advantage of the situation.

I'd hoped nothing would have disrupted our plans and that we could relish in the brief but cherished time together. But because of Tammy—that drunk of a bitch with split ends and burned, splotchy skin—that dream was now in danger of being completely upended. She had intentionally threatened my entire getaway, making me rue the decision of having heeded her call.

I shook my head, pushing away all the negative thoughts as my fingers trailed down Brett's back and around his sides. *Focus. I need to ask him. It's either now or never.* "Brett? Is this where you grew up?" I asked, locking my hands around his stomach and resting my chin on his left shoulder.

"Yes, and no."

"What do you mean?"

He turned to me, the look in his eyes worn and heavy; bags puffy. Damn, did those hours on the road take their toll on him. He was definitely in dire need of a nap. He yawned. "I mean, I was born and raised in Fredericksburg, which is three hours from here. But I spent my teenage years here in Huddleston. That's what I mean by yes and no."

"That makes sense." I released my hold on him and fell back onto the pillows, my hair pooling around my head like a puddle.

Brett followed suit, landing between my legs, his head on my stomach. We were both staring at the ceiling now, lying there in utter silence.

I ran my hand through his short, spiky hair as he massaged my foot. "I bet you were quite the player in high school."

"What makes you think that?"

"Oh, I don't know... your parents have this beautiful home on the lake, and you're quite the looker. I just assumed."

He let out a quick chuckle. "Well, I wasn't always this pretty. I did have my fair share of acne, like every other teenager."

"Well, it wasn't enough to keep away whoever you carved your name in that tree with."

Brett's grip on my foot suddenly tightened, his once tender touch turning harsh and agonizing as if I'd gotten my foot trapped in a batch of winding gears.

*Shit, this must be the secret; some ex-girlfriend he tried to forget about; one who'd done him wrong. Oh God the pain. Maybe they killed her...*

My thoughts raced as the pain grew more intense, spreading through my foot like a tidal wave, engulfing the shoreline. It became unbearable, numbing me to the core. "Brett, stop! You're hurting me!" I cried out.

And just like that, his grip on me vanished. It was as if he'd been in a trance, a spell of sorts, brought on by the mere mention of that tree. He turned to me with a blank stare as he lifted my foot and kissed it. Then his gaze trailed up my body and met with mine. "I'm sorry, Allison. You're right. My acne wasn't bad enough to keep away my first girlfriend... Christina."

"I'm sorry if I brought up a sensitive topic. I just came across the tree during my stroll earlier and wondered if it was an ex or best friend, perhaps even a—"

"You guessed right, Allison," he interrupted while gently running his hand up the inside of my pant leg and back down. "She was my girlfriend. But now you are. Someone who I cherish way more."

I smiled as he crawled his way up and kissed me, then rested his head on my bosom. As we lay there, our hearts beating as one, I thought back to the tree with the initials: B + C. *Perhaps Tammy is crazy or envies the Eldridge family. Maybe Christina was her daughter and Brett had done something to her that was unforgivable. Maybe he got her pregnant. Maybe she got an abortion.*

The thought was too unbearable to entertain, yet I couldn't shake the feeling that something far more sinister had occurred. Perhaps—

I hesitated. I couldn't bring myself to even think of the word. Yet, somehow, it still emerged. *Did he rape her? Could it be that he, along with his parents, had taken her life and buried the evidence on their property? Or worse, sold her into a trafficking ring? Here I go again, spiraling. Maybe Tammy knew they did it but just couldn't prove it. Maybe that's why she warned me. I better not mention her right now. I don't wanna make things worse. Perhaps it's best to wait until we return home. Wait until after the entire weekend blows over. Yeah, that sounds good.*

# Chapter
# 6

THERE I WAS DROWNING in assumptions yet again, letting the sickening thoughts of Tammy—a wicked stranger—penetrate my subconscious and ruin my mood, and potentially my future with Brett and his family. Whether he and his parents were hiding something, I didn't want to think about the matter anymore. I'd accomplished what I'd set out to do (question him about the tree). And he had told me the truth. But I couldn't ignore the accusations despite my best efforts.

I lay there, eyes wide and mind wired, staring at the empty whiteness of the ceiling. *Is this what they're hiding? There's no other reason why he squeezed my foot like he did if it wasn't. Something terrible happened here. But what?*

Suddenly, the chatter of footsteps and the slap of a door closing pulled me from my meandering thoughts. It must have been his parents. I looked down at Brett, at his bushy eyebrows and steadily rising chest to find he was out cold. He finally succumbed to the exhaustion the drive up here had caused. It made sense. Six hours behind the wheel with very few stops in between would tire even the most seasoned driver. Now, with him napping, I could take advantage of the time alone to investigate.

I slipped out from beneath Brett's imposing frame and tip-toed over to the bureau, where I believed they may have hidden something in the drawers, considering neither of us had stowed our clothes in it, but rather kept them in our suitcases and set them aside in the corner like a kid in timeout.

I opened the top two drawers and found them empty. I went for the second set and still nothing. Then I knelt and pried open the bottom two and uncovered a mysterious dark brown scrapbook in the left drawer. I wrapped my hands around it, clutched it tight to my chest, and snuck out of the room.

I gently closed the door following my swift exit and crept across the hardwood floor toward the sofa. I peered out the window to my right and found Brett's parents relaxing down on the boat dock, basking in the warm sun like a dog on a cool summer day. *Perfect. With them out there, I can read this book without any interruption just as long as Brett remains asleep.*

Settling onto the sofa, I examined the state of the leather-bound scrapbook. I traced my fingers along its weathered face, the small tears rough against my skin. *Hmm, no insignia or embroidery. Strange. And these cracks... this thing must be close to fifty years old. Maybe there's a date somewhere stamped inside. Seems highly unlikely though.*

When I peeled back the cover, a pile of loose sheets poured into my lap, many of which had yellowed from age. I didn't know what to make of them. Some were handwritten, others typed, as if done on an old typewriter. And as I scanned the pages, searching for anything remotely incriminating, I came up with nothing. Only random words and—

*Evaluations?*

I grew increasingly confused as I continued leafing through the pages.

*This is patient data. Why would they have this?*

A few trudging thuds just outside pulled my attention away from the book and I looked back over my shoulder and out the window to find Lydia marching up the walkway toward the deck steps like a staff sergeant about to reprimand a corporal. She was talking on her cell, one hand overly expressive as if angry, and her forehead was riddled with creases.

I ducked as she passed by and gritted my teeth, my heart thudding in my chest like a galloping horse. *God, I hope she didn't see me. She was clearly focused on whoever she was talking to. But still, I reacted slowly. Maybe I should've read this in our bathroom.*

To be safe, I set the scrapbook aside and cautiously peered over the back of the sofa in search of her. Thank God, she was gone. I wouldn't know where to stash the scrapbook if she'd caught me. Knowing I needed to be careful with my next move, I listened out for her footsteps. Tap, tap, tap. Once I heard them again, my heart rate slowed.

The deck door creaked open.

I took a deep breath and tip-toed to the base of the spiral staircase. Gripping the banister, I listened intently.

"What do you mean, he's gone?" Lydia asked in frustration, her voice echoing throughout the home like a school bell. "I can't believe you let him escape."

*Gone? Escaped? Who could she be talking about?*

"Yes, yes, I know, I know. I told you he'll try over and over again," she continued. "In the future, take more precautions. This is the second time already in six months. If he shows up again, I'll give you a call. Bye."

Silence fell.

"Hey," Brett whispered in my ear, his sudden presence making my heart skip a beat.

I spun to face him and whispered, "What the hell, Brett?! You scared the shit out of me." He'd come up behind me, his hand resting on the base of my back. "I thought you were still fast asleep. You know... exhausted."

He stretched his arms wide above his head as if doing a dance number. "What can say? All I needed was a quick nap. I feel pretty good now."

There he stood, wide awake and jokingly grinning, unsettling my nerves. *How long have you been standing behind me? Did you overhear your mother prattling on about an escaped prisoner? I bet he woke up to pee and noticed I'd left the room and came looking for me. That sounds like something he'd do.*

I was caught red-handed, with a book that was obviously meant for private eyes laying out in the open on the sofa just within arms reach.

"What are you doing?" he asked.

*Good. He doesn't know. I guess he wasn't standing behind me for long. What a relief.* With a death grip on the banister, I scanned the room in search of a believable excuse. As my gaze landed on the bookshelf, I said, "I couldn't sleep, so I came out here to take a look at your parents' book collection."

"Well, don't get too caught up in literature, okay? My mother has a busy schedule planned for us. And I know reading isn't on that list."

He grabbed my hand and brushed past me to lead me up the stairs. "C'mon, let's head upstairs and see what they're doing."

As he took the first step, I slipped from his grasp, stopping him. *I need to come up with a legitimate excuse quick. I don't want him questioning why I'm not following him. Someone's gonna find the scrapbook if I leave it where it's at. Think dammit, think. I can't imagine what they'll do to me if they find out I've discovered the book. They might kill me, carve me up, and serve me for dinner. Perhaps they'll tie me up and stow me away in some underground bunker until I'm nothing but skin and bones. Maybe they'll traffic me.*

I shuddered at the menacing thoughts, sweat forming under my pits. Everything was riding on this moment, and yet, I was mute. Finally, I said, "I'll be up in a second, okay? I need to pee first."

There I was, lying to the man I'd been dating for the past year; the man I'd shared numerous romantic dinners with at high-end restaurants, using it to relieve stress from our demanding jobs; the man I'd vent to whenever my boss would reprimand me for doing something I felt was right though it jeopardized the integrity of the hospital.

I never thought I'd lie to Brett, especially not to his face. But it was for a good reason. I felt endangered. And because of my traumatizing past, my safety was now my top priority. As I stood there, awaiting his response, I felt the sweat building on my skin. The bulbs of liquid steadily forming along my forehead threatened to out me. As unnerving as it was, I feared he'd see it soon enough if he hadn't noticed the rift in my demeanor already. And yet, as we stood there in what felt like an awkward silence for ions, my patience grew thin.

*Just hurry up and say something already.*

"Okay," he finally said, breaking the daunting silence.

He shrugged, turned, and continued up the stairs, allowing me to return the book to its rightful place.

# Chapter 7

*THAT WAS A CLOSE ONE*, I thought as I headed upstairs. *Now that it's back where I found it, no one's gonna suspect a thing.*

When I reached the top of the staircase, I peered out the window, spotting Lydia and Jeff basking out on the boat dock yet again. With the way the sun reflected off their bodies like polished armor kissed by dawn's embrace, I could tell their skin was glistening. A thirsty gulping sound drew me to look left. Brett was downing a tall glass of water.

"Do you think I should bother your mom now?" I asked. "I don't wanna interrupt her relaxation time."

He pulled the glass from his lips and let out a satisfying sigh. "Of course! She has all the time in the world to sunbathe, Allison. You're only here for three days. I'm sure she won't mind."

I shrugged, then headed outside. Stepping out of the

cool house and onto the baking hot deck surely made me second-guess coming out here to talk with Lydia. The sudden intense burning sensation along my heels felt as if I were walking across lava. *I shouldn't have taken off my flip-flops.*

I gritted my teeth and hurried off the main deck, hoping the shadowed part of the stone walkway below would be cooler. In my rush, during my descent, I tripped. Thankfully, I grabbed the railing in time to prevent a plunge. Once I landed on the breezeway, I looked at the sky and cupped my hand over my eyes to shield them from the light. No clouds were in sight, the sun intense, the sky bluer than ever. From the moment I set foot outside, I knew I'd made a mistake in wearing all black for the trip up here. It wasn't enough that I already looked like a thief. I was also going to sweat my ass off too.

I had already broken out in a light sweat from the trek down the stairs. I knew the longer I stayed outside, the more I'd perspire. Even with the help of the slight breeze coming off the lake, my skin refused to cool down.

I strode across the stone walkway down toward the boat dock. When I reached the end, where Lydia and Jeff sat, reclined beside a miniature cooler where they'd most likely stowed some ice for their colorful wine coolers that rest on top, I cleared my throat.

Lydia's ears perked up.

"Lydia?" I called. "You mentioned something earlier about some plans you'd made. Well, I'm ready to start on those activities now if you are."

She removed her oversized shades and sprang from the sun lounger like a gymnast. Her tropical flower sundress gracefully billowed around her. "Wonderful," she exclaimed. Then, turning to her husband, she added, "I'm going to take Allison inside. Hopefully, you'll survive without my company, honey."

"I sure will, dear," he replied without so much as a glance or change in expression. It seemed as if he were more focused on developing his tan to help insinuate his barely visible six-pack than being in the company of his wife, considering he was in a speedo, his arms outstretched behind his head and thin gray hair shining.

She grabbed her drink from atop the cooler, turned to me, and said, "Let's head inside."

We marched up the dock back toward the house. Once inside, we went upstairs, where she led me into a room that left me speechless. The walls were lined with shelves stuffed with books on every topic imaginable: cooking, psychology, self-help, and even classic romances by Jane Austen.

The collection was vast enough to rival a small library with how all four walls were encased in them, surrounding us in a sea of paper and color. Considering the sizable stock of literature here was larger than the ones in the basement, I'd say she had a true appreciation for reading. Far greater than mine. And perhaps, this was where she spent most of her days in her blissful retired life.

While exploring the room for other knick-knacks, I noted a large oak table in the center and an easel tucked away in the corner by the window. This had to have been an art room, a haven for creative souls given the remnants of paint covering the wooden structure.

"This is amazing," I said as I trailed the wall to inspect the collection of books.

"This is where I go to let my creative side run free," Lydia admitted. "It's my little art room."

I stopped, grabbed a book, and inspected its cover. It was a late 80s print about the history of painting in Italy. "Little is an understatement," I said absently before turning to her and adding, "I never pegged you as an artist."

She sat at the oak table and cupped her chin in her left palm. "There are a lot of things you don't know about me, Allison. But in time, you'll learn. From here on out, I suggest you take a better look at your surroundings because you would've noticed I was an artist if you'd paid more attention to the signs."

*Signs? What signs?* Returning the book to the shelf, I recalled my first impressions of their grand home; the tiny details such as the spiral staircase, brick fireplace, and the gleaming bamboo floors. *Perhaps she had a hand in the overall design of the house, not just the interior. This place is unconventional; with narrow passages leading to expansive sunrooms and observatory-like spaces, all offering unobstructed views of the stunning natural landscape. Maybe that's what she's talking about.*

As Lydia's words hung in the air, I racked my brain, trying to remember any hints that she may be an artist. Then, like a bolt of lightning, it hit me. *The artwork! That must be what she's talking about. The abstract paintings on the walls. They are vibrant and colorful. But something about them seems off.*

I recalled the figures in the paintings. They were of children who bore expressions of pain and despair, each of them teary-eyed and with a sullen pout. It was a stark contrast to the opulence and grandeur of the home, but perhaps it was an artistic commentary on the world's dark underbelly; conversation pieces to help spice up dull dinner talk.

*There was also the garden I'd stumbled upon earlier, mere moments before I traveled down the trail and met Tammy; a sprawling oasis of greenery and flowers, with a large sculpture in the center. Maybe that's what she's referring to. And God were those botanicals that encapsulated the fence line beautiful. I can picture it now; a vineyard wedding. But that sculpture was an eyesore. That angel with majestic wings looked so eroded.*

"You must be referring to the art around the house," I said, pulling out the stool from beneath the table and sitting across from her. "The paintings and the sculpture in the garden I mean."

She nodded.

"Well, I noticed them when you showed me the house. I just didn't comment on them because I figured you guys had purchased them. But now it's clear you possess artistic talents that extend far beyond the pages of a book. If you've authored one, that is." I laughed a little. "But then again, what do I know? My knowledge of art is limited, unlike my expertise in medicine. Not that I don't appreciate art or have a desire to create, because I do. Or at least did, but——"

"Did?" Lydia interrupted.

"Yep. Since childhood, I've been fascinated with art. For as long as I can remember, I wanted to draw comics for the newspaper. My dad used to read them to me every morning before school. I'd sit on his lap and eat my Pop-Tarts while he sipped his coffee. Whether it was Calvin and Hobbs, Garfield, or Peanuts, we'd always share a laugh over whatever stupid shenanigans the characters got into. And when I got home from school and finished my homework, I'd practice drawing them while my mom prepared dinner."

"Sounds like you have a great relationship with your parents."

I tucked my hair behind my ear and rested my elbows along the table in regret for how I'd ended things with them. "You'd think that but it's far from the truth. Don't get me wrong, I love my parents but as I got closer and closer to graduating high school, they discouraged me from pursuing art as a career and pushed me toward more profitable ventures. They often said, 'We just want you to have a secure future, dear. Not struggle like we did.'"

Lydia rested her right hand along my left as if attempting to comfort me; a great sign that signified she was a good person. That the family was good; loving; caring.

"For the longest time I hated them for it," I continued. "I believe they just wanted me to get a job that paid well so I could afford to take care of them once they became incompetent, you know? To this day I regret not standing up for myself and following through. After all, I could have been somebody; a caricature wiz with a career spanning thirty-plus years. Nevertheless, the past is the past and we can't change it. The best thing to do now is move on. Forgive and forget. After all, they are my parents. It's not like I can hold it against them."

"Well, you could."

I tilted my head to the side in bewilderment, prompting her to continue.

"It just wouldn't be right."

*Yes, it would. You just don't understand.*

I looked to my left, dismissing her comment. "You know what... life has a strange way of working out. Had I pursued my dream of becoming an artist, I might have never met Brett." *Or crossed paths with Ryan.*

"Or us," she added with a cheeky smile as she lifted her side of the tabletop and pulled out a puzzle. The image on the box was of the sweeping vistas of Africa; a golden sun in the distance descending upon a grazing herd of graceful giraffes and majestic zebras. It was a breathtaking scene that seemed like it had come straight out of a National Geographic magazine. She dumped the 500 pieces onto the table and they scattered like a herd of sheep to a wolf.

"Ah, this must be numero uno on the list you compiled before we arrived," I playfully suggested.

She grabbed a piece and connected it to another, creating the first corner. "It sure is. It'll give us a chance to talk more."

"Sounds wonderful. Let's continue with the art conversation then." I reached for a piece that looked like it would fit the corner she built, and absently asked, "Did you create all the art in the house?"

"What's ironic is that I've only created one piece out of everything you've seen," she answered. "The sculpture in the garden. The rest are from other artists. But we didn't buy them. If anything, they were gifts."

"Then how come you said I would've noticed you were an artist if I'd paid more attention to the signs if none of the art hanging on the walls is yours?"

Her gaze averted from the puzzle and her hands retreated, crossing her arms. "Because art is subjective, Allison. See, I gave each of those artists a prompt, which is why they all look similar. And though you are right, I didn't *actually* paint them myself, I still took part in the creation process, which technically makes me an artist as well. If anything, you could consider me, Geppetto."

"I guess that's one way to look at it."

"Yes, it is. However, your way of looking at is also correct. Since I didn't put paint on the canvas, some wouldn't consider me the artist. Much like yourself."

"Whoa, whoa, whoa," I said nervously, setting my puzzle piece aside. "I didn't say you *weren't* an artist."

"You didn't have to, dear. It was implied."

"Well, I didn't mean anything by it, okay? I was just a little bothered by your criticism of not having paid more attention to the—"

"Signs?"

I tucked my chin in embarrassment. "Yes."

Despite the tranquil activity of piecing together the puzzle, which obviously distracted me enough to forget about the scrapbook, I still couldn't get a read on Brett's mother. His father seemed okay, considering how laid back he was. Even though I hadn't gotten a chance to speak more than two words to the man since we'd been here. But his mother was different; a real challenge; something I found quite strange, considering I rarely experienced similar situations at the hospital from total strangers.

It seemed as if she were toying with me, trying to get a rise out of me for some odd reason. Was I that ignorant of my surroundings? Or was there something more sinister at play here? Falling deeper down the rabbit hole Tammy had forcibly tossed me in, I thought, *Perhaps Lydia isn't the artistic genius she appears to be. Maybe she's conniving, hiding the fact that each painting adorning the walls is a sinister reminder of each one of Brett's girlfriends they killed. Perhaps that's what they're hiding.*

The idea that she might ask me to create a painting with the same morbid prompt chilled me to the bone. *I most certainly won't paint. Not for her, or any of them. Not at least, until I can prove they aren't crazy. But after finding that scrapbook, I highly doubt I won't find more proof. God, I can't imagine contributing to their twisted collection. I wonder if they'll add me to their enormous patient list.*

Refusing to let my fear show, I refocused on the puzzle and tried to keep the conversation positive. I retrieved the piece I'd set aside and put it in place. "So what did you say you did for work again? You know, earlier... after you showed me the bedroom."

"I worked for the government. Jeff and I were at the Pentagon for several years. Hence the commute and traffic I'd mentioned. We worked in telecommunications."

"Then you retired and moved down here?"

"Not exactly. We just retired a decade ago. Lived here for fifteen. If anything, we're finally settling down."

"Okay."

I couldn't shake the feeling that Lydia was lying to me. And though I hadn't expected Brett's parents to have worked for the government, I did expect Lydia's explanation of what they did to be vague, simply because what they did in the Pentagon had to have been classified.

I did some quick mental calculations to test my theory on whether or not she spoke the truth. *Lydia's story about when they moved here, lines up with Brett's account of his childhood. So, that checks out. But there's still an unknown factor. Who called Lydia about an escapee? Who's the man she's so concerned about dropping in? Perhaps this is the secret Tammy was referring to.*

# Chapter

# 8

WHEN IT CAME time for dinner, my stomach growled with hunger. My body craved sustenance. So much so that I felt a headache coming on.

During our time piecing together the puzzle, our conversation remained focused solely on me; my career as a nurse and my aspirations to become a surgeon, my plans to get married and have two children (a boy and a girl), and how Brett and I met. Me, me, me. Every time I mentioned something more about the family, she'd quickly answer it, then divert back to me. The one-sided interrogation made me suspicious as if she was searching for something to use against me or searching for a reason NOT to kill me. I might have been over-analyzing it, but still, I hesitated to let my guard down.

As Lydia and I set the dining room table, the tantalizing scent of thyme and rosemary wafted in from the deck, where Brett and Jeff were grilling steaks. One of the windows along the back of the house was screened, allowing it to swivel open and let in air.

My mouth watered in anticipation of the upcoming meal like melting ice. The fine cuts of wagyu beef that Lydia and Jeff had thoughtfully thawed out for our dinner looked marvelous. The array of ribeye and T-bone steaks, along with the baked asparagus and mashed potatoes, were a feast fit for royalty.

I placed another silverware set on the table and relished in what good fortune I had to be treated to such a sumptuous meal, despite my feelings of being an intruder in their metaphorical castle. Nonetheless, this was the best I'd ever been treated by anyone. Even my parents. Sad to say, but it was true. Then, as I lay another silverware set on the table, a biting fear fell over me. *Are they buttering me up? Maybe Brett plans to propose over dinner. If he were planning such a thing. God, I sure hope not. Perhaps they aren't trying to butter, but instead fatten me up like livestock before sending me off to the slaughterhouse.*

I quickly pushed away the thought, not wanting to ruin the pleasant evening we were having. "You know you guys didn't have to do this for me," I said, returning to the kitchen and wrapping my hands around a bowl of mashed potatoes.

Brett and Jeff had just brought the steaks in and set the plate on a dish towel in the middle of the dining table, the smoke trail from the meat still lingering behind them like a mountain lion on the prowl.

Jeff grabbed the large cutting knife and sliced the meat. "Please, Allison, we do this every night. I see no other way to eat, especially after we fast until noon."

I brought over the bowl of mashed potatoes and set it beside the meat. "Well, I appreciate everything."

As Jeff continued cutting up the meat, I sat beside Brett, where we faced the deck and the beautiful view of the lake. Once Jeff and Lydia dished out the servings of steak and the sides, they sat across from us. We bowed our heads, said a prayer, and then began to eat.

While silently indulging in the delicious meal, I wondered what secrets this family held behind their well-mannered façade. The more they treated me with warmth and hospitality, the more suspicious I became.

*Curse that bitch, Tammy. She's the reason I'm not enjoying this as much as I should right now. It's all because of her opinions and lies. They're eating into my subconscious and sucking the joy out of me like leeches. I sure hope none of this shit is true. I sure hope Tammy's just crazy. God, please let her be crazy. I'd sure hate to break things off because they aren't. So far, I've scrutinized every word they've said; every nice gesture they've made; every attempt to get to know me more, all just to decipher some hidden meaning that doesn't seem to exist.*

"You guys sure seem to have it all," I muttered between bites.

"What do you mean?" Jeff replied.

"Well, from what I've discussed with Lydia earlier and from this beautiful home we're currently eating dinner in, I can confidently say you guys live in luxury. I assume you've enjoyed every bit of it too. I'm talking traveling the world, exquisite meals in five-star restaurants, pretty much what most people dream of." I felt a twinge of envy in my gut, drawing me to admit my depressing upbringing. "My parents were rather plain-jane folk who didn't want much from life. They barely traveled. And when they did, it was around the United States only; never out of the country. Barely ate out, even though home-cooked meals are the best. But still... that was only because they barely made enough to pay bills. So all in all, they barely lived."

Jeff set his fork aside and patted his mouth dry with his napkin. "I'm sure they had their reasons, Allison. They were probably looking out for your best interest; making sure you had the most opportunities. At least, more than they had when they were your age."

"Don't get me wrong, I appreciate everything my parents did for me. I'm grateful, but... but... it just seems like they could've done more for themselves, you know; could've been more selfish. That's why I left Colorado after college. I needed a change of scenery."

"Where'd you end up?" Lydia asked absently as she continued slicing a sliver from her ribeye.

"Texas. I wanted more experiences; more memories. I didn't wanna just remain in the same town, seeing the same people day in and day out. I especially didn't wanna settle on marrying someone I'd gone to high school with, you know. That wasn't in the cards for me, let alone my future children. There's a whole world to see, and an even larger plethora of divine cultures dying to be studied. Why should I neglect my right to experience such beauty?"

"That's quite the question," Lydia commented.

"It sure is," Brett chimed in. "I find it funny how long it's taken you to open up like this; how passionate you truly are about living life to the fullest." He playfully squeezed my thigh under the table. "I never pegged you for one of those hippie girls who travel the countryside of Switzerland in a Volkswagen bus."

I blushed and turned away. "That's because that was the old me; before we met. My dream of drawing comics and traveling the world got pushed to the wayside when nursing sick people back to health became the priority to pay rent. However, I never gave up hope. Traveling is still a possibility, babe. Regardless of whether things work out between us or not."

He released his grip on my thigh and his smile flipped to a bewildered gape. I knew I'd crossed the line saying such a thing, but I didn't care. It was the truth. One day I'd eventually enjoy the opulent lifestyles of the rich and famous because I deserved it as much as the next person. Perhaps even more after everything I'd been through.

"It sure sounds like you two got your fill while I was out baking in the sun," Jeff said to Lydia.

"We sure did," she answered.

"How come you didn't mention she's a nurse, Brett?" Jeff asked.

"I didn't think you guys needed to know," he strangely admitted.

*Didn't think they needed to know? What sort of response is that? Why would he not tell them much about me? I'm not a secret. At least, I don't think so. Perhaps they think he's a homosexual. Maybe this is the first time he's brought home a woman instead of a male partner. Maybe Tammy had it all wrong. Maybe he's—*

I pushed my rambling thoughts away, no longer wanting to question his sexuality. "Eh... we never really discussed my career that much besides how much of my time it takes up. That's probably why he hadn't mentioned it to you guys. Stuff like that kind of makes or breaks relationships, you know?"

"We understand, dear," Lydia said, taking another bite. "We actually wanted our baby to follow in our footsteps, but—"

"But I didn't want to," Brett exclaimed. "To be honest, I didn't want any part of what they did for a living. I don't necessarily agree with what they took pride in doing." He turned to me. "You only heard about it, but... I had to experience it."

"Experience what, Brett?" I asked. "You're being vague."

"That's enough, you two," Jeff interjected. "How about we change the subject."

Brett didn't stop. "A form of torture."

"That's enough, Brett," Lydia said this time.

Her tone clipped, but Brett still refused. His voice got louder and his tone became overbearing.

"Day in and day out, seeing the pain of—"

Lydia slammed her hand on the table, breaking

whatever trance Brett was in. The sound echoed like a gunshot, causing my ears to pop and my headache to worsen. Brett instantly shut his mouth, leaned forward, picked up his fork, and returned to eating. It was as if he were a well-trained dog, obeying its master, or maybe some form of hypnosis. His mother had slammed her hand so hard on the table it had to have hurt, but yet, somehow, she appeared unfazed, as if it were a fake hand. I watched as she slowly retrieved her silverware and took another bite like nothing had happened.

"What was that all about?" I asked Brett, resting my hand on top of his thigh under the table.

He took a second before responding, his gaze still focused on his mother. Then he lowered his head and continued eating. "Nothing. Just talking about the subject of my parents gets me a little worked up sometimes. That's all."

*Hmm. I guess it's best not to confront him about it in front of his parents. I don't wanna seem rude, let alone suspicious. I'll just keep my reservations to myself for now. It seems things are getting stranger as time goes on. And to think it's only been a few hours. I can't imagine what the situation's gonna be like by the end of the weekend.*

Throughout the day, I gained substantial knowledge about the family. However, I remained clueless as to what they were hiding. The strange scrapbook, the enraged neighbor, the carving etched in the tree, the dubious phone call, and Brett's abrupt silence following his mother's outburst sent me spiraling.

Various ideas regarding their secret clawed at the insides of my skull like an infant trying to escape its crib. My headache intensified and I clenched my teeth and squinted to numb the annoying throbbing pain. But the throbbing only worsened to where I swore I could hear an actual knocking sound. Knock, knock, knock.

The incessant pounding drowned out all other noises, such as the sound of teeth gnashing on succulent steak or the clatter of utensils against plates. The sole auditory experience was the irritating knock reverberating inside my head; a cacophony of discomfort that seemed to echo the rhythm of a relentless drumbeat, each thud synchronized with the relentless pulse in my temples.

The dissonant symphony of agony enveloped my senses, eclipsing even the most delicate of sounds, leaving me captive to the discordant cadence that had claimed dominion over my world. And then, unexpectedly, a moment of relief emerged, prompting me to open my eyes wide.

That was when the inexplicable occurred.

In disbelief at the surreal scene before me, I almost choked on the steak I chewed. My heart raced and my body went numb. *What the hell? Was I drugged? Could they have laced my steak with something, leading to these hallucinations? Wait a minute... I didn't prepare my plate. His parents assembled a diverse array of meats for me to sample. Maybe Tammy's warning had merit after all—the Eldridge family was plotting to murder me, extract my organs, and sell them on the black market. But wait... why would they drug me? Why run the risk of damaging the organs? Why not wait until I fell asleep? No, they wouldn't have drugged me. But what else can explain this?*

The image of Brett standing on the deck, staring back at me while knocking on the glass like a dog pawing to get back inside was proof of my delusion. Perhaps that was the source of the incessant pounding inside my head: Brett knocking. As I pondered this possibility, something seized my hand. I shifted my gaze to the left to find Brett squeezing as tight as he could.

"What's going on?" I demanded, breaking free from his grasp.

Brett remained unresponsive, and my attention shifted to his parents. Yet, no one seemed to acknowledge the perplexing event that had just occurred. I sat there in silence, completely bewildered by the entire situation. It was as if they were ignoring me. But then, to my surprise, Lydia rose from the table, strolled across the living area, and unlocked the door for Brett's doppelgänger.

*This can't be happening. This isn't real. Maybe I'm just having a nightmare. Yeah, maybe I'm still asleep in the car and we're heading up the Blue Ridge Parkway. No, maybe I'm still lying in bed with Brett on my chest, napping like an infant minutes after being bottle-fed. But if that were the case, then how'd I come up with this preposterous story? I don't recall falling asleep. But perhaps it's true and I didn't find a scrapbook.*

I rubbed my eyes to see if anything would change. But nothing did. It seemed implausible that the entire Eldridge family would be a figment of my imagination if I were experiencing a nightmare. I hardly knew them. But yet, I couldn't think of any other explanation.

In dismay, I watched Lydia open the deck door and let the strange man in.

"Thanks, Mother," said the man as he stepped inside.

"What are you doing here?" she asked contemptuously.

As the man scratched his elbow, seemingly in wonder to her question, my attention drew to his clothing. He wore a striped short-sleeved shirt and cargo shorts. I reached for my head as the pulsating pain intensified. Brett tried to comfort me, but I pushed him away. I didn't want to be touched by anyone at that moment because I still felt out of it; sick, as if I were about to puke.

*How can he be standing across the room and sitting beside me, simultaneously?*

"What do you mean?" the doppelgänger continued addressing Lydia. "I came to see you. I deserve to be free, just like the rest of you." Then he locked eyes with me and began his approach. "And I see you have company."

As the man passed by Lydia on his way over to me, my mind reeled from the surreal event that was transpiring. The pain in my head felt unbearable, and I was convinced that it must all have been a dream. The Eldridge family appeared to be embroiled in some unknown mystery, and I couldn't comprehend what was happening. While still lost in my thoughts, the enigma seemed to be fast approaching. *I wonder if he's gonna take a seat next to me and maybe even hold my hand, merging with Brett and becoming one.*

It was all so bizarre.

Trippy.

Psychodelic.

My mind must have been playing tricks on me all because of the talk I had with Tammy. When the doppelgänger reached the table and extended a hand, I winced, fearing what would happen next if we were to touch. But as my heart continued to race and my head pounded uncontrollably, nothing happened. I didn't wake from a dream. I didn't even pass out. It was then I realized this wasn't a nightmare, and that, what took place was actually real.

Finally, the man who stood before me said, "Hi, I'm Connor. What's your name?"

# Chapter 9

In a frightened rage, I stood, kicking out the chair from under me. "Connor? Who the hell are you?"

I turned to Brett, disoriented. "Allison? It's okay, I can explain. Just relax... please."

Connor spoke again. "It's a pleasure to meet you, Allison."

I looked him up and down with disgust, ignoring his hand that he'd extended. "I'm not shaking that."

He returned his hand to his pocket and smiled. The kind of a smile that weirded you out. The type of subtle grin that carried a hint of menace and mystery as if at any moment he'd open up and tear into my jugular, basing the floor in a sea of crimson.

Still feeling disoriented and confused, I put my palm to my forehead. *Wow, lukewarm. That's weird.*

I tried to make sense of the situation that unfolded

before me but couldn't. I stepped away from the table, struggling to stay afloat. But as I did, the room began to close in on me and spin. I struggled to maintain my balance as the darkness engulfed me. *Stay calm. This isn't real. It can't be real. Just take a deep breath.*

In a daze, I stumbled out of the dining room, my head pounding furiously. Then I stormed toward the bathroom down the hall. Considering everything I'd seen, I felt an enclosed space such as the bathroom would be ideal at that moment. A small, confined space where I could regain my composure at my leisure.

"Allison, wait?" Brett called out as he grabbed my arm, but I pushed him away and continued down the hall, hugging the wall for support.

The spinning sensation only grew more intense, and I could feel the pressure in my head becoming unbearable. Any more and my eyes would bulge; possibly even pop out. Finally, when I reached the bathroom, I turned the knob, opened the door, and barricaded myself inside. With my body pressed firmly against the thick wooden door, I felt my end was nearing. That, because of Tammy and my anxiety-ridden suspicions, I believed I would die. If not by their hand, then from a panic attack.

I whispered, "What's happening to me?" as I ferociously gripped the vanity and stared at my skewed reflection. Suddenly, a sinister voice answered, "You've been drugged. HAHAHAHA!"

In one frantic, swift motion, I gripped the faucet, turned on the water, and splashed my face, splashing water everywhere around the vanity. But it didn't help. I stared at my reflection again, my vision doubling. *Stop playing tricks on me dammit! I wasn't drugged. They wouldn't do that to me. It's probably just my sinuses adjusting to the mountain air or something. Or perhaps... No, I couldn't be having an aneurysm, could I?*

Suddenly, a wave of nausea hit me, and my stomach gurgled like a washing machine in overdrive. I leaped toward the commode, dropped to my knees, and vomited just as I latched onto the porcelain. I heaved and heaved as a slew of menacing thoughts circled my mind. After I evacuated my dinner, I fell onto my back and put my hand to my head again to check for a fever. And yet, it was the same result.

*Calm down. You're just overreacting. Breathe. That's all you need to do. Breathe.* I drew in a breath and exhaled. Then I did another. But my heart didn't slow. *Maybe I need to take another Xanax.*

But then I remembered my medication was in my bag, in our room. *I can't make it there before passing out or throwing up again. I just can't.*

I sat up and my gaze landed on the medicine cabinet. Immediately, I reverted to the thought of being drugged. Using the commode and the vanity as a crutch, I scrambled to my feet and opened the cabinet in search of the answer. The Eldridge family could have easily laced my steak with something, using whatever was in the cabinet as a part of their concoction. Though, as I pulled the glass open, what I found threw me askew.

Multiple orange medication bottles were inside; Tramadol, Morphine, Oxycodone, and Ambien. The labels on the bottles blurred before my eyes as my head still pulsated with constant pressure. I squinted, trying to make out which medication was which, but my vision refused to cooperate.

Throughout the minutes, the pounding in my head only grew more intense. With no regret, I popped the cap to the first bottle I grabbed and tossed two pills in my mouth. Then I turned on the faucet, cupped my hands, and took a drink. But the pain didn't cease. My head still spun.

Perhaps taking the pills was a mistake. I stumbled backward, hitting the wall and elbowing the painting they'd hung there. The faucet was still running, the sound echoing in the small bathroom like a waterfall. I slumped down to the ground, the cool tiles offering a small comfort against my clammy skin. *What's happening to me? Is this it? Am I gonna die now?*

I felt like I was losing my grip on reality as if I were dying and would soon be ascending to the heavens. But why? Why die? Why now? I exercised on the daily, lifting overweight patients out of bed and to the bathroom, then back. I also ate fairly clean. At least, whenever I did eat, considering I barely had the opportunity since I was one of the many trauma nurses in the ER. The Eldridge family, the strange scrapbook, the hallucinations, the medication...

It all swirled around in my mind, like a vortex sucking me under.

A gentle knock at the door startled me, and I flinched. I

cowered against the cold porcelain of the toilet bowl, my mind in total chaos. I didn't know what was happening or who was at the door. But what I did know was my overarching desire to be in the confines of my home, tucked under the covers of my bed like I had as a child. But unfortunately, I couldn't. I drew in another breath and exhaled to calm my sporadic heart rate. But it was no use. There I was, trapped in a sprawling lakeside mansion in Huddleston as my body forsake me. So much for a wonderful weekend getaway.

"Allison?" Brett called, his voice muffled by the wooden door. "Please come out. I can explain everything."

I didn't respond.

I flushed the commode, sending the stench of half-digested steak and stomach acid down the drain. And after the swirling gargle of water ceased, he spoke again.

"Allison, please... I know it doesn't make any sense to you right now. But like I said, just come out and I'll explain everything."

Hesitantly standing from the floor in disarray, I leaned against the vanity and wiped my mouth with the back of my hand to rid myself of the rancid taste of salt and acid. The thought of Tammy's claims left me uneasy. *What happened in the past for her to have such bitterness toward them? Something strange had to have happened. Considering how sick I am only adds to my suspicion. I can't open the door. If I do, something bad will happen.*

There was another knock. But this time it was heavier and more jarring as if someone were trying to break in.

"Allison, dear?" Lydia said. "Are you okay?"

I cracked open the door and lied, "I'm fine."

Though my head wasn't spinning anymore, I still had an immense headache, and didn't understand the rationale behind my discomfort. Perhaps it was the elevation that had gotten to me. That and a mix of allergies. But damn, was my headache a bitch.

"Why don't you come on out here so we can talk," she urged while pushing the door open gently.

I hesitated at first, knowing that if I did, it could be the end of me. But then I thought, *I'm making a fool of myself right now. They must think I'm crazy; an anxious pill popper with a traumatic past. God, they won't let Brett marry me. No one in their right mind would. I just need to relax.*

The cadence of Lydia's voice beckoned me out of hiding. It had a soothing quality akin to a mother's gentle lullaby. Once out, she gripped my forearm and led me down the hall into the kitchen, where Jeff, Brett, and his look-alike were huddled together around the island.

"I can tell you're a little disoriented, Allison," she said after releasing me and moving to her husband's side.

"A little?" I repeated begrudgingly. "I'm more than that." Then I pointed to the enigma standing across from me. "Now does anyone care to explain to me who the hell this guy is?"

None of them answered. They just stared at me as if I were a deranged patient in an insane asylum acting out simply because I hadn't gotten to watch my show. Then, amid the silence, it dawned on me.

*Connor is Christina.*

Brett had lied to me. B + C wasn't an arborglyph for him and his girlfriend. No, it was for him and his twin brother, Connor.

My blood boiled and I turned to Brett. "Why didn't you tell me?"

"I... I—"

"You what, huh?" I got in his face. "You didn't think you needed to disclose that you had a brother at some point?" I raised my hand to strike him, but Lydia intervened, grabbing my wrist firmly to prevent me from making contact with his face.

"He didn't tell you because we told him not to, Allison," she said curtly.

I snatched my arm from her grasp and rubbed my wrist. "What? Why?"

"It's because they think I'm mentally unstable," Connor opined. He leaned against the sink and crossed his arms, seemingly distraught by the words.

"Shut it, Connor," Jeff barked. "We don't think you're mentally—"

"Yes, you do, Father," he interrupted. Then to me, he added, "All three of them do. That's why they locked me away in that prison."

"Central State Hospital is not a prison, Connor," Brett disputed.

"Yes, it is! But now I'm free... and healed." He smiled menacingly, much like the Joker from Batman.

Lydia approached Connor and grabbed his arm as if to

lead him to the dining area. "How about we get you some food, then we can work on getting you back."

He pulled away in an instant. "I'm not going anywhere, Mother. Especially back to that wretched place."

"But—"

"But nothing," he finished. Then he crossed the living area and marched outside onto the deck, leaving the door to slam with a heavy thud.

Lydia sighed and walked off as Jeff followed her. "Every time. It's like he's getting worse," she muttered.

"Honey, that's..." Jeff's voice trailed off as they disappeared into another part of the house.

At that moment, the veracity of Tammy's claim dawned on me. *This must be their secret. They had twins; one of which they confined to Central State Hospital. But why? Do they really consider him mentally unstable? That seems unbelievable, as Brett and Connor share the same genetic blueprint. Science doesn't lie. If one twin is mentally unwell, the other would be too, right? Brett hasn't displayed any signs of cognitive impairment in the year I've known him. I highly doubt his brother's ill.*

The new doubts swirling in my mind begged the question: Why did they lock Connor away in a mental institution? Here I was again, spiraling.

Brett gently touched my shoulder, drawing me out of my rambling thoughts. "Allison, I know you're probably wondering what the hell is going on right now."

I shrugged his hand off and crossed my arms. "Yes, I am, Brett. Now please, explain." I gestured toward the sofa and he led the way.

We sat.

He drew in a breath and exhaled. "I can't tell you everything, but—"

"Why can't you? If you want me to be in your life, then I need to know the truth." That was my chance to verify my suspicion of whether B + C really stood for Brett and Connor instead of Brett and Christina. "Does the C in that carving in the tree even stand for Christina? Or does it stand for Connor?"

He hesitated to answer, opening his mouth to speak and then not.

He'd given me the confirmation. "That's what I thought. I can't believe you lied to me. You know what,"—I shot up from the sofa and headed toward the stairs—"I'm going to bed."

I marched down to our room, my rage propelling me to break free from Brett's every attempt to stop me from doing so. No amount of strength would prevent me from isolating myself from the lies I'd been fed over the past year. I feared what else he'd lied about. It could have been anything; where he worked, his age, whether there was another woman. The possibilities were endless. I'd experienced enough deceit in my life already. I refused to endure anymore.

When I finally reached our room, I slammed the door to showcase my aggravation and locked it. I didn't even bother turning on the lights, just sat on the edge of the bed in total darkness with my head in my palms, the moon casting a twinkle of light through the window onto the floor before me.

As I sat there in quiet anguish, emotionally hurt from the betrayal of the man I'd grown to adore, I remembered the tattered scrapbook. Though I wanted to retrieve it, I feared Brett would come knocking on the door at any moment to make amends. Or at least try to because I wouldn't let him in.

I knew that if I wanted to investigate some more, I'd need to do it when everything cooled down. When everyone wasn't on edge from the unexpected return of Connor, and when my head wasn't in agonizing pain. And so I grabbed a few things from my suitcase, changed into my silk nightgown, and popped an Ambien. Then I unlocked the door, slipped under the covers, and drifted off to sleep.

# Part Two:
# Mindfulness

## Saturday, April 15th, 2023

"The best way out is always through."
- Robert Frost

# Chapter
# 10

THE FOLLOWING MORNING, I awoke to the sound of mournful weeping. And as I lay there, eyes closed, trying to drift back off to sleep, I couldn't. His muffled sobs permeated the room, echoing faint hums like your neighbor's lawnmower at sunrise on a Saturday.

I opened my eyes and rolled over to investigate. Brett sat on the edge of the bed, huddled over with his elbows that rested on his knees with his face buried in his palms. He sobbed hysterically. I couldn't fathom why he was in such distress. *Am I the reason he's crying? I hope I didn't toss and turn all night, waking him over and over again like a newborn teething. Maybe I screamed myself awake again.*

I scratched the back of my head, failing to recall if I had. *Perhaps his parents expressed their skewed opinions of me after I'd gone to bed. Yeah, they probably deterred him from marrying me. It's not like I wanna get married right now anyway, but still... They probably said I wasn't a good enough prospect. That I'd come with a heap of problems. Was my behavior that questionable last night?*

Even if they said I'd come with a myriad of disorders, I had none. Parents hadn't possessed them either. My anxiety and insomnia derived from my traumas. Post-traumatic stress. Luckily, that couldn't be passed down. Not unless I were to traumatize my kids. No, post-traumatic stress could only be inherited through experience; a debilitating experience I wouldn't even wish on my greatest enemies.

As I slid out from under the covers, moved closer, and rested my hand on his shoulder, I thought, *Perhaps he's upset about the state of Connor's well-being. Maybe even upset about how we met; how jarring the situation was for me; for the entire family really. Maybe he thinks I'm gonna break things off just because he lied. I mean, I am angry with him. Even feel betrayed. But I'm not gonna end things just like that. At least, not until we talk about it.*

Did I feel hurt? Yes.

But only because lying eventually led to more lies.

More deceit.

More headaches.

Only a very few individuals could sustain such deviousness.

"What's wrong, babe?" I asked.

His body was warm to the touch, and his breathing shallow. Every whimper he let out traveled up my arm and into my chest. The sound of his cries echoed in the silence of the room, tugging at my heartstrings. It was as if his pain was my pain, his worry my worry, and his regret my regret. I felt like an empath, experiencing every emotion he was going through. And yet, I still had no idea what was bothering him.

"C'mon, babe... talk to me."

He turned to face me, his expression stone-cold, as if he'd retreated into himself; a foster child meeting a potential adopting couple for the first time. He didn't say a word, just held my gaze with a look of shame. Had he done something wrong? Was that why he was crying? His eyes were red and swollen, evidence of the emotional turmoil he'd been going through.

I had no clue how long he'd been sobbing. It could have been an hour or two. I craned my neck back toward the clock on the nightstand. It was 7:20 a.m. *If he'd been doing this for the past two hours, I surely would have woken up earlier. So, it couldn't have been that long.*

"Brett, please answer me," I pleaded. "What happened? Why are you crying?"

"He... he... Connor..." Brett sniffled and wiped his nose, unable to finish his sentence.

I shot to the edge of the bed and wrapped my arms around him, caressing him with a mother's care. "Connor, what? What did he do?"

Brett had given me nothing, leaving my mind to spiral with assumptions and accusations. I feared the worst. Connor had murdered his parents and fled. Perhaps he'd harmed an officer who'd tried to bring him back to the mental institution, and now there was a body bleeding out on the kitchen floor, a knife protruding from its chest, a puddle forming.

My aimless thoughts ran wild, and with Brett's continued silence, I felt like I was falling into an abyss of uncertainty.

"Connor killed himself, Allison," Brett finally croaked.

Air escaped my lungs. "What? No, he couldn't have."

"It's true. He must've done it overnight while we were all asleep."

Brett stood from the bed and wiped his face on his collar. That was when I noticed he was already dressed. Strange. I'd been so roped up in the situation that I hadn't even paid attention. And yet, when I circled my hand along his upper back to calm him, I hadn't felt the lush fabric of his peach polo.

Thudding footsteps overhead caught my attention as he exited the room. With the door left wide open, I could sense where they were and overheard the mumbling. It seemed as if they were in the kitchen or the living area. I could make out Lydia and Jeff's voices, but the others were unfamiliar. Despite the muffled tones permeating the home, I managed to make out certain words—phrases, not entire sentences. Things like, "Where were you at..." and "Do you have any idea..."

It was the police.

I'd heard those phrases many times before in the emergency room when officers questioned victims and their families in search of any possible information that could lead to the suspects responsible for their misfortune.

In my navy, silk nightgown, I reluctantly rose and left the room, ascending the stairs to find a somber scene unfolding in the kitchen. There were three officers; each with distinct features. One looked extremely older than the other two considering his face bore many wrinkles. Perhaps he was their commanding officer, teaching them the ropes. And with his graying hair and mustache, I assumed his retirement was underway.

They were gathered around the island, their expressions stern and heavy with grief. Tears flowed from Lydia's eyes, drenching her cheeks, while Brett and Jeff comforted her with gentle touches and tissues. All three officers suddenly turned to me. All but one turned back to the family as they were in mid-conversation.

He looked to be the youngest of the three. Also seemed to have stopped listening to his fellow officer ramble on about the supposed death I'd just learned about. His piercing gaze trailed down my toned thighs, past my stupendous calves, and to my white-painted toenails.

Perhaps he was fond of my fairly revealing nightwear, considering it insinuated I had wide hips with how snugly I'd pulled the sash to ensure it didn't flap open. I was disgusted by how he bore into me as if I were some dancer on stage at a strip club, satisfying his carnal fantasies. And so I turned toward the steps to head back to the room and change. I refused to be eye-fucked by some stranger who wanted nothing more but to see me naked.

But as I gripped the banister, he called out to me. "Wait!"

I tensed, my heart skipping a beat. *Why didn't I take my meds before I came up here?*

The weight of the situation settled on my shoulders as I braced myself for what was to come. I knew that being new to this family's troubles would lead me to be no help to the police. However, I highly doubted the family had disclosed I knew nothing of Connor and his mental illness, which meant I'd soon be questioned.

As I stood there, crippled by the fear of what I'd be asked, the officer who'd made me uncomfortable approached and said, "Ma'am, a word?"

I slowly turned and immediately demanded, "I want to see him. Connor, that is. Show me his body, then I'll answer your questions, okay?"

The officer drew in a breath and looked at me with a mixture of confusion and doubt, one eyebrow raised. It was as though he couldn't understand why I wanted to see the deceased. I assumed he'd already realized I wasn't a member of the family, considering I hadn't shed a single tear or acted distraught. I was just the girlfriend who got caught up in the chaos of this dysfunction. And yet for a moment, I too, wondered why I would even want to see the corpse. Maybe I was just in disbelief.

"You did want to question me to see if I knew of any reason why he'd want to take his life, right?" I asked.

He nodded, then raised his arm and gestured toward the deck door in heed of my request. "Now if you will, please follow me."

Though it was early in the morning, time hadn't

prevented the sun from shining down on the back of the home, illuminating the entire living room and part of the kitchen through the large windows that scaled the ceiling. I wasn't upset about it though. If anything I preferred it that way, because then the afternoons would be pleasant and calm, not scorching like the front of the house would be.

In bare feet yet again, I followed the officer outside, my hands tightly wrapped around my torso to prevent any mishap of my nightgown flapping open and flashing someone. Encapsulated by the sun's rays, I shielded my eyes, where I noted two more officers down on the boat dock, pointing at fish in the lake. Curiosity struck me. *I hope Connor isn't down in the lake.*

"Ma'am?" the officer called out to me. "This way."

I followed the man off the deck and down the breezeway onto the stone patio that led to the detached garage. When Brett and I first arrived yesterday, he hadn't shown me what was inside. Even when I'd spent time with Lydia, piecing together puzzles and discussing art, she never mentioned anything about that building. I assumed it was just another storage place. For their cars and maybe a jet ski or two. Yet, when we turned the corner, I found that the building also doubled as a living quarters.

Many people were coming and going from the side entrance above the garage; one officer and two paramedics. Who would have thought there would be an entire crew of personnel who'd come to a home following a death?

"I hope you're prepared," the officer said.

"I'm a nurse, so I've seen a lot. This shouldn't faze me."

Though many people passed away from natural causes and accidents, suicide was a rare occasion at the hospital. But that's because most of the time it happened away from the public eye in the confines of solitude. You never truly know what to expect to find in the event of a suicide. It's a whole different level of tragedy. The thought of someone intentionally ending their life was hard to comprehend. Nevertheless, I pushed myself to face the situation head-on, knowing I needed to see for myself to kill my disbelief.

We stopped at the door and allowed the paramedics to enter with the gurney. I turned to the officer after noting he didn't enter afterward. He peered down at me with his chiseled chin and modelesque cheekbones and gestured me in.

I had no clue what I was about to see. It could have been anything. Perhaps Connor could have slit his throat with a knife, painting the walls and carpet crimson. He could have cut vertically down his forearms and shed his skin like a snake, exposing his bones like a deranged person on drugs; or worse, sent a bullet right between the eyes, spraying the pleasant painting Lydia might have hung on the wall behind him with a combination of brain matter and blood. Unfortunately, each scenario ultimately ended with him dying. A painful sight to imagine for anyone.

As I entered the room, an immediate stillness fell over me. Connor had killed himself in a way I hadn't expected. Among the bed, beige carpet, navy-blue walls, and miniature kitchen, he was hanging from the ceiling in the middle of it all. He had hung himself along the exposed beam.

The place was a studio guest room with stairs off to the side that led down to the car bay below. In hindsight, it was the perfect place to take his life, away from everyone else given the seclusion. No one could stop him. He had absolute freedom to do as he pleased. Sadly, he chose this.

Disappointment swelled in my chest. Lydia and Jeff had made a mistake. They shouldn't have put him in here, hidden away from their supervision, knowing damn well of his acrimonious state. I couldn't imagine the mental strain he must have endured while locked up.

The fear.

The nightmares.

The mistreatment, if there so happened to be any.

Why would they not watch him?

The only sound in the room came from the paramedics as they went about their job, cutting the body down and moving it onto the gurney. The room was frigid, and the air felt thick and heavy. It was as if life had been drained from it, much like the life from Connor's body.

I tried to avert my gaze from the sight before me, but my eyes were drawn to it like a magnet. It was a gruesome sight, yet there was a strange sense of peace about it. His body was suspended and very pale; his expression dull. His eyes were closed, thankfully. It was a redolent vibe that calmed my nerves. *I wonder what led Connor to give up. What could have caused him to feel there was no way out?*

I quickly inspected the room, wondering if there were

cameras hidden somewhere in the shadows. That would have made sense. That would have made it easy for Lydia and Jeff to watch him. But I found none. Come to think of it, if there had been cameras mounted somewhere, they would have prevented this tragedy from happening. Would have allowed his parents to rush out of the house and storm up here just as he lost consciousness, cut him down, and resuscitate him before he drifted off into oblivion.

I exited the garage just as the paramedics zipped up the body bag. It was clear this weekend was turning out to be a disaster.

# Chapter
# 11

"H OW WELL DID YOU KNOW C ONNOR?" the officer asked me.

We were back inside the house, in the living room, sitting on the sofa with my back to the kitchen and the blinding sun to my left. Just me, him, and two other officers who lingered around the home. I hadn't a clue where the rest of the family had run off to. Maybe they had gone to cover their tracks on whatever secret they were hiding. If what they were hiding was connected to Connor.

"I just met him last night during dinner," I admitted. "I didn't even know he existed until then."

"Really? That seems strange, don't you think?"

For some reason, I felt his tone implied I had murdered Connor and feigned ignorance. "I do. But it's quite simple; Brett neglected to tell me he had a brother before we came up for the weekend."

The officer scribbled away in his notepad. "And the reason you two came up for the weekend was?"

"To celebrate our one-year anniversary and to meet his parents."

He scribbled some more in his notepad. "Tell me, did Connor seem odd to you, or acted weird in some way or another? Something that may have been a warning sign perhaps?"

I shook my head. "No. He seemed normal."

Immediately following my answer, a tinge of guilt bubbled in my stomach. I had lied to him, but it was for the best. Because of my altered state last night, Connor *was* acting weird. But not in the way one would think. Because I thought he wasn't real—a hallucination, a figment of my imagination—I believed everything was weird; off; odd. However, I knew better than to tell the officer that.

If I had, it would have made me seem like an unreliable witness, or worse, a lunatic. Which I was not. It might have even given the impression that I had killed Connor and hung him up like an ornament, framing it as a suicide. But I wouldn't do that. I had no reason to, let alone was creative enough to stage a scene such as that. I knew that much. Considering the unsettling situation, I was just struggling to come to terms with everything I'd experienced, much like the rest of the family. I just wasn't as bothered by it.

"Did you so happen to wake up at any point throughout the night?" the officer continued. "You know... to relieve yourself?" He shot a glance at my legs, then back to my face.

But we didn't lock eyes. Instead, he hovered around my lips. "Or did you hear anything that might have woken you up?"

I tucked a few loose hairs behind my ear. "No, unfortunately not."

I highly doubted I would have heard anything, given the distance between the garage and our room. Even with me being a light sleeper.

The officer drummed his pen against his notepad, signaling that we were getting nowhere. But what I could do? I wasn't going to tell him that Connor was acting crazy, simply because I was acting crazy. What I thought was weird might have been normal. Everything might have been perfectly fine, and I was just experiencing something I'd never experienced before. Some overly dramatic panic attack. A nightmare. Even an out-of-body experience. It could have been anything.

Not once in my life had I ever felt an immense headache such as that. Perhaps it was caused by my anxiety. I don't know why, but I couldn't make the distinction between Connor and Brett being twins at the time. Not until I had vomited and taken a random pill. And me being unaware of his existence, only exacerbated the situation.

"I know this might sound rude, sir," I said, "but what's the reason for all of this? Like... he's dead already. There's nothing else we can do."

As if to cop a quick feel of my shaved legs, he rested his hand on my thigh and said, "Ma'am, this is just standard procedure for something like—"

I pushed away his hand before he could even finish his statement.

"I apologize for invading your personal space. But to answer your question, we have to do a check to make sure there weren't any signs that could've prevented this unfortunate event from happening."

"Don't you think the biggest sign would have been him running away?"

The officer didn't respond. Perhaps he agreed with me. That whenever someone escaped from an institution, they were already on edge; ready to be free. That the simple act of rebellion conveyed their cry for help. A telltale sign of someone's intent to harm not only others but also themselves just to alleviate their suffering.

I often thought about how suffocating it would be to live in a place where my every move was under scrutiny, a mental prison that robbed me of control and autonomy, reducing me to a mere puppet. The thought of being denied the simple pleasures—like savoring a meal of your choice, venturing out for an early morning hike on a trail, or even indulging in a lazy morning—felt like a slow erosion of the soul. It was the yearning for freedom that resonated most with me.

But then, on the darker side of those thoughts, I'd sometimes find myself contemplating the concept of escape through the unthinkable. The notion of suicide as a means to liberate oneself from such confines is dark. It's a glimpse into the extent one might go to reclaim control; to reclaim their own life; to reach true freedom.

Wanting to be done with the discussion of death and sorrow, I stood, pulled my sash as tight as I could, and said, "Are we done, officer? I don't think I'll be of much help since I didn't know him."

"We're done here," he said, closing his notepad.

"Thank you."

After leaving the officer on the sofa, I headed downstairs to our room to get dressed and go for a quick walk to expunge myself from the sullen mood that begot the morning.

———

EXPERIENCING the gentle breeze flowing through my auburn hair as I stepped out the front door calmed me. The fresh air I thought for sure would help clear my head. I needed to get away from the craziness and peculiar events that had occurred at the Eldridge residence over the past day because everything seemed a little too much for me to handle at that moment.

It was strange enough that I'd uncovered lies within the family, and now a death. I feared what more I'd find if I searched. Distancing myself from it all to gather my thoughts seemed to make the most sense.

I made my way down the paved driveway and scanned the scene, noting the four police cruisers and the ambulance parked out front by the side entrance of the garage. The paramedics were loading Connor's lifeless body into the back of the van. As I continued walking, I also noted an unfamiliar pickup truck parked beside Brett's Acura.

It was a 90's Ford Ranger. White; single cab. I knew it was the second generation because my father had one just like it, right before I went away to college. Last I remember, his was in way better condition than the one that stood before me. This one showed signs of neglect, with surface rust around the back wheel wells and dried mud coating the front bumper. *I wonder whose truck that is. Maybe it belongs to Brett's parents. On second thought, I doubt it.*

The poor state of the truck couldn't have belonged to Jeff, simply because he didn't strike me as someone who would allow his vehicle to deteriorate to such a degree. But, if in the case it were his, where could it have come from?

When we arrived, the vehicle wasn't there, and his parents were out on a walk. Certainly, they wouldn't have gone anywhere and I not notice. Could they have? No. They were simply enjoying the weather out on the boat dock and entertaining me with food and puzzles. Then I thought about Connor. *Maybe he used the truck to get here.*

I pulled out my cell and Googled Central State Hospital as I continued onto the main road, heading away from the Eldridge estate. The hospital was located in Petersburg, two and a half hours away from Huddleston. *Connor couldn't have walked, let alone taken a train since the map shows no train station nearby. Perhaps he purchased a bus ticket. But where could he have gotten the money? I highly doubt he stole cash from one of the staff before his escape. Maybe he robbed someone after breaking out.*

I imagined him dressed in some thin light colored sweatsuit and barefoot, walking into a gas station a mile or two away from the hospital, wielding a rusty knife he'd found somewhere behind a dumpster in a back alley, and holding up some poor middle-aged woman who worked behind the counter.

I almost turned back and inspected the white pickup, searching for keys or any signs of forced entry or altering, like hot wiring, but ultimately decided against it. I suspected Connor had enough know-how to steal a vehicle, just as I'd learned from my college roommate, who had a penchant for trouble.

She came from a large family, with four older brothers who had all been in trouble with the law for various offenses, including theft and burglary. This poor example set by her siblings influenced her to follow in their footsteps, leading her to spend many nights in lockup at the local sheriff's office. It wasn't uncommon for her to disappear for days at a time. And to think, I hadn't seen her since we graduated.

As I strolled along, lost in my musings, the stillness of the moment was interrupted by the sudden rumble of several patrol cars speeding past me, closely followed by the ambulance. The sight led me to think of Lydia and how distraught she must have felt, knowing one of her sons was now dead.

The emotions that were etched on her face were a clear indication of her distress; a mix of regret, disappointment, and grief. Despite trying to empathize with her, I couldn't fully comprehend the pain of losing a loved one; a child, a parent, or even a cousin. Sadly, my grandparents had passed long before I was born, so I never experienced the warmth of their love, the comfort of their embrace, or the grief followed by their passing. And my parents were thankfully still alive. I just hadn't spoken to them in years.

*Losing a son must be tough. The emotional weight of regret and guilt for not having done better at raising them must be unbearable. I'm kind of surprised that his parents took such a drastic step and institutionalized him, given his charming demeanor. I wonder what he did to deserve such treatment.*

Lydia's demeanor was one of distress and sorrow, but yet, I couldn't shake off the feeling that there was something more to the story as if she was playing a role, putting on a façade for the police, and possibly me. Anything was possible.

*They locked Connor up like a rabid animal. But why? Perhaps uncovering the truth will tell me. It may even be somewhere in the scrapbook. Even though, deep down, I don't wanna know, something tells me it needs to be done. I just hope my secret doesn't come to light in the process.*

# Chapter 12

I'D BEEN WALKING for a while now, but couldn't say for sure how far I'd gone or where I was. I must have been walking for at least twenty minutes, and at my urgent nurse's pace, I'd lost sight of the house completely. Nothing but a shroud of greenery surrounded me.

In the distance, a stop sign at the intersection of a T-shaped road about twenty meters ahead offered some solace. But not much. Considering I was asleep when we arrived the day before, I had failed to pay close attention to the path we took on the way in or the surrounding houses. As I continued walking, I worried I might end up lost and have to knock on a stranger's door to request directions back to the Eldridge estate.

Though I had only made two turns so far, I was unsure if I'd find my way back easily. Hopefully, Brett wasn't worried about me, wondering where I'd run off to. I'd hate to give him a reason to come looking for me much like a concerned parent would who feared their child had gotten kidnapped by a pedophile in a sprinter van, never to be seen again. That was the last thing he needed.

*Though if Brett does search for me, it'll surely prove he cares about me; more than his parents cared about Connor, I'd imagine. But that's beside the point. I need to get back. I've been gone too long. It's time to enjoy the rest of the weekend.*

I turned to head back and took a few steps. Suddenly, a shiny Cadillac sedan screeched to a halt beside me and I jumped into the grass. It was dark gray with heavily tinted windows, giving it a mysterious and sleek appearance. It looked like it had just been washed, with a polished sheen that was hard to miss.

*What the hell is their problem?* I thought as I strode on. But with every step I took, I found the car creeping in the same fashion; crawling like an infant, slow and steady. The hairs on the back of my neck shot up as I wondered who could be inside. *This is it, isn't it? They're gonna kidnap me and traffic me. I guess Tammy was right. How could I have been so naïve?*

I rubbed my clammy fingers along my black leggings nervously as I feared who may be inside the Cadillac, watching me with prying eyes. And though I'd taken my anxiety medication, I still pictured the worst; the backdoor springing open and a tall, muscular man jumping out and groping me in a bearish grasp, pressing a white raggedy cloth laced with chloroform against my face in an attempt to subdue me. I'd flail like a fish, hoping another passing car would see the event and stop to prevent them from kidnapping me but, with my luck, that car would never come.

The winding sound of the passenger's window rolling down caught my ear and I glanced over at the vehicle. Though I wanted to remain fixed on the road ahead, my curiosity got the better of me. And when my gaze landed on Tammy sitting in the driver's seat, my nerves settled.

"I'm glad to see you're still alive," she said with a grin.

She was wearing her sunglasses again, so I couldn't see all of her smug expression.

*Still alive?*

Her arrogance was despicable. The way she seemed to derive pleasure from making me uncomfortable and anxious was sickening. I was certain she reveled in the fear she instilled in young women whom she met with her twisted scenarios of betrayal, violence, and exploitation.

I balled my fists and prepared to give her a piece of my mind. "Where do you get off?"

She tapped the brakes, bringing the car to a halt. "Excuse me?"

"You heard me. Because of you, I haven't enjoyed one minute of this weekend!"

She scoffed. "It's not my fault you're dating a psychopath."

I rested my hand on the roof of the car and leaned in through the window. "You've got some nerve."

"Honey, I'm just looking out for your best interest.

That's all. Nothing else. Now have you done any snooping yet?"

Her sudden change in topic caught me off guard. I had assumed she was just taunting me for her own amusement as she'd done with every other woman whom Brett had supposedly brought home. I even half expected her to speed off, running over my trainers in the process. But yet, she didn't move an inch. Rather stared at me with intrigue.

Tammy seemed genuinely interested in my response. Perhaps she had a soft spot for me after all. Or maybe she just wanted to know if I had for some twisted reason. Either way, I indulged her curiosity.

"I found out Brett had a twin."

"Had?"

Tammy averted her gaze from me to out her front windshield. I turned to find a patrol car approaching us from the opposite direction. It must have been the last one, knowing the ambulance and other officers had gone already.

I raised my hand and waved as it passed, then looked back at Tammy as she repeated herself once more.

"Connor died," I said. "Killed himself last night."

She gasped. "But he was locked up."

"He escaped from Central State Hospital yesterday. This must've been the first place he visited." Then something clicked, which led me to ask, "Wait... how'd you know about Connor? You didn't mention him before."

"I... I..." She couldn't get the words out. It was as if she was trying to come up with something on the spot.

Something that would have convinced me to stop asking questions or change the subject. Then, finally, she said, "I can't explain it right now. Just know that I've done my own snooping, okay?"

She anxiously looked in her rearview mirror as if she was checking to see if she'd been followed, then refocused on me. "Well, I've got to get going." Leaning across the armrest, she popped open the glovebox, pulled out scrap paper and a pen, and wrote her number while saying, "Give me a call if you ever feel unsafe, okay?"

"Unsafe?" I repeated, wondering what she meant.

Without a word, she reached out and handed me the piece of paper before quickly rolling up the window and speeding away. Watching the Cadillac disappear into the distance, I wondered, *What the fuck was that?*

———

UPON MY RETURN from my walk, the house appeared deserted. I entered through the front, much like I'd done when I left, and now I stood in the grand foyer. I managed a sweeping panorama of the entire space—from the living room to the kitchen, the back deck, and the dining hall— and yet, no one was there.

I headed toward the living room and stumbled upon a room with a swath of plastic covering the opening. I couldn't resist the urge to peek inside as if I were a child exploring the depths of a makeshift fort. I pulled back the plastic and peered in. The space was stripped bare, devoid of decor, and the curtains were drawn, allowing no light to filter in. After straining to get a better view, I made out the scaffolding on the far end of the room and an assortment of tools scattered across the floor. The burgundy walls added to the darkness. I drew in a breath, catching the sweet scent of fresh lumber. Then I spotted them off to the side.

*Hmm, this wasn't on the tour. I guess Lydia decided against showing me this part of the house. I wonder why they're undergoing a renovation though. This place doesn't need it. It's flawless. Why make a change? I guess I'll ask Lydia later.*

I stepped back and let the plastic curtain fall back into place. Then I wandered over to the floor-to-ceiling windows that overlooked the deck and found Brett down on the boat dock fishing.

Despite the recent tragedy, he appeared to be at ease, reeling in his line with practiced ease. I placed my hand along the glass and thought, *There's no way he's come to terms with Connor's death already. It's only been a few hours. Maybe he witnessed enough of Connor's agony over the years and is relieved that his suffering has ended. Whichever, I should check up on him.*

I stepped out onto the deck, descended the steps, and headed toward the boat dock. I knew a cloud of grief billowed over Brett like a hook to a fish, trying to find the meaning of it. Connor's death was a subtle reminder that in the journey of a relationship, there's no shortcut more valuable than the path of shared vulnerability. The exchange of confidences, the seeking of opinions on troubling issues—whether good or bad—it's in these moments that we truly bridge the gaps that hold fears, resentments, and pains. These conversations, where walls break down, become the foundation of something stronger. And when I finally reached Brett, he'd caught a fish and whipped it out of the water.

"Nice catch," I said, coming up behind him as he started to unhook it.

"Not as nice as they used to be," he replied absently before tossing the fish back into the water.

"So much for lunch." I tried to joke, but it seemed to fall flat. And when he turned to face me, he bared a cold expression, which assured me he was going through a difficult time.

As he loaded another worm onto the hook, I thought, *He's still hurting. Maybe if I can convince him to take me out onto the water, he'll open up. Yeah, that sounds promising. I can see it now, both of us sitting on the back of his parents' boat and basking under the sun as the water flows through our toes. I know I'd enjoy that. Why won't he?*

Brett released the hook, pulled back his arm, and absently said, "Watch out. I don't want to hook yah."

I grabbed the end of the rod before he tossed his line back out, grabbed his arm, and caressed his side. "Let's go for a ride around the lake, babe. I want to see how fast your parents' boat goes."

"I'd rather just fish."

"I don't care. Fishing's boring. But you know what isn't?"

"What?"

I gazed deep into his eyes and smirked. "Sex. And we can do that out on the lake, where no one can see us."

He looked out at the water for a moment as if in careful deliberation. Then he turned back to me and smiled. "Well, that does seem more fun than fishing. Let's go." Brett put away his fishing gear in the small shed attached to the dock, then approached the miniature yacht, where he untied the rope from around a large cleat bolted to the dock. When he finally boarded the cruiser, he turned to me and extended a hand with a gesture of invitation. "Watch your step. I don't want you falling in."

"You don't want me falling in?" I repeated playfully as I gripped his hand. "Are you not gonna jump in and save me if I do?"

"You know it," he answered, hoisting me onto the boat with ease.

In fear I'd fall back, I wrapped my arms around him, sending our gazes to meet. "That's not funny," I muttered.

He grinned. "Good, because I wasn't trying to be. Now, have you ever been on a boat before?"

"No."

"Well, then"—he reached into one of the side compartments under one of the seats and fished out a life jacket—"you need to wear this, in case you fall overboard."

He handed me the flotation device and I slipped it over my head. Afterward, I got comfortable on the seat nearest the helm. "This is quite the boat, Brett."

He turned the key in the ignition and fired up the engine, sending a rumbling roar to the fiberglass beneath us. "It sure is. My father bought it a couple of years ago." He pulled back on the throttle and slowly reversed the yacht away from the covered dock. "He loves being on the water, and I don't blame him. Being out here is like a different feeling altogether."

While looking out at the water, I absently said, "I can only imagine."

Brett turned the boat away from the house and aimed the bow toward the mountain. Then he glanced back at me. "You ready to see how fast this thing can go?"

I sent him a chipper nod.

"Hang on!"

He jammed the throttle forward and the motor roared to life, creating a deafening sound that resonated across the lake like a wolf's howl in the woods. Within seconds, the boat picked up speed, and the force of the motion jerked me back into my seat. We glided across the water's surface as if we were Jesus himself, walking on water. We passed by a neighboring yacht where a group of kids were at play. I turned back to look at them as we sped by, waiting to see the small waves our boat created disturb their pleasant gathering. I laughed as each kid got smacked in the face by the rushing waves.

After doing a giant loop around the lake, passing by many anchored boats, we started going in a straight line. Despite the constant bumps and ripples of the water, I got to my feet and clung to Brett's side. I thought if only I could get to the bow of the boat, then maybe... just maybe I could be like Rose from the Titanic, hanging off the edge as the wind encompassed me. But I knew at the rate of speed at which we were going, I wouldn't be able to manage it. I'd most likely fall overboard before making it to the front. So, instead, I remained put, smiling at what fun I was having.

Eventually, after following the shoreline for a while, Brett pulled back on the throttle and slowed the boat to a gentle stop. Once we were stagnant, he turned to me where I noted the sudden change in his expression. *He's smiling now, thank God. I guess it didn't take much convincing to get him to do that. Now let's see if he'll open up.*

"What a rush," he exclaimed, cutting power to the engine.

He came up to me and we locked lips.

"You sure seem chipper now," I said, pulling off my trainers, removing my socks, and balling them up before tucking them in my pocket.

"Yeah, I am," he answered. "And I'll be even better once this weekend is over."

I asked, "How so?" as I headed to the stern, sat on the edge, rolled up my leggings, and dipped my feet in the water.

"Because then I'll have you all to myself."

I giggled and kicked my feet, creating ripples. I was beginning to think this weekend was looking up. That, despite all the loss and strangeness I'd experienced so far, the remaining two days would be perfect, devoid of any mishaps or strange occurrences.

I looked back over my shoulder and found Brett smiling at me.

Infatuated by his gleaming smile and hazel eyes, I flirtatiously smiled back at him. "What?"

"Oh, nothing."

"Aren't you gonna join me?"

He removed his socks, then he came over and sat beside me, also dipping his feet in the lake. I leaned my head against his shoulder, finding comfort in his closeness. It was as if were finally alone in a place where we could both be vulnerable.

The serene backdrop of the mountain and the lake on a cloudless day brought on such a sense of calm that I couldn't help but say, "I'm sorry, Brett. I'm sorry you lost your brother. I can't imagine what you're feeling right now."

"A mix of emotions and a stir of regret," he absently admitted while staring out at the thick brush that lined the shore. Then he peered down at me. "For the longest time, I wished I was an only child. Not someone who had to share their toys. But I guess in a way I got what I wanted." He looked back out at the water. "Now I resent that wish. Because I know I can't take it back."

I gently grabbed his chin and pulled him back toward me. "Did you ever visit him?"

"I'd hate to say it, but no, he didn't... I didn't visit."

"How come?"

He drew in a deep breath, then sighed. "To tell you the truth, I have no reason."

"That can't be true."

Brett broke from my grasp and used his hand to shield

his face from the sun. "Well, if anything, I just didn't want to see him. Didn't want to entertain the thought that he was actually ill. It was already hard enough knowing my brother had undergone such hell in the past. Perhaps you could say I just couldn't bear to see him in that light."

"Yet somehow, you were okay with your parents locking him up in the first place," I opined.

Brett jarringly pulled his feet from the water, turned, and stood. *Ah, shit. I shouldn't have said that. Stupid, stupid, stupid. So much for having him open up.*

I'd pried too hard and now he'd closed himself off like a dam. How could I have been so callous and naïve to his feelings? I slipped my feet from the water, spun around, and watched him return to the helm and restart the motor.

"I don't want to talk about this anymore, Allison. Now let's change the subject, okay?" he barked over the chugging engine.

I shot up from the deck and stormed up to him. "Well, I don't want to, Brett. I'm sorry that he killed himself. I'm sorry that this entire weekend is probably ruined because of it. But I brought you out here for a reason. So we could talk. So I can make sure you're okay. Not brush things under the rug like most people do. It's important to address moments like these in a relationship. We need to have open and honest communication if we're going to make this work. We need to work through things together, not just ignore them and hope they go away. Remember, I'm here for you. I always have been." I reached for his forearm. "Now please, talk to me. I beg of you."

Brett was unresponsive. He just stood there, with his back to me, as if I'd done something wrong. As if I had hung myself from the top level of the boat and he was scared to look toward my lifeless body. Then suddenly, he started sniffling.

When he finally turned to me, his eyes glistened in the bright sun, tears streaming down his cheeks like rain on a window pane. "I'm sorry, but I'm not ready to talk just yet."

*I poured my heart into that speech, and all he can say is, "I'm sorry." What the fuck!* I felt the Brett I'd come to know over the past year was slowly slipping away, fading into dust before my eyes.

"I've never seen you like this before, Brett. I get it, you're hurt, but—"

"But nothing. I don't want to talk about it right now. Now just drop it already."

"Okay, okay," I said, slowly backing away and returning to my seat.

I leaned forward, sank my chin, pressed my elbows to my knees, and fell deep in thought, allowing the silence of the lake to envelop me. *Perhaps this weekend isn't going to end well. I guess Connor's death changes things. If Brett can't open up about this brother's death, then maybe he won't open up at all. Well, maybe he just needs some time. Yeah, everybody needs time. But time alone. Away from me. We might just break up.*

# Chapter 13

*THIS IS SO RIDICULOUS*, I thought, sitting with my arms crossed as Brett docked the boat and shut it off.

He'd given me the silent treatment the entire ride home and it infuriated me. The deceit was one thing. But the emotional disconnection between us was too much. I blamed myself for not having noticed sooner that Brett was a nice guy, who was clearly dealing with some deep-seated issues that required addressing. Perhaps I didn't notice sooner because we hadn't experienced such a devastating feat, such as his brother's suicide, together. Something like that certainly would have caught my attention if it had. But then I thought, *Maybe I'm being too harsh on him. After all, he did just lose his brother. Perhaps he does need more time.*

Brett left the helm, stepped onto the dock, and tied off the boat. I followed after him after returning my life jacket to the cubby below my seat. I thought to help him, to possibly cheer him up, but didn't, considering I knew nothing of the proper boating procedures and practices. I'd be damned if I were to improperly tie off a cleat and be the cause of how the yacht ended up damaged. So instead, I headed inside.

As I climbed the deck steps, I felt the best way to mitigate my frustration was to resume my quest for the truth. The truth that would hopefully uncover the underlying reasons for Brett's behavior, and possibly Connor's death.

I pushed open the deck door, set my trainers and socks aside on the floor, and looked around for Lydia and Jeff but they were nowhere to be found.

"Hello?" I called out into the silence. "Is anyone here?"

No response.

I peered back out the windows toward the deck and found Brett retrieving his pole from the small shed so he could return to fishing. *Well at least he's doing something that calms him*, I thought. *Hmm... Maybe now's the best time to look through the scrapbook again.*

I headed to the kitchen to grab some water to quench my thirst. After sifting through the cupboard for a glass, I filled it from the tap on the refrigerator. As the water trickled into the glass, I noted a clattering sound coming from outside. I turned toward the commotion on my left, leading me to peer out the window above the sink.

There, was a direct view of the side entrance of the garage, the same doorway I'd entered earlier when I'd asked to see Connor's body. Jeff and Lydia were coming and going, stacking cardboard boxes and milk crates outside on the walkway. Some of the boxes looked old and dusty like they'd been in storage for many years. Others bore stains in some places as if they had suffered water damage.

*I wonder what they're filled with. It could be anything; magazines, clothes, even Connor's old belongings. If I search through those boxes, I'll surely find something. Secrets or even—*

Droplets of water splashed onto my bare toes, pulling me from eavesdropping. I'd been so engrossed in my thoughts about Brett's parents and my unrelenting urge to uncover the truth and unravel the web of deceit that I'd forgotten about the glass I was filling. I yanked away from the tap in a knee-jerk reaction, sending water cascading onto the floor.

"Shit!" I muttered.

I set the glass on the edge of the counter and rushed to grab some paper towels to sop up the water. As I dropped to my knees to clean up the mess I'd made, a moment of déjà vu overtook me. A memory that dated back to around six months before I'd ended things with Ryan. This was before my realization that he was exploiting me, and before I came to terms with the fact he was resistant to change.

I'd walked into our home after a grueling double shift at the hospital.

"Ryan?" I called out, closing the front door and setting the lock.

No response.

"Ryyyyannnn?" I called again. "Where are you?"

His car was in the driveway. So, with no response, I

assumed he was just in bed; asleep. Considering the time of day—being quite early in the morning—I had no doubt he was. And so I set my overnight bag down near the door and kicked off my clogs, then headed toward the kitchen to cook myself breakfast.

I left the foyer and stumbled across the mess Ryan had left behind in the living room; a mountain of empty beer cans, a whiskey bottle that had leaked onto the carpet, and a half-eaten box of pizza resting on the coffee table. *What a mess.*

But that wasn't the worst of it. When I finally reached the kitchen, I found him passed out on the linoleum, head slack, and another empty bottle of whiskey beside him. In nurse mode still, I rushed to grab a glass from the cupboard, flicked on the faucet, filled it from the tap, and set it on the counter above him. Then I sat him up and pressed two fingers to his throat. Thuwwmp, thuwwmp.

I let out a sigh of relief. *Thank God you're still alive.*

I tapped his face a couple of times, but he didn't budge.

"Come on Ryan, wake up!"

When I tapped his face a second time, his eyelids flickered. Suddenly, his eyes sprang open like a jack in the box. He startled and jerked back, slamming his head into the cabinetry behind him. Not a second later, the glass I'd poured tumbled to the floor and shattered like a grenade. Water and shards flew in every direction.

Ryan was drenched.

Upon my tired return, I hadn't paid attention to where

I'd placed the glass (it having been set toward the edge), and as a result, it fell when he bumped the cabinet.

In a rage, he struck me upside the head and yelled, "You, stupid bitch! Clean that shit up."

I was in disbelief. And as he got to his feet, I couldn't respond. He'd hit me yet again for simply checking on him and making sure he was still alive. Had I intended for him to get wet? No. Yet, somehow, it had happened. That still didn't call for a means to hit me. But, me being as naïve as I was, I stood, grabbed the dishtowel I'd draped over the oven handle and got cleaning.

Ryan left the kitchen to change into something dry as I was on my hands and knees. I couldn't fathom how I was reprimanded for something he did. For simply caring about him. *How inconsiderate of him,* I thought.

I wasn't angry then because I was naïve and ignorant to his ways. But I felt differently about the whole situation the following day. More so, because I had to lie to my coworkers when they asked about the bruise he'd given me, using generic excuses such as, "I slipped and fell," or, "I got in a car accident," because it was still visible under the copious amounts of makeup I'd put on to cover it. And it had remained as such for a week until it eventually healed. I knew they had their reservations about the situation, but I didn't care.

I was in love at the time.

A surge of warmth within my chest snapped me back to reality. I'd almost finished drying the floor now, which led a smile to tug at the corners of my lips. It was a gentle reminder of how I'd managed to escape the abuse and rid myself of the burden and ceaseless discord that had plagued me for years.

The night I left, I'd made a vow—to never again bear the weight of another's violence. *No longer will I surrender my power, tip-toe on eggshells, and fear punishment for the slightest misstep. I've embraced my freedom, shattered the chains that held me, and reclaimed my strength. Because only in times of adversity do we truly find ourselves. I am free. I am strong.*

My smile erupted into an even bigger grin, knowing Ryan had gotten what he deserved. The only reason was simply because I believed in karma. That what goes around comes around. I knew that in death, Ryan would get a taste of his own medicine; that he'd spend an eternity in the fiery depths of hell, suffering excruciating pain at the hands of demons, repeatedly being poked and pried with pitchforks until beaten to death, then revived again to receive the same treatment; a perpetual cycle.

When I finally finished cleaning up the mess I'd made, I tossed the paper towels in the trash and peered out the window above the sink in search of Lydia and Jeff. To my surprise, they remained in the garage, unpacking.

From there, I continued to the basement, to our room, and locked the door.

# Chapter

# 14

I RETRIEVED the scrapbook from the bureau and carefully opened it. As I analyzed the notes and readings, it became clear that Lydia and Jeff were not who they said they were. Based on the information in the pages before me, I concluded they bore at least some responsibility for Connor's death.

I turned the page and discovered a piece of loose paper that had been redacted. Lifting the page toward the ceiling, allowing the light to brighten it, I squinted to get a better look. But even after inspecting the page, I caught only a glimpse of all the information that had been written. The paper was too thick and the black ink too dark. However, I still managed to pick up one word in particular: Psychiatry.

I thought back to yesterday when Lydia gave me a tour of their home. Every bookshelf carried quite a few psychology and psychiatry books, alongside other

literature. *I bet Lydia and Jeff are psychiatrists. Or at least...
were. They probably used cruel and inhumane methods to treat
people. And the names and social security numbers in the
scrapbook are the proof. Despicable.*

I slipped the page back in where I'd found it and
scrutinized other pages filled with patient data. Only then
did I realize what I held in my hands. *This isn't a collection of
records, this is a collection of trophies. It can't be anything else. It
makes no sense to keep records like this out in the open for
anyone to see. Such private information would be locked away in
a filing cabinet. If they had any respect for the oath, they
would've properly disposed of the files or kept them at the
establishment in which the operations were held. Yet, they're
here. Why? No one in their right mind would allow them to hold
onto these files. No one!*

I recalled Lydia and I's conversation in the art
room. *How could she've lied straight to my face like I'm some
idiot? Perhaps they never worked for the government. No. They
probably worked for themselves. That's the only thing that makes
sense. The government surely wouldn't allow this.*

I remembered the eerie paintings and how she admitted
she hadn't painted a single one. That they were
commissioned. *Perhaps they're from a few of their patients. The
ones that were the most disturbed. Or maybe they were from
every girlfriend Brett brought home. Everyone made a patient at
least.*

I rubbed my temples in agony, knowing that I was
completely out of mind at this point. Tammy had

successfully gotten to me, fucking up my entire weekend, and there was nothing I could do about it.

With that idea in mind—the patients who had painted the disturbing images that adorned the walls of the home—I skimmed through the list of names, searching for female ones. I started counting; one, two, five, ten. I gaped in shock as I counted more and more female names in the scrapbook. It seemed like Lydia and Jeff had a twisted fascination with their patients and their ailments, almost as if they enjoyed causing harm to them.

I shuddered at the thought of someone I knew being treated by them. It made me sick to my stomach to think of all the pain and torment they must have caused. *How could they've gotten away with this for so long? And why do they feel the need to keep a record of it?*

I continued flipping through the pages until—

*No way...*

My breath caught in my throat. I'd guessed right. The Eldridge family had experimented on their own kids, using them as guinea pigs for their psychiatric treatments. It was sickening to think that a family would go to such lengths, especially to their flesh and blood. My stomach churned as I read through the descriptions of the treatments they had subjected Brett and Connor to. *No wonder Brett is so troubled and conflicted and how Connor committed suicide.*

I wallowed in a stew of anger. In a way, Brett had succumbed to the same trauma I'd also endured. Though vastly different, our traumas were still similar.

"What did they do to you two?" I muttered as I ran my finger along the edge of the page.

There was some chicken scratch beside their names. I tried to decipher it, but it was too difficult to make out. I couldn't tell whether it was a code or a note. I turned the page, and an old photo fell into my lap. I picked it up, ran my fingers along its yellow fringed edges.

*Must've gotten burned at some point. Luckily, it's still clear.*

It was a picture of Lydia and Jeff dressed in white lab coats, standing beside a young boy dressed in a patient gown, strapped to a chair with some metal contraption attached to his head. He carried a look of distress—gritted teeth and wincing eyes—as if he were being tortured. The boy had to have been no more than twelve years old.

As I gazed at the photo in horror, my mind raced with questions. *I wonder who the kid is, and what are they doing to him. I hope he isn't Brett or Connor. How can Lydia and Jeff live with themselves after doing this? This must be what Tammy was talking about.*

The idea that Brett had brought me out here for a sinister purpose resurfaced. *Perhaps he didn't bring me out here to connect on a deeper level but to feed his parents' sick hunger for torture. To add another name to their ever-growing trophy list.*

I shuddered, slipped the photo back into place, and closed the book. I couldn't fathom what sort of nefarious acts they had done to those people. I also couldn't think of a reason for what could have sparked such madness in them. All I knew was that I needed to leave ASAP. I needed to escape this hellish environment. I couldn't take the chance for them to torture me like they had countless others. It didn't matter how I'd escape or where to as long as I got far away from this wretched family.

I set the book back in the bureau and rushed to the bathroom, grabbed my toiletries, and haphazardly stuffed them in my duffel bag. My makeup bag slipped off the edge of the bed and hit the floor with a thud. When I knelt to pick it up, someone knocked on the door and my heart leapt out of my chest. I pressed my hand to my mouth to prevent a gasp and listened intently for who it may be.

"Knock, knock. Allison? Are you awake?" a voice asked.

It was Lydia.

I froze, unable to move, my heart pounding as I struggled to keep my breathing under control. *Now how the hell am I gonna get out of here if she's blocking the door?*

I didn't want to respond, letting her know I was awake and of sound body and mind. I feared she might have come down to check on me or to tell me lunch was ready even though it was still morning. I needed a means of escape, but I didn't have one.

I swallowed the lump in my throat as the doorknob jiggled. I was stuck in a room with only one exit, trapped like a cornered animal. Yes, I had the large window behind the bed, but how long would it take to break it before she'd burst through the door and tackle me to the ground like a lineman?

I scanned the window, considering the prospect. It could be done. It was a possibility, yet the glass was a hefty three inches thick. *There's no way I'll break through it before she breaks through the door.*

I had to remain calm, despite what I now knew about them; about the lies they told and the atrocities they had committed. It was the only way I could hope to escape unscathed and in one piece. I only had one option at that moment: to heed her call. And so I went for the door and opened it.

"Sorry, I was napping," I lied, scratching my head, acting as if I'd just woken up. "What's up?"

"I didn't mean to wake you, dear. I can come back if you want to get more—"

I shook my head. "There's no need. I'm awake now."

"Oh, well... I just came to ask if you'd be interested in painting?"

*Painting?! Oh God, no. Maybe if I abandon my bags then I make it to the car. But I'll probably run into Brett and Jeff before I can get away, especially since I don't have the keys. Dammit, why'd I put myself in this situation?*

My plan was impractical. I had little confidence in my ability to maneuver that quickly, considering I was barefoot and feeling a little sluggish. Thus, I had no other option but to adhere to her request, to eliminate any suspicion of my will to leave. And so I regrettably said, "Of course. I'd love to paint."

# Chapter 15

WE TRAVELED upstairs to the art room, where I found a canvas resting on the easel by the window she must have laid before having come gotten me. The faint sound of a melodious instrumental tune played in the background at a low volume, gently humming like industrial powerlines.

I gazed upon the canvas, and recollections of various paintings created by her patients sprang to mind. Images of despondent children haunted me. *I hope she doesn't pry into my past. Or at least try to. Oh, what am I thinking? I'm a fortress. She can't break me. She won't learn shit about my life.*

My attention was momentarily diverted as she crossed the room, approaching the closet. She extracted a palette and several partially used tubes of oil paint as I sat on the tiny stool.

"Have you ever painted before?" she asked, coming up beside me.

"A few times," I hesitantly admitted. "But it's been a while. I think the last I painted was back in college. You know, in one of those extra electives."

She handed me the palette and set the paints in the small cubby below the canvas. "I think that was the last time I painted too. Oh, how those were the days. Well, I'm not much of a painter myself, so I'm not one to judge. Just try your best, okay?"

She smiled, and I smiled back to be courteous.

I felt she was feigning amiability to manipulate me. For all I knew, she might have planned to ambush me while I painted, striking me across the head and rendering me unconscious. Then, call out to Brett and Jeff to come pick me up and bring me to some offbeat location so they could—

"Allison?" she called.

I quickly gathered myself. Upon my narrowing thoughts, I'd tuned her out. "Hmm? Sorry, I just spaced out for a second. What did you say?"

"I said... do you have an idea of what you'd like to paint?"

"No, not really. I do like the view of the garden out there, though. I might paint that."

"How about you do a self-portrait instead?" she suggested. "You can paint your story."

There it was, the question I anticipated she'd ask me at some point. But her tone was not as I'd predicted. It had taken on a softer, gentler quality. The request for a self-portrait, coupled with the deceptions and scrapbook, cemented the fact the Eldridge family had been committing abhorrent deeds for countless years and remained unrelenting.

What concerned me more, though, was my belief that they had no intention of stopping. And that I would soon be their next victim. They were going to torture me, then kill me. Upon my death, they would add my name to their roster and retain my painting as a macabre trophy.

*Lord, what have I gotten myself into?*

I stared at the blank canvas and was at a loss for words. A part of me wished I had the fortitude to stand up, strike Lydia across the face, and flee. But I remained motionless, entranced by an inexplicable force. It felt as if I'd been placed under a spell. It was like my body was trapped within a never-ending loop akin to the rhythmic beating of a maternal heart.

The melodic, wordless tune filled my ears, enchanting me like a snake charmer, lulling me into submission. As I pulled my focus from the canvas, Lydia had disappeared from my peripheral. I strained to catch a glimpse of her but to no avail. I was powerless to resist; couldn't turn my head fully.

"Think back to when you were young... vulnerable... scared," she slowly muttered as she rested her hand on my shoulder.

A sudden wave of emotions overcame me, causing tears to build in my eyes. A few streamed down my face, then my body went numb. A prickling sensation in my toes, hands, and head, like static electricity, flooded my body. Darkness crept in, enveloping me in its abyssal embrace. The feeling was akin to being stuck in a state of sleep paralysis, where my mind was conscious, but my body was immobile. In the background, the music continued to play, growing louder with each passing moment. Though the increase in volume was slight, it was enough to warm my entire being.

I had become one with my environment.

"What do you see on the canvas?" she asked.

"I... I..." I couldn't answer Lydia's question.

It wasn't because I was unable to speak, but because my mind had gone blank. My vision only consisted of the blinding white void of the canvas before me. Nothing more. In a sudden, unexpected turn, darkness enveloped me, as if I'd closed my eyes. But I hadn't.

Blackness.

Suddenly, my mind was inundated with memories and scenes that played out like a movie. An array of images bombarded me. They appeared and faded so fast, they resembled flickers of light. Stars in the sky. Some were steeped in bleakness and despair, while others oozed serenity and vibrance. My lower lip trembled in fear.

Out of my control.

I didn't know what was happening. And even though I dreaded what experiences would surface, I was along for the ride. Eventually, the flashing images slowed to a jarring stop, showcasing a scene from my past.

My childhood home: the kitchen.

My parents were entrenched in a heated argument. Their

voices crescendoed screams, and the air crackled with tension. My mother radiated anger as she hurled a glass at my father, which missed him, and shattered against the wall. In response, he retaliated with a fist, striking her with brute force.

My mother dropped to the floor with a thud.

"No, stop!" she yelled, holding her arm up to protect her face as he struck her again.

I tried to scream, but my voice wouldn't come out.

Silence.

I was a mere observer, watching my past unfold before me. The memory of that moment had been seared into my mind from inception; the vivid recollection of my mother's blood streaming from her nose, and a broken blood vessel in her eye, giving it a red hue had scarred me.

Then, much like an influx of water rushing from a fire hydrant, my tingling receptors picked up every single ounce of sensation I felt at that moment. As a child, I'd watched from afar—while cowering behind our sofa and clutching my teddy bear tightly—as my father beat my mother incessantly; my breaths interrupted by mere sobbing. Sniff, sniff. The horrific scene frightened me.

My mother's tears cascaded down her cheeks as she pled with my father, but he was beyond reason.

Irate.

Manic.

Her words were impotent, and he continued to unleash his fury upon her, striking her mercilessly, his fists connecting with her flesh over and over again.

"That'll teach you to talk back," he yelled, hitting her some more.

As if I'd become one with my father, I could feel his rage and frustration. The burning fire from within; the elevated heart rate and adrenaline. It was a memory I'd buried deep within me; one I dreaded thinking about. But there it was, in vivid detail, right before me. And there was nothing I could do to look away.

Suddenly, my father turned and locked eyes with me, and I gasped because he was coming for me next.

"No, Daddy, no! No, Daddy, no! No, Daddy, no!" I screamed.

That was all I remembered from that day; him snatching me out from behind the sofa and beating me senseless as if I'd personally thrown the glass at him.

After that, everything went black.

While reflecting on that painful memory, another image emerged, superimposed over the previous scene. It was a similar kitchen, but the players had changed—this time, it was Ryan and I, bickering over a trivial matter weeks after I'd moved into his place. He had come home from work expecting dinner to be ready, but I'd not yet prepared it.

"I don't want to hear that you wanted to relax," he yelled. "I don't care if it's your day off. You knew I was coming home at this time!"

"But I have a life too, Ryan!" I shouted back at him. "I wanted to go out and hang with my—"

He slapped me across the face and shoved me against the wall. "I don't want to hear it, bitch!"

Regret had flooded me, engulfing me like a tidal wave as I lay there, sprawled on the cold, hard linoleum, caressing my face tenderly, while he towered over me like some ominous figure. The realization hit me like a mack-truck— the cycle of abuse had never ended. The wounds of my past, inflicted by my father upon my mother and me, had followed me relentlessly, digging deep into my psyche, carving out a cavernous hole within the very depths of my soul.

Amid the darkness of my epiphany, I envisioned the overwhelming sense of pain and injustice that had engulfed me for years through vivid colors. Reds, blues, greens. A full spectrum of insanity.

My misguided attempts to come to terms with the horror of domestic abuse, hoping it would be a passing phase I could overcome, ended up being a permanent stain, an indelible mark on my soul. One that I feared would also taint the lives of my future children if I failed to choose the right partner. And then, in a moment of clarity, I saw the path forward. The light at the end of the metaphorical tunnel. By finally relinquishing the past, accepting the harsh reality of my abuse, and extending forgiveness to my father, I regained control of my life, my body, and my soul.

I anxiously drew in a heavy breath as if I'd been drowning, bringing forth a new life.

"What did you feel?" Lydia asked. Both of her hands gripped my shoulders.

"I felt... scared; betrayed; hurt. Like everything I've experienced up until this point has been a looming cloud."

"But now you feel… relieved?" she suggested.

I nodded.

"Good."

I lifted my arm and retrieved the paintbrush from its holder. Lydia stood in the background, silently observing my every move as I loaded the thick oil onto the palette. Then, with each dip of the brush, I felt a sense of catharsis and began to paint with purpose.

The canvas was a blank slate, a vast expanse of white waiting to be transformed. I started with a dark, shadowy triangle that dominated the space, then I dipped the brush in a cup filled with a cleaning solution and dried it before selecting another color to outline the figure of a child. Slowly but surely, I created a masterpiece—a visual representation of myself through the eyes of my father.

A little girl; scared, curled up into a tight ball, clutching my beloved purple teddy bear.

*Whiskers! That was his name.*

I wore a white and red polka dot dress, with my hair pulled back into two short pigtails. My eyes were filled with tears, and my cheeks glistened under the overhead light.

*Is this how I see myself? Is this how I've always felt inside? Has Lydia done this same exercise with her other patients? And possibly Brett's other girlfriends?*

Just as quickly as the thought had come to me, I shook off the hypnotic state Lydia's exercise had induced and took back control. *I'm no longer a victim of my past traumas or fears. I'm no longer a victim of my past traumas or fears. I'm no longer a victim of my past traumas or fears.*

A half-painted image stood before me, which led me to finish it. With each brushstroke, I continued to pour myself onto the canvas, creating what I believed to be my greatest work of art yet. I painted and felt a newfound sense of courage building within me—a boldness I'd never felt. I wondered why Lydia had done such an exercise with me. I felt as if I'd overcome a great force that had ruled over me for many years; a debilitating weakness that had held me at gunpoint, threatening to pull the trigger. And yet, my past still haunted me.

"Lydia?" I absently called.

"Mhmm."

"How many patients have you done this exercise with?"

"Say again?"

I lowered my paintbrush and turned to face her, finding her carrying an expression of sheer astonishment, her mouth agape, and forehead riddled with creases. "It's just the two of us in here. There's no need to repeat myself."

As I spoke those words, I wondered whether I'd made the right decision in confronting her, knowing that by revealing I knew the truth about her profession, I'd put my life in jeopardy.

She took a step backward, retreating to the central table in the room without response.

Silence hung in the air for far too long.

I waited for her response, half-expecting her to stick me with a needle she'd hidden behind her back or somewhere around the room. Yet, she simply sat at the table in utter silence, prompting me to ask another question. "How many?"

"The number is inconsequential, Allison." She let out a quick snicker. "I didn't expect you to realize it this soon. I guess I mistook you for someone broken."

"Broken?" I set the paintbrush and palette aside. "Though I might've been broken before meeting Brett, and still might be, there's one thing I know for sure—your entire family is just as broken as I am."

She scoffed. "You don't get it. You might be a tough cookie, but you're no Sherlock Holmes, dear."

I stood and stormed the table. "Then enlighten me!"

I towered over Lydia, expecting her to cower at my outburst. But she didn't. Instead, she stared me down with a deathly glare.

"Why bother? You'll be nothing come tomorrow."

Her tone clipped and I gasped. My heart stopped once I realized my reaction had given her power over me. I'd been overthrown like a dictator, a mistake I quickly regretted. I wondered what would happen next. Would I be tortured? Harvested for organs? Or sold to be sex trafficked?

With Lydia knowing I had an inkling of what was really going on, I highly doubted I'd be spared, free to go back to the life I once knew, to an empty apartment in a city where I'd run away. I knew too much. And because of that, they wouldn't let me leave. They wouldn't risk me going to the police.

Fearing I wouldn't make it out of this place alive, sweat beaded up on my forehead like condensation on a cold glass. *Great, I have no leverage now. No trust to rely on. No blackmail or bribery. Nothing. There's no doubt she's gonna do everything in her power to shut me up.*

I could tell Lydia had a plan. But I had no clue what it was. And as her stately gaze bore into me much like a woodpecker to a tree, a regret surfaced. *I shouldn't have said a thing. What's gonna stop her from killing me now?*

The mere thought of her entering my room at night and injecting me with a lethal dose of morphine made me tremble. She could say I died of natural causes the next day with no need for an autopsy. She could instruct Jeff to strangle me, then hang me up in the studio above the garage, much like their son, Connor, and claim I committed suicide. She could even hogtie me like swine, dump me in the lake, and leave me to drown and rot until I bloated and rose to the surface.

However, I wouldn't let that happen. I'd lock the door and place a chair under the knob for extra security. But then I remembered Brett and how Tammy had mentioned he lured all his previous girlfriends here. *What if Lydia included him in her plans? He could administer the drug, slit my throat, or strangle me in my sleep without even a peep from her. Keeping her out wouldn't matter then.*

"So, what now?" I asked, calmly sitting across from her as if I were no longer afraid.

She rested her hands on the table like a detective starting their interrogation. "I recommend you enjoy what little time you have left, dear. But I highly doubt you will now that you've opened up Pandora's box."

She was taunting me.

Tormenting me.

Playing twisted mind games to entertain herself.

But I refused to allow her to have the satisfaction. In a heat of rage, I said, "If you even breathe a word of this conversation to Brett or Jeff, I'll kill you."

She smiled menacingly and picked at her fingernails as if not impressed by my attempt to inflict fear. "That's mighty bold of you, Allison. I commend you for trying to instill fear in me. Sadly, it won't work." She stood and went for the door. She opened it and looked back over her shoulder, adding, "Don't forget to clean up when you're done, okay?"

Then she left the room, closing the door with a heavy thud.

# Chapter 16

Lydia's unwavering demeanor left me bewildered and in a state of shock. Despite my threat to end her life, she displayed no fear or hesitation as if she were aware of my bluff. I found myself at the hands of God now, in a foreign territory and without access to any lethal weapons.

I recalled the steak knife set we'd used during last night's dinner. It rested on the kitchen counter next to the microwave. *If I can get my hands on one, it'll surely do the job.*

I exhaled all of my anxieties, rose, and approached the easel. A radiant sunbeam streamed in through the window, illuminating the canvas with a warm glow. An overwhelming sense of admiration overtook me as I looked at what I'd painted. During our time together, I'd created a striking masterpiece; an image of a frightened child taking refuge behind a sofa, clutching a teddy bear. The colors I'd selected—a blend of rich reds, browns, and blacks—created a mix of earthy tones that warmed my heart.

Though I'd grown angry at Lydia for portraying herself and her family as wholesome, I couldn't disregard the fact she'd actually helped me. Despite everything she put me through—*is still putting me through*—she'd helped me overcome a deep-seated wound; a darkness that had followed me for many years. But now, knowing their dark truth, I had another obstacle to overcome: escaping this place alive.

I pulled the slip of paper Tammy had given me from my pocket and dialed her number. She answered on the first ring. It was as if she had expected me to call, waiting by the phone.

"Allison?" she said. "Is everything all right? Are you hurt?"

I opened the door to the art room and peered out before answering, ensuring Lydia wasn't eavesdropping. Then I re-closed the door and pressed the phone tightly to my ear. "I'm fine, I'm fine. I just need your help."

"With what?"

I ventured over to the easel, peered out the window, and whispered, "I need a gun."

"A gun? Allison, what on earth do you need a gun for?"

"I can't explain right now. You told me to call whenever I felt like I was in danger, right? Well, just know that I feel unsafe. Okay? I have a gun at home and I know how to use it. The thing is... I didn't bring it with me. Didn't think I needed to."

The line went silent as if Tammy was in a state of deliberation. I wondered what went through her mind. Would she alert the authorities? Comply with my demands? Or God forbid, hang up and leave me for dead? I highly doubted she'd do the latter, knowing she was the one who had warned me about the family in the first place. Yet, it was still a possibility. Because anything in life is possible.

"You know what... I don't know why I'm calling you. I'll just call the police."

"You can't!" she exclaimed.

"Why not?"

"You just can't all right. Now tell me, what did you find out?"

"What do you mean, 'what did I find out?' You were right. They are fucking crazy and have done things to Brett's previous girlfriends."

The silence resumed.

I couldn't comprehend what had motivated me to contact Tammy. Perhaps I sought comfort in the fact I had someone to call; someone who could relate to my ordeal. But it was her actions that had instigated this whole mess to begin with. She caused me to unravel, instilling the belief the family had conspired to kill me, much like the many other women before me. It was all her fault. Nonetheless, it was true. But if I'd never stumbled upon the trail and trespassed onto her property, then I wouldn't have been privy to the impending danger.

*Maybe that might've been a better way to go Yet, knowing is a blessing in disguise. I guess it's true what they say. Knowledge is a blessing and a curse.*

Amid the silence, another grim realization set in, and I gasped. Perhaps, Tammy *wasn't* crazy after all, but a part of the whole thing; the ploy to convince all the women Brett brought home that something was afoot, creating a chink in what little armor we had left to guard us by so we could be transformed.

I recalled the picture of the kid. I imagined being in his place, strapped to the chair with the metal contraption on my head, as Lydia stood before me with a menacing grin. However, that wouldn't transform me, only torment me. *Maybe this whole thing is a setup; a sick, twisted game they all play with each victim before their untimely deaths.*

I shuddered at the thought, believing it wasn't true. "Tammy, are you still there?" I asked, filled with dread, knowing if my accusation were true, I'd surely be in for a world of hurt.

Finally, she broke her silence. "Come over. We need to talk."

"What? Just talk now, over the phone. I just can't up and leave. They'll stop me."

"Allison, if you want to give the Eldridge family what they deserve just as much as I do, then I highly recommend you come over... *now*," she said demandingly.

"But—"

Tammy ended the call on me abruptly, giving me no other option but to adhere to her request.

By the time I arrived at Tammy's front door, it was ten a.m. I stood on the stoop, nerves frayed, as I waited for her to answer my knock.

I pondered how I'd snuck out undetected. For all I knew, they could have been watching me the entire time as I snuck out the front door, traveled down the narrow driveway, and along the road over here. And though Jeff and Lydia were outside in the backyard, while Brett was in the basement doing God knows what, I still feared they'd heard the creak of the front door open.

A slew of thoughts and fears raced through my mind as another minute passed. *I hope they don't notice I left. They'll probably come looking for me if they do. And if they find me over here... eh... I don't even wanna imagine what'll happen. But what if Tammy is involved with them? What if, as soon as she opens the door, they ambush me? What then?*

The idea filled me with dread and I nervously clenched my fists. Every whistle of the branches and slap of water against the rocky shore didn't help ease my edginess either.

Suddenly, the door swung open, and Tammy appeared like a magician. "Are you alone?"

I nodded.

"Good."

Without warning, she grabbed my arm and pulled me inside as if we were fugitives on the run. I stumbled over my feet, barely missing the door as she slammed it shut. I never thought I'd be crazy enough to enter the neighbor's home with how this weekend had gone so far. Yet, somehow, I was there, putting all my trust in a stranger I'd just met the previous day. If this were two days ago, I surely wouldn't have gone inside her home. Yet, things were different now.

Tammy led me through the foyer, quickly skimming past the living area that was shrouded in modern decor. The layout of the home was quite different from the Eldridge's with its open floor plan. Despite its wondrous modern and minimalistic design, it lacked a certain personal touch as if Tammy didn't truly live here. Only a handful of black and white paintings adorned the gray walls, a few magazines scattered on the coffee table, and an espresso machine and fruit bowl in the kitchen finished off the living space. The entire layout resembled a spread similar to an IKEA showroom display, not a real place where someone would actually live.

We headed straight down a narrow hallway.

"How long have you been living here?" I asked when we stopped at a door at the end of the hall.

Tammy turned to face me with a look of intrigue as if she wondered why I'd ask such a question. "About two years. Why?"

"Eh… no reason. The real question is, why am I here?"

"To show you this."

She opened the door and flipped on the light switch. Immediately, a sight that I thought only existed in movies greeted me. The entire room was covered in hundreds of family photos, newspaper clippings, and missing person's reports, all pinned to the walls from floor to ceiling. The desk across from the door was cluttered with yellow sticky notes and other various items. Then, my gaze shifted to the bulletin board to my left, where I found a large picture of a young woman with the caption: 25-year-old political activist missing.

I turned to Tammy. "Who are you?"

Her fingers dug into my shoulder, and she pulled me inside the room and closed the door. There, hidden behind the door, was a green velvet wingback that she gestured for me to sit in. Once seated, I crossed my legs and arms and waited for her answer.

She stood before me, directly under the dim overhead light that cast an unflattering shadow on her, and said, "I know this is going to sound crazy, but I'm a PI."

"A what?"

"A private investigator, Allison." She pointed toward the large photo of the woman on the wall. "I was hired to find that girl two years ago. Her name is Kathleen Otterman. I tracked her here, to the Eldridge residence not long afterward."

"I see now why you warned me that they were hiding something, and to be careful," I said, my voice low and intense. "You knew what they were hiding the entire time. And yet, you still allowed me to stay there for the night!" My voice rose in anger as I gripped the arms of the chair. "Why didn't you just tell me from the start?"

"Would you have believed me?"

"Eh—"

"Exactly!" she interrupted, pulling away from me and

walking over to the bulletin board. "I warned you. You just decided not to listen." With one hand on the bulletin, she studied one of the many photographs, absently adding, "And I couldn't simply tell you everything because it would've jeopardized my whole operation."

"You really think so?"

She spun on her heels. "Of course, it would've. You could've even gone as far as mentioning me to one of them, saying something along the lines of, 'You know you have a crazy neighbor, right?' And then that would've blown my cover. But I get it. You're upset that I didn't tell you. You have every right to be angry. To be honest, I don't think I would've believed me either if I were in your shoes."

"So, now what?" I asked. "Why are you showing me all this now? Aren't you afraid I might still tell them and ruin everything?"

"No. Not one bit."

Tammy went to the desk, sifted through the papers, and retrieved a spreadsheet, which she then handed me. I scanned the page but could barely make out anything because of the lack of light in the room. Bringing the page closer to my face, I found the document listed numerous female names. Kathleen's name appeared third from the bottom. I continued down the list, gasping after stumbling upon my name at the very end.

"I invited you here for a reason, Allison," Tammy continued, sitting in the desk chair and rolling it over to me where we faced one another. "The last girl I spoke to—the name before yours—disappeared out from under me without a trace. I didn't even get a chance to tell her the truth; the reason I'm here. I tried calling her phone, but it's been turned off. Now when I call, I get nothing but the voicemail. I have no clue if they destroyed it or simply powered it off. Either way, I've lost contact with her." Tammy leaned back, clasped her hands behind her head, and looked up at the dark ceiling as if in deliberation. "All I know is that one day she was there in that house, and the next day... gone."

## Chapter
# 17

TAMMY'S REVELATION about the Eldridge family and their involvement in the disappearances of young women left me littered with anxiety. For some strange reason, I felt I couldn't trust her though her admission and plea for help seemed genuine.

At that point, I concluded she couldn't have been working with the Eldridge family. The idea was clever indeed. Instilling more fear within their victims, using Tammy as just a means to an end was possible. But I doubted their sick game would extend to such depths.

After Tammy finished explaining how she had lost contact with the last woman she'd tried to save, and also utilize, I wondered how could she have spent two whole years near the Eldridge family without drawing suspicion. It seemed implausible. Despite the peculiar situation she was in, I questioned her competency as an investigator.

"Tammy, why has it taken you this long?" I asked.

"What do you mean?"

"Surely you would've befriended them by now. Infiltrated their inner circle. Maybe even accept a dinner party invitation or two just so you could gather intel. Why didn't you just break into their house while they were away and dig around for evidence? It seems like you could've done any number of things while you've been here for the past two years. And yet, all you've done is remain cooped up in here like some chicken, frightening every girl Brett's brought home. What is it? Were you afraid to get too close to them, fearing they might find out who you are? Or was it that you were afraid you'd start liking them?"

She stopped shuffling through the papers on her desk and turned to face me. "There's a lot that goes into investigating, Allison. It's not that simple."

I was out of my element when it came to private investigations. As a medical professional, I had limited knowledge of police procedures and the tactics used to solve cases. While I had heard of search warrants and undercover stakeouts from TV shows, I didn't know the intricacies involved in such operations.

But that didn't stop me from asking, "But can't you just break in and search their place while they're not home? Question them? Issue a warrant? Something?!"

She scoffed. "You watch too much TV. I'm a *private* investigator. Not a cop. I'm paid to do things and go places where the police won't. You know... in a place where they have no jurisdiction or after they find no leads and shelve the case. Stuff like that. However, that also comes with a caveat. I can't do any of those things you mentioned. Yes, I can break into their home and ransack the place. I could even question them, but that would only tip them off. And since I live next door, there's a good chance that if I had, we wouldn't be speaking right now."

"You believe they killed that girl, huh?"

"That list in your hand has the names of ten women who have gone missing along the East Coast within the last four years. All of them in which have dated their son, Brett. When Kathleen disappeared two years ago, her parents hired me. After I—"

"They must be well off to afford to pay you for that long."

"Now's not the time to discuss their financials or social status, Allison. Just know that they are Kathleen's parents."

I rolled my eyes as she continued.

"After I questioned her friends, I found out she was dating someone."

"And that someone was Brett?"

She nodded. "So, after some digging, I tracked him here to the lake."

"You track his phone?"

"I'd rather not say how I did it exactly, just know that I had to get awfully close to him."

I had no clue what she meant by that. It could have been anything. Perhaps Tammy had resorted to some unethical ways. Maybe she'd followed him to his car after work, sneaking up on him and deftly planting a device under the bumper. The more I thought about it, the more I realized the sheer amount of risk and danger she'd put herself in just to get here. There was no telling what she might have done to get in this position.

"Regardless, I did what I had to do," she continued. "And it got me here."

"But *here* is not far enough," I opined. "I swear you could've done more instead of sitting here, hiding away like some—"

"Allison, the only thing I can do is a citizen's arrest." She pointed to the cuffs on the end table beside me. "Plain and simple. I'm limited. Even if I was employed by the state and broke into their home and found something, the evidence would be inadmissible in court because it had been obtained illegally."

Tammy slid her chair over to me, grabbed my hands, and looked me in the eye. Hers were as brown as chocolate. "I need a second person," she croaked. "Someone on the inside. That's the only way we'll catch them. The only way we'll discover the truth."

Slipping from her grasp, I sighed and fell back into the plush leather. "I guess that's why I'm here."

"Yes, exactly."

"So, what's the plan? You want me to record some audio, a video, or—"

Tammy lowered her head and laughed. "You and these TV shows. Tell me... what did you find in the house?"

"I found an old scrapbook with tons of patient files in it, dating back to the early nineties, and some pills. I'm also under the impression that all the paintings in the home were done by the women they've murdered, and they've kept them as some sort of memento."

Tammy stood and reached for the black mug on her desk. "That scrapbook sounds promising." She went to the door. "You want something to eat? I've got some breakfast on the stove."

The thought of a hot breakfast made me salivate. My stomach had been grumbling since I arrived. I looked up at the round clock that hung above the desk. It read 10:35 a.m., which meant I had another hour to wait before Lydia and Jeff would start cooking.

The idea of waiting until noon for my first meal seemed foreign to me. I was used to eating on the go, grabbing a granola bar or a handful of peanuts whenever I could. It wasn't ideal of course, but my work schedule left me with no choice. Unfortunately, I never really had time to eat them. I was always on the go, with barely a moment to spare, and my hunger often took a back seat to my hectic lifestyle.

Considering the time I might spend at Tammy's, conspiring with her to uncover Kathleen's whereabouts, while brainstorming tactics to endure this distressing and gut-wrenching ordeal I'd found myself in, it seemed counterintuitive to eat. If I ate now, I wouldn't eat with the rest of the family, which would only draw suspicion. And I didn't want that.

"Thank you," I said. "But I think it'll be best if I eat with the family."

She shrugged. "Suit yourself."

As soon as she left the room, a wave of uncertainty fell over me. Recalling just how twisted their sick game was, left me with a nagging suspicion that perhaps my food would be spiked to incapacitate me, ultimately leading to my demise. Remembering how I'd reacted after eating dinner the previous night, it seemed risky not to indulge in the offer. So instead, I stood and chased after Tammy.

"On second thought, I could eat. I don't trust them with feeding me anymore."

Tammy's eyes widened as if she'd gotten the gist of what I meant. Even though I'd not explicitly mentioned my slip-up to Lydia, how I'd inadvertently revealed my knowledge of their sinister plot, or how I'd undergone some sort of hypnotic experience that led to a painting of me being displayed on the walls of their home upon my demise, I got the sense that Tammy was aware of it all. The way she looked at me as if impressed by my decision to eat, gave me the impression that she too had concurred it was a wise choice.

I grabbed a seat at the island in the kitchen as Tammy pulled a plate from the cupboard and created a simple spread for me with the remaining scrambled eggs, crispy bacon, and roasted potatoes she'd left out on the stove.

"You want toast or a bagel?" she asked.

"A bagel please," I answered.

She passed me the plate, and a fork and knife from a

drawer on the opposite side of the island, then went for the bag of bagels above the refrigerator. As I took my first bite, she split a bagel, put it in the toaster beside the microwave, and pushed down the lever.

"So, what kind of patient files did you find in that scrapbook?"

"Oh, you know... regular information; names, socials, age, height, weight, mental status."

"Mental status?" she repeated. There was a note of uncertainty in her tone as if the concept I'd mentioned was foreign to her.

"Yes. There are assessments done on people through evaluation; things such as general appearance, behavior, any unusual or bizarre beliefs and perceptions—you know... delusions, hallucinations. Things like that. There's also mood. It's mostly done to distinguish neurological disorders. Especially in psychiatry."

"You don't say?"

Tammy grabbed the butter from the refrigerator just as the toaster popped. She unplugged it from the wall and brought it over to me so I could retrieve my bagel. When I grabbed the two pieces, they were so hot I almost dropped one of them on the granite countertop.

Once the bagel was on my plate, Tammy returned the toaster to its designated spot. "How many names did you say were in this book?"

"A shit ton. Like hundreds. Maybe even thousands, I'm not sure. All I know is that it's pretty thick and pretty old."

I buttered my bagel as Tammy fell silent. I couldn't

quite discern whether she was lost in thought or had completely disengaged from our conversation. She leaned against the counter, her gaze unfocused as if she were lost in reverie.

"What's on your mind?" I asked.

"I don't know exactly. But you know what... after you're done, I want you to go back to the house and look through that book again."

I bit my tongue, almost choking on my food. "What for?"

"Were there dates beside each name?"

I was taken aback by what she'd asked. I had no clue what she was plotting. "Yes. There were dates as well," I answered. "Why?"

"Good. Look through that book."

I set my fork down. "How? You haven't told me what I'm searching for."

"I need you to check and see if Kathleen's name is in there. If there are dates, then her name should be near the end of the book. That'll prove that they kidnapped her."

Suddenly, I understood. The tome I'd previously assumed was merely a collection of trophies could very well contain damning evidence, implicating the family in the crimes they had committed. If Kathleen's name was inscribed in that book, then Tammy could use it to alert the authorities, leading to the arrest of the family for the abduction and murder of her and all the other women they had taken.

At that moment I knew exactly what I needed to do;

retrieve that book. As I took another bite, an immense weight lifted from my shoulders, relieving the pressure that had been bearing down on me ever since I woke up. I exhaled a sigh of relief.

*It looks like I will make it home alive.*

# Chapter 18

When I returned to the Eldridge residence with a plan in mind, I headed down the spiral staircase toward my room. My body tingled with liberation as I knew once I retrieved the evidence needed to help Tammy conjure the presence of the police, I'd be freed from this crazy family. And afterward, I could return home to Charleston. All I had to do was find Kathleen's name inside that scrapbook and give it to Tammy.

I reached the basement and found Brett watching something on the TV. "Hey, babe," I said nonchalantly as if nothing fishy was going on.

He looked back over his shoulder and said, "Oh, hey."

I walked past the sofa and he reached over the top and grabbed my hand. "Come check this movie out."

He tugged my arm and guided me around the sofa, forcibly sitting me beside him. Given the importance of the situation at hand, I couldn't bear to waste a single second on frivolous activities like watching movies with someone who'd proven himself to be untrustworthy. I couldn't fathom why he even bothered with such pursuits, let alone why he wanted me to join him. Perhaps he felt lonely. Or maybe he was trying to get back on my good side after what had happened out on the lake.

In light of what I'd uncovered about his family, I had no intention of continuing our relationship. But for the time being, I had no choice but to play along. So, with my arms crossed, I reluctantly indulged him, knowing that slipping away to my room to reread the book without his notice was out of the question.

"Why are you down here?" I asked.

He took his eyes off the screen. "What do you mean? I'm relaxing."

"Relaxing?" I repeated, thinking that rewatching a movie he'd already seen was far from a form of relaxation.

His lack of a meaningful response was palpable, as was the childlike grin he wore. It was almost as if he'd never seen a movie, much less one we had already watched together a long time ago. Was he simply passing the time while his parents prepared brunch? Or was something more sinister at play? A menacing thought crossed my mind. *This must be a trap. Lydia and Jeff are probably behind us, waiting with a knife in hand to slit my throat.*

I shuddered at the thought. The gruesome image of blood gushing from my neck like water from a hydrant and covering the walls and floor in a grotesque red stain was too much to bear. *No, they're way too calculated for that. That's something an amateur would do.*

Suddenly, another image surfaced. An image of them securing a rope around my neck and pulling me over the sofa and up the stairs, where they would hang me in the garage much like Connor. Just to be safe, I glanced over my shoulder.

No one was there.

I exhaled a sigh of relief.

My mind was a labyrinth of torment, the mental anguish surpassing even the physical abuse I'd endured from Ryan and my father. I would have taken the physical pain over this mental agony any day, even though I wished for neither. Pushing the menacing thoughts away, I snapped back to reality just as an idea ensued.

"Can we talk?" I asked.

"About what?"

"Earlier on the lake, when I was trying to—"

He raised his hand, silencing me. "No need to bring it up. It's water under the bridge now."

"But I need to make sure you're okay, Brett. After all, he was your brother."

He patted my thigh, his eyes remaining on the screen. "I appreciate it, Allison. But I've done my mourning."

"Brett, surely you—"

"I said I'm fine." His tone clipped, and my heart skipped a beat.

There it was again, his tone overbearing and demeanor unappreciative. Perhaps Lydia had told him about our little conversation in the art room, and he now knew everything. Knew that I'd threatened her, him, and his father. Knew that he'd cunningly lured me here to my death. I highly doubted that was the case. Lydia wouldn't dare do that to spite me. It would be a waste of her efforts.

I stood and marched toward the bedroom, determined to follow through with my plan.

"Where are you going?" he asked.

"To go lay down," I shot back, my tone sharp as if annoyed.

He grabbed the remote and muted the TV, then readjusted himself on the sectional. "What, why? Did I do something wrong?"

He'd fallen right into my trap.

I turned to face him. "Yes! I tried to apologize, but you wouldn't let me. And now this is the second time you've spoken to me like you've done earlier. So now I'm going to go lay down."

"But brunch is almost ready."

I opened the door, stood within the frame, and said without a second glance, "Well, come get me when it is."

Then I entered the room and spun to close the door. But that's when he rushed over. He pressed his hand on the door, slightly pushing it open just as I'd closed it.

"Wait, I'm sorry. I didn't mean to upset you."

"Well, you did!" I yelled back.

I braced myself against the door, trying to hold Brett at bay. But he was too strong like an ox. Stalwart. For a moment, I feared he'd break through, strike me, pin me down on the bed, and call out for his parents to come and tie me up.

My heart fluttered as I struggled to prevent him from entering the room, my breaths shallow. All I wanted was to flee from this deranged family and put them where they deserved to be; in prison. Better yet, a mental facility much like they'd done Connor. But it appeared my efforts would be for nothing if I couldn't secure the proof needed for Tammy's plan. Eventually, Brett overpowered me and entered the room, leading me to cower in fear before him.

"What's the matter?" he demanded. "Why are you so uptight and stressed?"

"Uptight? Stressed? What are you talking about?" I sat on the edge of the bed, crossed my arms, and sank my chin. "The only reason I'm like this is because of you and your fucking family."

Silence followed.

I raised my head and met Brett's gaze, surprised to find a look of genuine sincerity. It was as if he empathized with what I was going through, regretted bringing me to this place, and shared in my emotional turmoil. I knew he and his brother had endured some harrowing experiences in the past, considering what I'd discovered in the scrapbook. But why would he care about me now, especially after deceiving me and luring me into this deadly trap?

"I understand things are weird," he said. "It's been like this since I was a kid, so I understand your confusion."

I tilted my head to the side in wonder as he sat beside me and grabbed my hand.

"Being born into this family was nothing but a death sentence."

"That's quite the statement," I said.

"But it's true. Ever since my brother and I were born, my parents toyed with us. They didn't buy us gifts like the other kids. Instead, they gave us things like mental games and tests as if we were chimps in a lab."

"Like memory games and crosswords?"

"Sort of. They were more complex than that. Things like completing a specific number of tasks within a minute, not acting on our impulses, and high-grade math."

"And they did all of that while shocking you with a helmet?" I cautiously suggested.

His eyes darted to mine in shock. "You know?"

I'd expected him to pin me to the bed upon that statement and holler for his parents, but he didn't. Instead, his hand tightened around mine and didn't let go. *Perhaps Lydia didn't tell him yet. Or maybe he's not even in on their sick game. God, I sure hope he isn't.* I recalled my time spent in the art room with Lydia, how I'd fallen into a trance and lost all control. *Perhaps Brett was under some form of hypnosis. Maybe he unknowingly led each girlfriend down here to be murdered. But is that really possible? Surely, he'd notice each one disappear.*

I recalled last night's dinner; how passionately he'd spoken about not wanting to follow in his parent's footsteps, how he'd stopped and went mute upon his mother slamming her hand on the table. *Perhaps Brett didn't want to get involved but did so because he was hypnotized. Maybe that's why they locked Connor away in Central State*

*Hospital. Because Lydia couldn't keep a hold of him. Because he was mentally stronger than Brett.*

The possibility of hypnosis seemed absurd, yet it was the only explanation that made sense. And though I didn't know much about hypnosis, I remembered hearing stories of people being able to control others with just their words; weird sayings that weren't used in everyday settings. Repeated three times. Even sudden jarring sounds such as her smacking the table. Perhaps that was what had happened to Brett. Perhaps he was a victim too, just like me.

The thought of him being a victim made my stomach churn. I couldn't believe that someone who was so physically imposing and seemed to have everything under control could be a victim of anything. Perhaps—

"Allison?" he said, waving his hand before my face.

"Yes, I know what your parents did, and... are still doing as a matter of fact."

His hand tensed up even more.

Any more pressure and my knuckles would have cracked.

Within the sorrowful look in his hazel eyes, I believed he'd been imprisoned, left to live out the rest of his days, watching every girlfriend pass him by like a seagull in the wind. But then, with that in mind, I felt a glimmer of hope. *Perhaps Brett isn't like the rest of his family. Maybe he's just like me and wants a change of scenery. Maybe we can escape this nightmare together.*

I slipped from his grasp and dropped to my knees before the bureau. "I found a scrapbook with both you and

Connor's names in it. I saw pictures of what they were doing to you and tons of kids."

After retrieving the book, I returned to the edge of the bed.

"Electroshock therapy," he muttered.

Tears welled up in his eyes as I opened the book.

"That's what they call it?"

He nodded.

"Why would they do such a thing?"

"Why else do people do bad things? Either for money or for notoriety."

I flipped through the pages in search of their names, absently saying, "I guess that explains how they're living in this mansion."

"It doesn't explain all of it, though." He stood from the bed and went to the window behind the headboard. "They—"

"Brett, Allison? Breakfast's ready!" Lydia shouted from upstairs.

I closed the book and put it back in the drawer as Brett opened the door. He turned back to me before exiting the room. "We'll continue this later, okay?"

I nodded and followed him upstairs.

# Chapter
# 19

"WHAT WERE you two getting into down there?" Lydia asked playfully as we entered the dining room. She had just set a plate of bacon and eggs on the lazy susan in the center of the table.

Brett and I exchanged glances.

"We were just eh... bonding," he said, cheesing at me.

"So, what do we have for breakfast today?" I asked as I sat.

"Oh, nothing special," she answered. "Just a simple spread."

"Ah, there you two are." Jeff entered the dining room with two plates in hand: one with sausage, the other held biscuits. "I'm glad you could join us."

"Where did *you* two disappear off to?" I asked. "Since we're asking questions."

Jeff and Lydia looked at me with blank stares. They

exchanged glances, then Jeff answered as Lydia returned to the food he'd set on the table. "Well, I was tidying up things in the garage. Lydia was—"

"Hopefully, you didn't throw away any of Connor's stuff," Brett interrupted.

I turned to him. "No, they wouldn't do that."

"You don't know them like I do."

A wave of anger and frustration crashed over me as Brett's words sank in. *He's right. I don't know anything about them. Every interaction, every conversation, every moment I've spent in this house has been built around a carefully constructed lie. For all I know, they probably did throw away a lot of Connor's stuff. Wait... the boxes!* "I saw them throwing out a few boxes earlier."

"Don't tell me you guys threw away his—"

"Stop with the nonsense," Lydia exclaimed. "Your father and I did *not* throw away your brother's stuff, okay?"

Brett sighed and grabbed a plate, poured scrambled eggs onto it. "Whatever."

Everyone began to eat, yet I didn't. Awkward. I'd already eaten at Tammy's, so I had no desire to eat here. But given how they'd not prepared individual plates like they had the previous night, I believed I was in the clear. *There's no way they could've tampered with the food this time. There's too much of a risk.*

I grabbed a plate and ate to avoid arousing suspicion.

Minutes passed.

The soft murmurs of everyone eating filled the silence.

I took small bites here and there, watching Lydia and

Jeff like a psychopathic stalker. *It seems so strange how calm and collected they are. Like... are they not mourning? Lydia was definitely a mess this morning. Perhaps they did kill Connor. Maybe they staged the whole thing, simply to avoid sending him back to Central State Hospital. Save themselves on another recurring bill.*

I slowly chewed on a crispy piece of bacon, trying to make sense of it all. *Perhaps Connor was a source of constant frustration for them and they saw an opportunity to be rid of him for good. What an impulse; a deep, dark, desire. I get it though. They thought it was the best way to rid themselves of the headaches and disrespect. Especially, since this wasn't the first time he escaped. They were probably sick of it. Just sick of it.*

The mere thought of Jeff and Lydia murdering their son sent shivers down my spine. But without concrete evidence, I was left to my suspicions. *Maybe I should confront them and test my theory. But they're therapists or psychiatrists or... whatever. Surely, they'll see through my amateur psychoanalysis, won't they? Ah, what the hell. After all, Lydia already knows I know the truth. What's the worst that could happen?*

"It must be difficult losing a son," I said.

"We lost him a long time ago, dear," Lydia replied, not sparing a glance. "This was no surprise to us."

Brett slammed his fork down as if outraged by her comment. "I can't believe you two." His tone was sharp. He kicked his chair out and rose from the table in anger. "It's like he never existed. Like you hadn't birthed him, let alone carried him for nine months!" He stormed off, leaving an unfinished plate behind, muttering, "You guys make me sick."

I stood to go after him, but Lydia motioned for me not to.

"He's just upset, that's all," she said before taking another bite. "Give him some time. He'll calm down."

"You're okay with him acting out like that?"

Jeff grabbed more sausage from the plate across from me. "Everyone grieves in their own way, Allison. It's not smart to get upset at him for reacting in such a way. After all, they were brothers."

"They shared a deeper bond with each other than we did with them," Lydia finished.

Her words were strange and off-putting. But I understood them. *Everyone grieves in their own way. We can't blame them for how they do it. Brett's just upset because his brother committed suicide. Well... supposedly. However, what's strange is his parents' reaction. They just seem too calm. Maybe Lydia was just putting on a show this morning.*

"You must not be hungry?" Lydia asked, drawing me from my rambling thoughts.

*And you must be taking notes, studying me like a frog you're about to dissect.*

I gazed down at my plate and noted how much of it was still there. During breakfast, I hadn't eaten much. Even with what little food I'd put on my plate, I still couldn't finish it. Just moved it about the plate with my fork like a stubborn child who refused to eat their vegetables. *Maybe I shouldn't have eaten at Tammy's. No. I made the right decision. Tammy would also think so. At least, I think. No, she would.*

"I'm not really feeling well," I lied. "I think the steak from last night didn't agree with me."

"Oh dear, you poor girl. If you'd like I can give you something for—"

"No, thank you." I stood and held my stomach as if I felt sick. "I'm sorry, but I don't feel up to doing any more activities today. I'm just gonna go lay down." Then I turned and headed to our room.

Brett sat out on the patio, shrouded in the cool shade beneath the deck as I brushed past the pool table in the basement. But something about his demeanor gave me pause and I stopped by the bookshelf, one hand caressing the wall. *There's no way he's finished mourning. Perhaps he's struggling with something deeper, something like... a secret. But what could it be? I get he's angry with his parents; that he resents them for the manipulation. Shit... I'm angry with mine. But maybe, just maybe, he's hiding something.*

I entered our room and locked the door. I wasn't going to give Lydia the chance to find me looking through the only thing I believed would save my life and many others. But when I opened the bottom drawer of the bureau, the scrapbook was gone. I gasped in shock and fell back, bumping my head against the bed's footboard. *Oh no! Where could it have gone? It was right here. Certainly, Brett didn't take it, did he? Lydia and Jeff couldn't have. They were in the dining room with me the entire time. Dammit, Brett must've taken it. This is what I get for trusting him.*

I frantically scoured the room in search of the book. My hands trembled as I checked every remaining drawer, under the bed, under the bathroom vanity, and even in my bag, hoping that I'd simply misplaced it. But alas, it was nowhere to be found, having seemingly vanished without a single trace.

Panic gripped me as if I were on an airplane experiencing engine failure. *This is just perfect. Without that book, Tammy has nothing. What else is there for her to use to build a case against the Eldridge family? C'mon, think.*

Suddenly, the patio door opened on the basement level and I froze and listened intently. Brett was coming back inside. *I wonder if he's gonna come in here. Maybe lie down. Hopefully, he goes back upstairs. Perhaps, even return to the movie he was watching before brunch.*

The doorknob jiggled followed by a thud as if he'd bumped into the door thinking it would open.

*Dammit.*

"Allisonnn... you in there?" he called.

I shot up from the floor, adrenaline coursing through my veins. "I am."

"Let me in."

"I'm not descent," I lied, trying to conjure up an excuse to keep him from coming in.

"It's nothing I haven't seen before, babe. Now come on, open up."

"I'm just..." I felt I couldn't tell him what I was actually doing, as if he already knew I was searching for the scrapbook that he'd taken and hidden somewhere.

Instead of fighting the urge to lie to him, I went for the door and opened it. It swung wide and then, like a porno, he put his finger to my lips, silencing me, and groped my ass. I was unsure of his intentions.

*Whoa! Is he really doing this right now? This is so weird, given the current circumstances. Oh wait… maybe he's just using sex to distract himself from the grief. I did promise him sex out on the boat.*

He kissed me.

I pondered about the consequences of our actions as he felt me up. *What are we doing? Are we really about to have sex amid this madness?*

My thoughts quickly faded as his lips trailed down my neck, sending shivers down my spine. The thrill of being caught only added to the excitement. I glanced at the door, hoping it was locked. I didn't want his parents interrupting our intimate moment, even though I was tempted to put an end to it. But when Brett pushed me back onto the pillows and lowered his jeans to the floor, I gave in to my carnal desires.

He climbed on top of me and kissed me again, the taste of salty bacon lingering on his lips. It was an odd but not entirely unpleasant sensation.

I tore off my shirt as he unzipped my jeans. Then he pulled down my pants as I stared at the ceiling in wonder. As much as I wanted to give in to the pleasure of the moment, I couldn't ignore the nagging feeling in the back of my mind. The feeling of manipulation. *No, no, no! Don't give in. Brett's just trying to distract me; take my focus off the scrapbook he moved.*

As those thoughts lingered, my arousal only grew. I couldn't escape the sensations that were washing over me. With his mouth traveling down my naval, I licked my lips.

*Oh, that feels goooood.* "Kiss my feet," I said, my voice barely above a whisper.

Suddenly, his actions ceased and he pulled from my stomach. "What?"

I averted my gaze from the ceiling, locked eyes with him. "You heard me, big boy. Kiss my feet."

He pulled away, sliding to the edge of the bed in a disturbed manner. "Eww, no."

"No? What do you mean, no? You love my feet, Brett."

I toed my way out of my socks and shoved them in his hands, but he gently pushed them away.

"I'm not kissing your feet, Allison."

I scoffed and grabbed my shirt, pulled it over my head. *So much for getting some.*

Don't get me wrong, I didn't want to have sex at that moment anyway because it wasn't the right time. If anything, I was thankful that he stopped. Yet, I found the reason we stopped strangely concerning.

I slid to the edge of the bed and sat beside him. "Okay, what the hell is going on, Brett? Why are you coming on to me? One day you're hot, the next you're cold. I get that you just lost your brother and all, but this just doesn't make any—"

"Allison," he interrupted, grabbing my arm in a jarring motion. "You need to calm down. I can explain."

"Yeah, just like how you explained you had a twin last night?" I retorted.

"That's not the same and you know it."

His grip tightened and I panicked.

"Get away from me," I yelled, yanking my arm away like an angry child.

I shoved him with all my might, then bolted out of the room toward the patio. It felt like the world was closing in around me, suffocating me with its secrets and lies, my heart beating incessantly. The book was my last hope, my only chance to uncover the truth about Kathleen and the Eldridge family's dark secrets. But now it was gone, vanished into thin air. The weight of defeat settled heavily on my chest, suffocating me with its crushing force. The plan to search the book for Kathleen's name was simple, yet somehow, completing the task seemed impossible.

*How could I've let this happen?* I thought, bursting through the door onto the patio. *I was almost there. All I had to do was look through that book.*

"Allison, what's wrong?" Brett called out to me.

I ignored him because it was the easiest thing to do to eliminate my troubles. I felt I couldn't trust him anymore.

I stormed down to the boat dock in search of fresh air and solace. I didn't want to have anything to do with him anymore. Believing he was responsible for the book's disappearance led me to scour the heavens in search of a reasonable doubt. However, I couldn't conjure one.

"Allison, please, what's this all—"

"Don't! I just can't right now," I hollered. "I need a moment, okay?"

By the time I reached the end of the dock, the cool breeze from the water basted my skin like a chicken. I looked back over my shoulder to find him standing right where I'd left him; the patio. It was as if he was waiting for something. Waiting for me to walk right back up to him and discuss what had set me off. But I wouldn't. His eyes bore into me like a predator stalking its prey. It was as if he was toying with me, much like his mother had earlier.

Despite my desire to be alone, his presence made it impossible for me to relax, even though we were hundreds of feet apart. Then, amid the gentle breeze of the summer air and the soft rustling leaves in the trees, Brett's overbearing glare turned to a look of compassion. Immediately following that change in expression, he turned and headed back inside the house.

I looked back out at the lake and the wondrous mountain. I shed a tear, knowing my hope for survival was quickly diminishing. I had nowhere else to turn. I couldn't even gather my thoughts with the amount of cortisol racing through my veins. And despite the elegant landscape before me, I still couldn't keep myself together.

*Everything I've been through, everything I've experienced up until this point has been for nothing now that the scrapbook is gone.* I dried my eyes with my shirt collar. *I should call Tammy. She needs to know. God, what is she gonna say?* I pulled my cell from my pocket and pressed redial. *I hope she doesn't flip out.*

As soon as Tammy answered, I came out with it.

"What do you mean you lost the book?" she exclaimed. "How could you misplace it when you just had it?"

I groped my head in frustration and sat in one of the reclining chairs. "I don't know. One minute it was there, the next minute... gone."

"Well, you need to find it, Allison. That book's our only hope in getting justice for Kathleen and every other person they've killed."

"I know it is, I know it is. But I've looked everywhere for it, and I still can't find it."

Tammy exhaled a sigh of frustration.

I could sense her weariness and her disappointment from my failing her. Despite the tension in the air, I forced myself to take a deep breath and try to approach the situation with a calm and rational mindset.

Tammy said, "What about those pills you found? Could they be prescribed to one of the previous victims?"

I tried to recall the images of the orange bottles I'd stumbled upon in the medicine cabinet the previous night, but it eluded me. My mind was a jumbled mess, broken. I couldn't make out the labels on the bottles. It was as if my headache was so overbearing that it caused me to have a temporary lapse in memory.

"Possibly. But I don't remember," I regrettably admitted. "However, I do remember where I found them."

"Great! Go check them out. They're our last chance at getting what we need."

With a burst of energy, I lifted my chin with promise, feeling ready to continue my search "Copy that!"

Then I ended the call.

# Chapter

# 20

After I ended the call with Tammy, a soft voice spoke.

"Who were you on the phone with, Allison?"

I whirled around in utter amazement to find Lydia standing behind me. In my dismay, my foot slid out from under me, sending me tumbling off the dock into the water, my phone disappearing.

I flailed my arms about as the lake enveloped me, the sky overhead turning from a peaceful hue of blue to a forbidding gray. I slammed into the unyielding shore rocks and a sickening thud echoed throughout my body like a shockwave. My spine had taken the brunt of the impact. I was wracked with pain as I sank, my body paralyzed. The memory of Lydia's vicious attacks flooded my mind, making me hyperventilate and exacerbate the situation.

*Is this it? Am I gonna drown now? Is this how I'm going to die?*

I was certain my fate was sealed, considering my lack of movement. Only my eyes could scan the blurred heavens. And as the murky water engulfed me, Lydia's menacing silhouette loomed above like a harbinger of death. *I can't believe that bitch pushed me off the dock. Or did she? I didn't feel her hands. Maybe I stumbled off. Regardless...*

I feared they were going to succeed in taking my life, leaving yet another tormented soul to perish in their wake. Someone who had only ever sought to live an honest and unburdened existence.

Suddenly, I regained my mobility and shot upward until I surfaced. I gasped for air. Struggling to catch my breath, I looked around frantically for Lydia, but she'd vanished. Water poured off my skin as I climbed back onto the dock. I collapsed onto the stained wood, my body shaking with fear and my heart sputtering like an engine without fuel.

I wanted to leave. Wanted to escape this hellish place and return home where I could lock myself away from everyone and cuddle beneath my blanket where I'd then watch detective shows on TV. Not only was I drenched in the freshwater of the lake, but I was also in imminent danger. Even if I had to walk it and hitch rides from a few strangers just to make it back home, I was going to leave.

*But the job's not done*, a rushing thought surfaced. I regained my balance and walked toward the house with my head held low. *I can't leave yet. Not until the job's done. I'd be doing every single woman a disservice if I dropped everything and left. No, I can't. I gave Tammy my word. The manipulation, the physical torture, the mental strain, it would've been all for nothing if I left now.* I stopped and turned to face the lake and the blaring sun. *I won't be able to live with myself if I don't help Tammy.*

I gritted my teeth, balled my fists, and marched back inside the house in search of the pills. I knew the sooner I found them, the sooner I could get out of dodge. When I stepped inside, I locked eyes with Brett on the sofa in the basement. He still carried the same concerned expression as he had before he left me to be alone.

"Why are you wet?" he asked.

"Like you would wanna know," I shot back, storming off to our room, droplets of water trailing behind me like footprints in the snow.

Deep down inside, I felt he already knew why I was wet. Knew that his mother had pushed me into the water in a dastardly attempt to off me. Anger and agony coursed through me like a raging river, my entire body pulsing with every heartbeat as if I'd struck my sciatic nerve.

I entered our room, locked the door, and shed my clothes, then headed to the bathroom to rid myself of the muck I'd gotten covered in. *I can't wait to get this crap off me.*

I turned the faucet below the shower head and waited for the water to heat up. During my wait, I examined myself in the mirror, where I discovered a small gash on my lower back. I ran my hand over the wound and my body tensed. I gritted my teeth from the pain as I inspected it some more. *Dammit. I drew blood. I wonder if she has any antiseptic in here. Oh wait, there's no alcohol or peroxide in here. If there was it'd be under the sink.*

Steam began to encircle me and I entered the shower. The hot water cascaded down my skin, soothing my discomfort like a Swedish massage. I pressed my hands against the wet tiled walls and dove deep in thought. *Just breathe. You can do this. You're strong. You've overcome a lot of trials and tribulations already; you can overcome this. It's simple. All you have to do is stay calm and grab those pills. There's no need to resort to your old ways. At least, not until you have to.*

———

WHEN I FINALLY EXITED THE shower, I was a brand-new person ready to take on the day. The steam had opened my pores and washed away any lingering doubts I had, leaving me feeling invigorated and hopeful.

I wrapped myself in a warm towel and headed into the room. *Who knew something as simple as a shower could uplift your mood? I guess it's the little things that matter.*

With a renewed sense of purpose, I got dressed and headed upstairs in search of the medication. When I reached the main floor, I looked to my right, discovering Brett's parents out on the back deck. They lounged in the midday sun under the covered patio set. Lydia's gaze shifted from her reading material to me with a look of suspicion. It was as if she knew I was up to something, plotting against them to end their twisted game once and for all.

*She can't know it was Tammy, right? There's no way she can. I didn't mention her name. I didn't even say I was looking for the pills. But then again, could she've heard Tammy on the other end? I have no clue how long she eavesdropped for. Her hearing could be immaculate. Maybe she heard what we were talking about.*

You'd think she would have had the decency to speak up. Yet she didn't say a single word. She was like a fly on the wall; always around, lingering in the shadows. And just when you think you're alone, the buzzing returns. The belief that Lydia knew our plan to report them to the authorities and that I'd misplaced the scrapbook and was now going to scrum up the medication as a Plan B, made me shudder. And yet, as I stood there, a few feet away from the piece of evidence needed to lock them away for good, her piercing gaze returned to her piece of literature, as if no longer concerned with me or my desire to out her and her family.

Suddenly, another fear emerged, and with a burst of energy, I rushed to the bathroom, thinking, *Still be there! Still be there! Still be there!*

I entered the bathroom and hastily shut the door behind me. Then I leaned against the vanity and braced myself for the moment of truth. With my breathing heavy, a multitude of fears raced through my mind. I prayed the mix of medications were still where I'd found them. For if she'd disposed of them, I'd have nothing to hand over to Tammy. Nothing that would secure my safety from them, and end this charade.

*Tammy's counting me. I can't fuck this up. Please be there. Please be there. Please be there.*

I gritted my teeth, gripped the mirror, and pried it open.

Pressure hung in the air as I hesitated to look at what lay inside. It was a feeling that unnerved me to the point where I could almost puke. Knowing that if the medication was still there and the labels on the bottles didn't match the Eldridge family's names, meant I'd struck gold. But if they were missing, vanished like a capsized boat at sea, I would have reached another dead end, with the last lifeline for my safety and that of countless others gone as well.

The moment of truth.

I opened my eyes and my heart sank.

The cabinet was empty except for the extra container of hand soap and a bottle of lotion. I reached for my cell, thinking, *I guess it's back to the drawing board. Tammy's gonna be pissed.*

But when my phone was nowhere to be found, I panicked. I quickly felt around my remaining pockets but to no avail. It had disappeared.

"Dammit," I muttered, striking the vanity in spite. "It's at the bottom of the lake. Fuck! How could I have been so careless? Now I have no way of getting in contact with her. If only I hadn't thrown away her number after calling her. If only I could remember what numbers she wrote on that piece of paper. If only I hadn't fallen off the deck, then I wouldn't even be in this predicament."

I struck the vanity again, knowing I'd failed. I had failed not only Tammy, but myself and the countless other women the Eldridge family had supposedly murdered. In defeat, I made my way back to our room, my head held low and my body aching.

I didn't know what to do next. With the scrapbook and medication missing, I'd lost hope. The future seemed bleak and uncertain, and I was filled with hopelessness and despair. My every will to survive was being drained out of me like a leaky faucet, drop by drop, until I was left feeling empty. The weight of my struggles had become too much to bear, and I could feel myself losing the strength to carry on. Though it wasn't over yet, I felt as if it were.

Then, amid my sullen return to the bedroom, I had a moment of clarity. *The garage! I'm sure they've got some evidence in there. I just need to find it.* But then, I remembered seeing Lydia and Jeff throwing out boxes earlier, and doubt crept in. *Shit. They probably discarded everything. At least everything that could be used against them. That would explain the missing medication. But would they actually do it? Get rid of their life's work? No. They wouldn't. I sure hope they haven't. But there's only one way to find out. Maybe they left something behind. God, I hope they left something behind.*

I couldn't risk getting caught in broad daylight, searching through the place like a burglar looking for something valuable to steal. I had to be strategic about it if I were going to pull it off. So instead, I waited until nightfall when the sky was black and the moon was high.

Then, and only then, would I sneak out in search of the evidence needed.

---

AFTER AN AWKWARD DINNER with the family, I went back to the room and waited for the right moment to strike, using the novel I'd brought to pass the time. I'd gotten halfway through my book before Brett barged in.

I'd expected him to jump in the shower and wash up after all the sweating he did while out fishing and grilling. Yet instead, he sat on the edge of the bed and ran his hand along my covered feet.

"Allison?" he asked nervously. "Are you ready to talk about it?"

I shifted my feet from under his hand and turned a page. "You know there's nothing to talk about. Now go get in the shower, so we can go to bed."

"I'll kiss your feet." His tone was soft and promiscuous as if he was trying to entice me.

I shifted my gaze from the pages and sent him a look of aggravation. When I noted his seriousness and how it seemed like he wasn't going to stop, I drew in a breath, slammed the book shut, and set it on the nightstand. "Let's just go to bed, all right? I don't wanna talk about it."

"Fine."

Brett stood and undressed. After a quick shower, he switched into his nightwear and got under the covers, prompting me to turn off the light. At first, he slipped his hands around my waist and pulled me closer, but I quickly deflected his advances by pulling away and saying, "That's not gonna work tonight, buddy."

Minutes passed as I watched the clock turn. Tick tock, tick tock, tick tock. Within the still of night, I lay there, unable to fall asleep, pondering the reason why he'd moved the scrapbook. Questions circled my mind. *Was it manipulation? Did he trick me into thinking he was on my side? Could he be just as evil as his mother?*

I rolled onto my back, my gaze landing on the ceiling in disbelief. I felt the need to wake him and ask. But I feared doing so, not knowing what the consequences would be.

Brett let out a roaring snore, snatching my attention away from my meandering thoughts. I looked at his calm face. His expression was of pure bliss. *He must be dreaming.* I turned to face the ceiling again and fell deep in thought. *The entire year I've known him, he's never snored. But we don't live together, so maybe he does and I just never noticed whenever he stayed over. Well, whenever he did, we would stay up late. Perhaps, I fell asleep before him. That would explain why I've never heard him make such a racket. Or maybe I'm just losing my mind.*

As I lay there, being serenaded by Brett's snoring lullaby, I counted the minutes until it was time to sneak away. I glanced at the clock, watching the numbers tick away. One by one, I counted, eventually drifting off to sleep.

# Part Three: Resilience

Sunday, April 16th, 2023

"And here you are living despite it all."
— Rupi Kaur

# Chapter
# 21

I awoke with a gasp.

My chest was drenched in sweat and my body quivered uncontrollably. My heart raced faster than a cheetah. Yet, my mind was in a haze. *I guess I had a nightmare.*

I tried recalling what caused my sudden revival but couldn't. I glanced at the clock on the nightstand. It was two a.m. Somehow, I'd fallen asleep, perhaps because of the amount of stress I'd been under, which I believed led to my indefinite crash. Regardless, I rubbed my eyes clean of the dried crust that had formed and carefully slid out from under the covers in search of the truth.

I tip-toed to the door, gripped the knob, and slowly turned it until it opened. I only had one chance to achieve what seemed like the impossible, or else the weight of every woman after me would haunt me until the end of time. Even in death.

I gritted my teeth and left the room, being careful to keep the knob turned as I shut the door so as not to awaken Brett. *This place is such a maze*, I thought, maneuvering the premises in total darkness. No amount of confidence would make me feel better about sneaking about the place without knocking over a vase or bumping into a wall. However, I couldn't risk getting caught by turning on the lights.

I crept down the hall, my hand tracing the walls until I reached the living area. There, I made out the spiral staircase from the moonlight shining in through the back porch windows. I traveled upstairs to the main floor. *If I leave through the front door, I might risk waking Lydia and Jeff.*

I craned my neck to the second floor in search of a bedroom light.

Nothing.

Blackness.

*It doesn't look like they're awake. I still can't take the chance though. I think it's best to go back downstairs and leave through there. It is closest to the garage.*

I tip-toed back downstairs toward the back entrance and slid open the patio door. I stepped out onto the frigid stone and almost changed my mind about pursuing the feat. *Damn, that's cold.*

I continued, blindly stepping out and closing the door behind me, leaving it slightly ajar so I could reopen with ease. I followed the chilling stone pathway until I reached the garage, where I then noted an old silver tin security light shining down above the bays. *That must stay on all night.*

I surveyed the area for a means to sneak inside. Assuming the garage doors would open, I slid between the Ranger and Brett's TL, wrapped my hand around the lever, and pried. But no luck. I tried the other, but still the same result. *So much for taking the easy route.*

I ventured along the side of the building, assuming using the same door I'd come through when I was shown Connor's body would be unlocked. And though I knew it was in direct view of the kitchen and possibly Lydia and Jeff's bedroom upstairs, I didn't care. I had no other choice. It was my only way in. When I reached the door, I turned the knob, and strangely enough, it opened. *Hmm... why leave it unlocked?*

I knew this was a secluded lot, shielded from the rest of the neighborhood. So the chances of someone breaking in were slim to none. But still, why not lock it? I couldn't grasp their logic. It could have been a trap; something to lure me inside so they could catch me with my guard down, then render me unconscious, ultimately leading to my downfall. But I also knew if I didn't enter, this nightmare would never end.

And so I held my breath and stepped into the darkness. The door closed behind me and nothing but the blackest black surrounded me. I ran my hand along the wall nearest the door in an attempt to locate the light switch that I'd seen on my first visit. *Ah, there it is.*

A flicker of dim light flashed overhead for a second until

it settled. The fluorescent tubes hummed in the silence like buzzing bees. There I was, standing in Connor's old room, shivering from how cold it was. I pulled my sash tight, but it didn't lessen the chill. I inspected the area, expecting it to be dull and barren like a wasteland. But it wasn't. *Hmm, it doesn't look like they got rid of anything. Where'd those boxes come from then?*

I crossed the room in search of anything that could contain evidence. I checked the bookshelf in the corner near the bed first. I ran my hand along the vast selection of literature, looking for anything that stood out. After a thorough scan, nothing piqued my interest.

The bed was second.

I dropped to my knees and ran my hand under it. I grazed a rugged object and jolted back in fear. It could have been anything; another book, a hilt to a knife, hell... even a gun. I drew in a breath, reached back under, wrapped my hand around it, and pulled, praying that what I was about to find was exactly what I needed.

My discovery threw me for a loop.

A thin, short rope tied into balls at the ends lay in my hand. *What the hell is this... a chew toy? But they have no pets.* Then I gasped. *Is this what Connor used to help him figure out the slipknot? God, that's horrible.*

I carefully laid the rope back under the bed and continued my search for more evidence. After checking the bathroom, under the kitchen sink, and in the cabinets, I came up empty-handed. *Fuck! I'm getting nowhere. If only I hadn't lost my phone—and if Brett hadn't moved that damn scrapbook—I wouldn't be in this predicament. I should've just asked him why he moved it. Maybe he had a good reason. Maybe if I go back and wake him he'll tell me. NO! I can't. I'm so close, I can't take the risk. If I wake him, he might wake his parents.*

I exhaled a sigh of aggravation as I thought of other ways to obtain what I needed without having to include Brett. I gritted my teeth and clenched my fists as I stood in the middle of the room, surrounded by everything that made up a decent place to stay. There was nowhere else to look. No other evidence I could find.

I pressed my palms to my face and tilted my head back, thinking, *I don't have time for this shit. Tammy's counting on me to find something she can use against them. Why does everything have to be so difficult?*

Suddenly, I remembered the crates I'd seen Lydia and Jeff removing alongside the cardboard boxes. I quickly checked the closet beside the bathroom, only to find a collection of towels, washcloths, and a plethora of other toiletries inside. *Where else could they be storing those crates?*

In defeat, I turned to leave, but then I spotted the staircase. *I haven't checked there yet. Maybe they're down there.*

Somehow, the thought of inspecting the car bays eluded me. The idea of only vehicles being stored down there was what had caused me to dismiss any possibility I'd find the evidence I was searching for. But I wouldn't be certain unless I witnessed it myself; saw it with my own two eyes. So instead of returning to the house to suffer a tragic demise, I took to the stairs.

With my left hand tightly gripped around the railing, I descended the narrow stairwell. The wood creaked with each step I took. And, the further I got away from the light, the darkness seemed to press in around me, suffocating me with its weight. My chest convulsed, up and down, inciting panic. I tried to calm my nerves by reminding myself, *You're just being silly. No one's down here but me. Now relax.*

When I reached the cold concrete of the garage floor, I realized nothing about this situation was anything short of scary. A chill ran down my spine. I stepped away from the stair rail into the dark abyss, the lingering odor of gasoline storming my nostrils. Then I took another step. *This is too weird. Too quiet. But maybe this is where everything is.*

I reached out into the darkness and took another step.

*Nope. No cars here. This must be where they're keeping everything.*

I took another step and grazed what I believed was a thin chain that hung from the ceiling—one that led to a pull chord for a light. A faint ringing sound echoed in the silence as if someone had flicked a coin against an old tin jug.

I reached out for what I'd touched and pulled it. Lo and behold, the darkness before me had dissipated upon a simple tug of the chain, and I was now surrounded by a horrifying sight. Before me stood a wall of floor-to-ceiling high shelves filled with plastic crates, a TV mounted on the far wall, and a computer, resting on a desk in the middle of the room.

# Chapter 22

*Yes, I found it!*

I believed this was the evidence Tammy had been tirelessly waiting two years for. If only I could have contacted her, informing her of my discovery, so she too, could join me in unearthing the truth behind Kathleen's disappearance. Unfortunately, I was alone, left to carry out the rest of this journey solo.

I approached the shelving and found that each of them carried a yellow label that had a specific year written, dating back to the early 90s. I scanned the crates in search of the current year, until my gaze landed on one nestled at the bottom, near the floor. I dropped to my knees, pulled the crate from the shelf, and brought it over to the metal desk, where I then pushed a few things aside, set the box on the table, blew off the caked-on dust, and began my search.

I was filled with anticipation as my fingers sifted

through the folders with lightning speed. Name after name, I passed until—

"What the fuck?" I muttered.

I'd passed over a folder that had my name on it. I pulled it from the pile, opened it, and discovered it contained all of my medical history over the past five years, including past ailments, and prescribed medications. A shiver ran down my spine. The invasive nature of it all was overwhelming. *How did they get this?*

I shuddered at the thought of catching Brett rummaging through the drawers of my computer desk and looking through my personal emails on my laptop like a thief. The realization hit me like a ton of bricks; the Eldridge family was more than just a little twisted. They were deranged, consumed by their delusions, and completely out of touch with reality.

I felt completely violated and exposed as though they had peeled back the layers of my soul like an onion and left me naked and defenseless. This was not just a matter of criminal behavior now; it was a matter of survival. I needed to get out of this place, and fast.

I slipped the folder back into place and continued with my mission. Resuming my search for Kathleen's name through the pile of folders in the crate was all I needed to do to completely upend all of this scrutiny. But doubt washed over me as soon as I continued. I knew that at any moment I could be caught, and the uncertainty of knowing I might fail to locate the evidence needed to put the Eldridge family away for good beforehand gnawed at my insides like an upset stomach; faint but there, rumbling just below the surface.

Suddenly, there it was: Kathleen M. Otterman.

I removed her folder from the batch and studied her file. My heart sank at the sight of the word: rape. She, too, shared a similar pain, a history of physical abuse, and a rape that had left her with crippling anxiety. My breath caught in my throat at the thought of her pain. And the Xanax prescribed to ease her suffering only added to it.

I perched against the table and sifted through the papers with growing unease. I felt like an intruder as I read through Kathleen's medical history. The notes were detailed, documenting everything from her physical health, political views, and emotional state. It was like reading a diary that was never meant to be shared; a list of personal information that could be used against her to help break her down even more. The guilt of invading her privacy made my stomach churn. But simultaneously, I felt relieved that I'd finally found something that could help build a case. It was clear to me that Kathleen had suffered greatly before she was brutally murdered. It was a tragedy that could not be ignored.

I turned to leave and bumped my foot against a cardboard box under the desk. Setting the folder aside, I knelt and inspected its contents, where I found a bunch of mini DV tapes piled on top of one another. How nostalgic.

I estimated at least 200 tapes in that box, which led me to think the worst. *They aren't stupid enough to document their murders, are they? Then again, there's no other reason why they'd have this camera equipment. How disgusting. These people are so sick.*

It was one thing to partake in disturbing practices in the privacy of your own home, but to record it on camera was just despicable.

My gaze trailed back up to the desk, where I found a Sony Digital 8 camcorder and a few more tapes. Cables ran from the camcorder to the computer. My first inclination was that Jeff and Lydia were converting the tapes over to digital means so they could better store their documentation in less space-intensive ways.

I was familiar with the process, but only a little. My coworker had spoken about it months before after her father passed. She'd mentioned finding his old camcorder and a few tapes within the junk he'd left behind and had asked if I knew how to convert them. I didn't at the time. And so one day after work, she invited me over and we worked on it together. The few remaining tapes beside the camera must have meant they hadn't finished converting all the footage yet, and the ones in the cardboard box beneath me were soon to be trash.

I inspected the tapes and uncovered that each one was labeled with the names of the last few women on the list Tammy had shown me—including Kathleen. I grabbed her tape first and put it in the camcorder. Then I flipped open the LCD screen and powered it on. I pressed the rewind button, and it clicked immediately. The tape had already been rewound.

I pressed the play button and the tiny screen came to

life. A hue of a blue screen emerged, then instantly went black. I bit my fingernail as I waited for the video to play, wondering what I might witness. Within seconds, the image of Kathleen constrained to a chair with a metal contraption strapped to her head came on screen.

I gasped in shock at the horrid sight, dropping the camera onto the desk in reaction. The blunt impact forcibly tilted the screen in my direction, allowing me to view Kathleen being electrocuted, much like the child I'd seen in the picture from the scrapbook.

I turned away from the unsightly images playing on the small screen and shielded my eyes. But I couldn't escape her muffled screams that echoed across the garage. Wanting the incessant screams to end, I quickly stopped the camcorder and powered it off. I couldn't bear to see any more; to hear any more. It was just too sickening.

Then, my eyes widened in fear. *Thank God Tammy warned me. If she hadn't I'd be dead right now.*

An immense sense of gratitude fell over me, and my heart warmed, knowing that this nightmare would soon come to an end now that I'd found what she needed to put them away for good. Tammy had been a true blessing in disguise.

# Chapter 23

With the folder needed to help Tammy gain the police's assistance in hand, I turned to leave. But when I looked at the staircase, Jeff stood before me, his towering frame frightening.

I dropped the manilla folder in a jolting scare. Its documents cascaded across the floor like lava. During my search for the truth, I'd left the light on upstairs, which might have emitted a beam of light inside the house, possibly signaling to Lydia and Jeff that something was afoot.

I gritted my teeth as Jeff stood a few feet from me, his beady eyes boring deep into my soul as if he were death himself coming to take me to the afterlife. I was caught red-handed and now faced an uncertainty only God knew. Tightness gripped my chest as I stood there, agape in shock, with the only evidence that would save my life—and many others—now resting haphazardly on the floor between us.

"Well, now I guess you know the truth," he said, his tone low and menacing.

I swallowed the lump in my throat and tried to keep my composure, but the fear was too great. His gaze made me tremble. If it had been Lydia who stood before me, I probably could have taken her down, considering her petite stature. But since it was her six-foot-three husband, I knew I wouldn't stand a chance in hell fighting back.

"What did you do with Kathleen?" I demanded.

"Why are you asking me?" he answered. "You've seen the footage. You've read her files. Seems to me you already know what happened to her."

I stepped back as he approached, fearing what he might do.

Jeff knelt and picked up a single sheet, then skimmed over it as if searching for something. "Oh, well, maybe you didn't read it all." His gaze averted from the page, landing back on me. "Tell me, Allison, why have you felt the need to investigate the whereabouts of Kathleen?"

I remained silent, ignoring his question.

"I won't ask you again. This is your last chance to come clean."

Again, I didn't respond. I was too frightened and too concerned with how calm he was during our heated exchange to even bring myself to speak another word.

Jeff dropped the paper and came even closer, his strides short and slow. "I get that you're frightened. Many have been. However, only a few have gotten this far. So, I'm not upset with you, Allison. If anything, I'm elated, because this is where the fun begins."

I trembled in fear at the thought of not having been the only one to have uncovered their secrets. That some women before me had also done the same and failed. My heart sank to the pit of my stomach upon the realization that the end had come, and I would soon be another victim added to their ever-growing list. That my painting would be a macabre trophy they'd hang somewhere in the house, showcasing it for the world to see.

My mind spiraled with hundreds of ideas on how they tormented us. How they strategically broke us down using specifically crafted experiences catered to our pasts. The idea that they could make us think we were crazy, anxious, tripping balls—hour by hour, day by day—until they finally took the last step in procuring our lives, made my stomach churn.

*Perhaps this whole thing is a part of their sick game. Maybe they purposefully left the scrapbook for me to find. Maybe they did everything for a reason, so I could notice the discrepancies. But what if I'd contacted the police? What if I informed them of the murders? No, they're smart. They probably have people at the station they pay in case something like that were to happen. On second thought, I'm glad I didn't. That would've only made things worse. A lot worse. There's no telling how far back this goes; how much control they have. Jesus Christ! I'm gonna die. Mhmm, I'm gonna die.*

Instilling a sense of false hope within the minds of every

mentally broken woman they crossed paths with was the perfect way to lure them into submission. To break them down. To get them to submit. But then I remembered how I wasn't the same as those other women. I'd done something that had changed my life. Something I highly doubted any of the other women had done.

By now, Jeff stood inches from me, his body towering over my petite frame like a skyscraper. Now that he was also aware of the truth—that I knew they were psychiatrists who had tortured children, eventually advancing to adults before killing them—I didn't know what was about to happen.

My heart did backflips in my chest, pounding endlessly, causing my hands to go numb, and my vision to blur. Everything in my body changed within seconds as I realized what I had to do. I wrapped my hands around the camcorder on the desk and swung it at Jeff's head. Ka-thunk! The camera cracked against his skull, sending him stumbling a few steps back into the shadows.

I wanted to run for my life—up the stairs, out the door, and down the street, screaming, "HELP! HELP!" until one of the neighbors heard me and either called the police or came outside to inspect the commotion. But for some reason, I couldn't. In some way, my body had turned to stone like I'd seen Medusa.

Jeff regained his stance and emerged from the shadows. He had a small cut above his right eyebrow; big enough to create a stream of crimson down his face. And though I'd drawn blood, the force I'd used with the camera was ineffective. He was still conscious, standing, and now angrier than ever.

His forehead creased and his brows furrowed, his steely gaze overbearing. He stormed toward me and struck me in the stomach.

I crashed to the floor and groped my core.

"That'll teach you to hit people," he muttered.

Jeff had hit me so hard in the stomach that I felt like I was going to vomit. And as I lay there on the floor, I watched him dig into his pocket and retrieve a syringe. He popped the cap on the needle and came toward me. *NO! NO! NO!*

He injected the syringe into my neck. I didn't know what drug I'd been given, let alone how I'd allowed myself to fail at escaping. I'd screwed up. I'd failed Tammy and all the countless women the Eldridge family had supposedly murdered before me, and the ones they planned to do afterward. All I could do now was accept my fate.

I lay on the floor, Jeff still towering over me, my face pressed against the cold concrete. My eyes got heavy and the room started spinning. The dim light transformed into darkness. Hundreds of thoughts circled my mind now. One in particular was the words Jeff had said after he struck me in the stomach. "That'll teach you to hit people."

I hadn't heard those words since I lived with Ryan. It was the first time we got into an argument—one week after I'd moved in. I'd just gotten a promotion and was now making an extra dollar and fifty cents an hour at the hospital. So, we went out to celebrate. Steak and lobster were our dishes of choice. Ryan ordered a nice T-bone, and I got the lobster. The dinner was delightful, the service was excellent, and the weather was even better. There were no problems until we returned home.

The car eased into the driveway at eight-thirty. The neighborhood was quiet and fairly dark. Our neighbors were watching something in the living room. The faint LEDs from their TV shone through their front window.

"Tonight was amazing," I said, rubbing my hand along Ryan's hairy forearm as he put the car in park. "And you know what'll make it even better? Sex."

He shot me a look of disgust, then pulled his arm away and kicked open the car door.

I followed suit, asking, "What's wrong? Did I say something to upset you?"

He remained silent as he marched up the steps and put his key in the front door.

"C'mon, why're you upset? What did I do? Something happen at work? You didn't seem bothered earlier before we went out."

He ignored me.

"C'mon, babe... why're upset?" I climbed the front porch, grabbed his arm, and spun him around. "Babe... talk to me."

He turned and shoved his finger in my face. "I enjoyed my food," he said. "But what I didn't enjoy was *you* eye-fucking the shit out of our waiter."

"What?!" I exclaimed, my voice echoing across our entire block.

Ryan grabbed my arm and yanked me inside as if to prevent an atrocious scene for all our neighbors to witness. He closed the door, locked it, and then dragged me down the hall toward the living room, all while muttering, "You heard me. You were eye-fucking the shit out of our waiter."

He sat me on our burgundy sofa, crossed his arms, and glared at me as I pled. "What are you talking about, Ryan? I did no such thing."

He towered over me as if he were a giant and I a child, his beady eyes boring deep into my soul. "I saw how you were talking to him. Saying things like, 'Thank you, sir,' and, 'You're so funny.' You even touched his hand once."

I kicked off my flats and stood, my forehead coming to the height of his chin. "I was just being nice. And when we touched, I was reaching for the bread rolls. You're just overreacting. Now calm down."

I turned to walk away, but he grabbed my arm and pulled me in. It wasn't a sexy pull-in either like the kind you see in the movies where it was followed by a kiss. No. Instead, it was more so a dramatic pull-in like in a horror movie where the killer grabs you right before slitting your throat.

"Where do you think you're going?" he demanded. "I'm not done talking to you yet."

I tried to pull away, but his hold on me was too tight. "I told you I was just being nice. Now let go of me. I've gotta pee!"

Yet, he didn't release me. Instead, his grip tightened even more. That was when I peered deep into his brown eyes in search of an ounce of mercy, remorse, or even a sense of compassion. Unfortunately, I found nothing but darkness; a void so deep and all-encompassing that it felt as if it were sucking the very life out of me.

"Jesus, Ryan, you're hurting me," I cried out.

"Oh, calm down. Now you're overreacting. You know I wouldn't have to do this if you weren't such a slut."

Hearing that word made me flip a switch, and in a sudden reaction, I gritted my teeth and slapped him across the face. He released his hold on me and I marched away down the hall, toward the bathroom to relieve myself. Once I finished and washed my hands, I opened the door, where I then received a punch to the gut, leading me to cower over in pain.

"That'll teach you to hit people," he said sharply.

That was the start of it all—my three-year-long relationship with a sadistic psychopath; one that I was lucky enough to have escaped. Even though it left me scarred, worse than when I was abused by my father. And to think, just when I thought I'd freed myself from the binds of abuse, the lies and deceit, and the mental strain, I was met with it yet again.

# Chapter
# 24

WHEN I FINALLY REGAINED CONSCIOUSNESS, the only things I experienced were darkness, stillness, and a biting chill that crept through my bones. My mind was hazy and my body groggy, as if I'd been injected with a numbing agent.

I was no stranger to the feeling, having experienced it on many late nights during my high school years when I would indulge in substances in the privacy of my bedroom to spite my parents. The telltale signs were all there—the heightened sensitivity throughout my body, the accelerated pulse, and the throbbing pressure behind my eyes which threatened to split my skull open like firewood.

As the cold seeped into my core, I trembled uncontrollably. I scanned my surroundings for any sign of light but found none. *Where am I? What time is it? How long have I been out?*

All I knew was that I was in a strange place, completely alone and disoriented.

"Hello?" I called out into the dark abyss.

No answer.

I attempted to move, but couldn't. My hands and feet were bound tightly to an unknown object. It wasn't until I thought about it that I discovered I was in a chair. I expelled a sharp gasp and pondered my predicament. In that instant, the lights flickered on, illuminating my surroundings. I squinted, allowing my eyes to adjust to the bright lights. Then I looked around the room.

Nothing but cold concrete walls and a black metal door stood before me. A chill ran down my spine. *Wait a minute... this is the room with the black door!*

I frantically examined the room to find it empty, except for the blue electrical box affixed to the wall on my left, which seemed out of place. My gaze then fell on the helmet that sat above it on an attached rack. It looked the same as the one the boy in the photograph had worn. I peered down at the thick brown leather straps encircling my wrists and noted they were makeshift belts cast with holes and configured with metal hooks. The chances of escaping those binds were slim. Yet, I still felt the need to try.

I wiggled a little, but they didn't budge. Another slight chill came over me, and I let out a quick shiver. I gazed past my binds and found I was dressed in a blue hospital gown with a square pattern running down the length of the fabric. *That explains why I'm so cold.*

I tried to piece together the events that led to my

current situation. But they were fragments; broken pieces; splotches of black and white with a hint of color. I was still too drowsy to remember how I'd gotten here, let alone who'd changed me into this hospital gown, leaving me exposed and vulnerable. It could have been any of them; Lydia, Jeff, or even Brett.

The thought of Brett and his family being capable of such sickening acts made my blood boil. *He's such a liar. This whole family is a joke.*

It was sickening to think about. And the more I dwelled on it, the angrier I grew. They deserved the harshest punishment imaginable. But what could I do? My hands were tied; literally. And my fate resembled a ball that was now on their side of the court.

Suddenly, the black door swung open, and Lydia appeared. The time had come. They were going to torture me now, just like they'd done to Kathleen. I didn't know for how long, or with what. But I knew the pain was underway.

"Ah, I'm glad you're awake," she said with a menacing smile. She was wearing a white lab coat with a navy stethoscope slung around her neck. "I was beginning to think Jeff gave you too much."

"What the hell did give me?" I demanded.

She crossed the room, heading straight for the electrical box in the corner behind me. "Oh, just a general anesthetic. Something *you've* given many patients during your stint in healthcare; something that's considered a simple sleeping aid."

Instantly, an image of the many medication bottles I'd

found in the medicine cabinet popped into my head. One of them was a sleeping aid. I sighed and lowered my head in disappointment. "You gave me Ambien?"

"Sure did. Now I know what you're feeling right now, Allison..." The ping of metal on metal hit my ears as her voice trailed off. I turned to look to find she had lifted the helmet from its holder and was heading toward me. I looked her dead in the eyes as she continued speaking.

"Stress; neglect; wronged; anguish—"

"And you're the cause of all of it!" I interrupted. "Now that I know the truth of what fucked up things you guys have done."

Lydia's cold demeanor never faltered as she continued preparing me for whatever sick experiment she and her family had in store. I watched her every move as a mix of fear and defiance coursed through me. I had no clue what horrors awaited me. But I knew they were coming.

First, Lydia pulled a stretchy headband from the pocket of her lab coat and tied up my hair. Then she retrieved a tube of sticky gel and applied the translucent substance around my hairline. She secured probes to my temples, then, despite my resistance, placed the helmet over my head and tightened the thin leather strap around my chin. But when she pulled out the plastic mouthpiece from the other pocket, I drew the line.

"Open up, dear," she urged, holding out the mouthpiece.

I refused to open my mouth.

She wasn't going to get the satisfaction of shocking me.

The thought of her probing my mind for personal secrets sent shivers down my spine.

I spat in her hand.

*Smack!*

Lydia had retaliated immediately following my rebellious act, striking me across the face as she said, "Mind your manners, girl."

The force had caused my head to jolt and slam back into the chair. My eyes watered and my vision blurred for a moment. When I looked back, I saw the triumph in her eyes, the sick pleasure she got from exerting her power over me. To her, I was someone who couldn't defend themselves. Someone who had no power; a pawn.

"As if you mind yours," I said after licking my lips to see if she drew blood.

Lydia grabbed my face, puckered my cheeks. I tried pulling away, but her grip was too tight, almost suffocating. She forced the thick plastic into my mouth and I gagged because it touched my tongue.

*What is that taste? Salt? Ugh, disgusting. When was the last time she cleaned this thing?*

When Lydia took a step back, I spat the plastic out onto the floor.

"If you don't wear it, you'll only bite your tongue off." Her voice echoed in the silence as she continued walking around me.

"Fuck you!" I shouted.

I tried to catch a glimpse of her, but she had moved so

quickly that I couldn't see her in my peripheral anymore. She stood directly behind me.

"Suit yourself."

Her words were followed by the distinct sound of a click and a rising hum. The machine's lights flickered to life, illuminating the entire room. I braced myself for what was to come, knowing this was just the beginning.

Panic engulfed me, overwhelming every fiber of my being. All the hard work I'd done until now seemed pointless. I'd uncovered the truth about these psychiatrists who had turned to torture, using their son to lure women to this place of horrors. Yet, having uncovered all of this, I still couldn't fathom their twisted motivations.

*What do they want from me? Why am I caught up in their sick and twisted delusions? What's the point of all this?*

<h1 style="text-align:center">Chapter<br>25</h1>

A JOLT of electricity coursed through my body, wrenching a bloodcurdling scream from my lips. My muscles spasmed uncontrollably as if possessed by a malevolent force. My skin sizzled and blistered, as though I'd been plunged into a cauldron of boiling oil. And then, as quickly as it had come, the feeling had gone.

I gasped for air once it stopped, and looked down to inspect my body.

No burns.

No blisters.

But I could taste iron.

*Fuck, I bit my tongue. I shouldn't have spit out that mouthpiece.*

The black door swung open again, the squeaky noise like nails on a chalkboard, piercing my ears with its sharpness. I hoped it was Tammy and the police coming to rescue me. But when I looked at the door, I found Jeff, dressed in a matching lab coat and holding the camcorder on a tripod, walking in with his head held high. His grin was predatory, a wolfish expression that chilled me to the bone.

I let out a weary sigh as my will to fight drained away.

"How's our patient doing?" he asked Lydia as he set the camera up in front of me.

"She's being a little difficult, but it's nothing we can't fix," she answered.

He powered on the camcorder, then peered down at me with a look of disappointment. "Oh dear, the more you fight back, the more difficult it'll be for us to help you."

I spat blood onto the floor, landing right at his feet. Then I met his gaze. "Who said I wanted your help?"

He knelt and retrieved the mouthpiece I'd spit out, then gestured for me to open up. I complied without thinking as if some primal instinct had taken over. Jeff inserted the plastic in my mouth with practiced ease, his fingers brushing my lips in a way that sent me shuddering.

"Your actions are what told us, Allison," he said calmly. "You didn't have to ask."

He shifted his gaze to Lydia and nodded.

"No, no, no—"

Lydia flipped the switch, and the room was bathed in an eerie glow again. The shock came, wracking my body with convulsions that threatened to tear me apart. I bit down on the mouthpiece, my teeth grinding against it with a fierce intensity. The current surged through me as if it were a tidal wave of pain. And then again, it stopped.

"Why are you doing this?" I managed to get out through panicked breaths.

"To help you," Lydia said plainly. She came from behind me and stood by her partner in crime. "We know that you're lost, that you're hurt, that you—"

"There's nothing wrong with me," I screamed. "HELP! HELP! HELP!"

Lydia struck me across the face a second time, putting an end to my pleas. "There's no use in screaming for help, dear. You're surrounded by a foot of concrete in every direction. No sound escapes this room. Please... conserve your energy."

Tears welled up in my eyes, threatening to spill over at any moment. *I'm not gonna die. I'm not gonna die. I'm not gonna. Just hang in there. Someone will come to your rescue.*

I'd always been the victim, a punching bag for life's abuses. Nothing more. From my violent father to my drug-fueled past, to my toxic relationship with Ryan, it seemed like I'd never been able to catch a break. I thought I'd left it all behind, that I'd finally found my footing in life. But now, as I stared into the eyes of these sick people, it all seemed like a cruel joke, the final act of a tragic play. But it wasn't over yet. Not until I sang.

I sat there, bawling like a dog who'd been hit by a car.

Jeff leaned down in front of me to be eye level and rested his hand on my bare thigh. "Allison? Stop crying. Please.

Everything will be all right. All we need you to do is listen for a second, okay?"

I sniffled and nodded.

"We're going to ask you a series of questions. Depending on how you answer them, you'll either get a shock or a treat."

Immediately, my frustration boiled over like a pot on the stove that had been left unattended. I bucked at Jeff to frighten him, but the straps around my feet and wrists held me firmly in place, rendering my efforts futile. It was infuriating to be so powerless, to have no control over my fate. "What the fuck is this?" I yelled, wondering what treat they were going to give me. "I'm not a dog."

"You're right, you're not," he retorted. "But that doesn't mean we can't give you something nice in return for doing a good job now."

I gave him a sullen glare; a death stare beyond that of the Grim Reaper before suggesting, "Well, you could set me free after I answer all your questions."

"Now you know we can't do that," Lydia chimed in. "That goes against everything we stand for."

"And what is it that exactly?"

"The truth," Jeff said, standing. He returned to the camera and tapped the record button, and a little red light illuminated. Then he turned to face me and added, "Now, let's begin."

Jeff walked out of my line of sight as Lydia asked, "What is your name?"

I didn't answer.

Jeff rested his hands on my shoulders. "Come on, Allison. This one's easy."

I looked into the camera and sniffled, hesitantly answering. "Allison Sellers."

"Good."

He extended a hand, offering me a small piece of chocolate. I turned away from it, unwilling to indulge in whatever twisted fantasy these people were into. I couldn't imagine what kind of pleasure they derived from torturing me. From torturing many souls that didn't deserve it.

"Go on, eat it," Lydia urged.

I didn't want to, but I did anyway.

"Now, how old are you?" Jeff asked.

"Thirty-one."

He held out another piece, and I ate it.

"Why did you come here?"

I tilted my head to the side, puzzled by their question. "You already know the reason why I'm here! What type of question is—"

That was as far as I got in my thoughts before the shock sent my entire body to seize up in agony. I clamped down on the mouthpiece again, gritting my teeth against the pain. But this time, it felt worse.

Longer.

Stronger.

I wondered if they had increased the voltage, and whether they would continue to do so until my brain was fried. The thought of being reduced to a mere puppet, a shell of a person to be pushed around in a wheelchair for the rest of my days, terrified me to my core.

Lydia flipped the switch and the electricity ceased.

"What did I tell you before we started, Allison?" Jeff asked.

"That I'd get shocked if I answered incorrectly," I said miserably.

"Exactly. Now, why did you come here?"

"I came here because I wanted to meet my boyfriend's parents."

"Yes, but *whhyyy*?" Jeff came from behind me and held out another piece of chocolate. "Think wisely before you answer."

I was at a loss for words. Brett had asked me to come. I had no intention of meeting his parents. Did I want to? Of course. Who wouldn't want to meet their significant other's parents? But it was more than that. I wanted to break free from the monotony of everyday life and move on from what I'd escaped. And if that meant having sex on a boat in the middle of a lake, well, so be it. But I knew that wasn't the answer they wanted to hear. They wanted to know the real reason I'd come. Why I'd committed a year of my life to Brett.

I struggled to find the right words to explain myself. Then, suddenly, a jarring pain lanced through my head, making me grit my teeth. It must have been a delayed reaction to the shocks.

"You're taking too long," Lydia said in a high-pitched granny tone.

Silence hung heavily in the air as I kept my mouth shut, afraid of the consequences of speaking up. My mind raced with thoughts of the painful shocks and mental anguish that I'd endured since I arrived in this hellish place. All I wanted was to escape this nightmare and return to the safety of my home, away from these sadistic individuals who derived pleasure from my pain. Was that too much to ask?

I tucked my chin and braced myself for the next round of torment, slowly becoming convinced that this was how my life would end: strapped in a chair, at the mercy of my captors, with no hope of rescue. Fear and hopelessness washed over me, causing me to shudder. Then, on a whim, I blurted out, "I came here because I saw the potential to become part of a family that was truly loving and caring, not abusive drunks who beat on their loved ones."

I closed my eyes, fearing they would shock me for such a crude statement, but the electricity never came. When I reopened them, Jeff's hand was out, bearing another piece of chocolate.

I was correct.

I sat there, bound and helpless, my mind wondering how Brett could set me up like he had. Anger and frustration stewed within me. I'd trusted him—had begun to love him—and yet he'd betrayed me in the most heinous way possible.

Based on this experience, everything changed. I no longer wanted to be a part of this family anymore. Perhaps I didn't want to be a part of *any* family. Regardless, I strongly believed I'd never trust a soul again. I couldn't bear to take the risk of getting hurt; of being mistreated and beaten; of getting cut deep and scarred. And so I took the chocolate and chewed slowly as I waited for the next round of questioning to begin.

"What reason would you have for feeling that way, Allison?" Jeff asked.

"Because of my history."

"What history?" he urged.

I was lost in a fog of confusion. The memories of my childhood abuse weighed heavily on my mind. It was a never-ending cycle of torment, fear, and degradation. My abuser had stripped away my innocence, leaving me with nothing but scars. Physical and mental. The only thing I was spared from was rape.

I exhaled a weary sigh, feeling a knot of frustration form in my gut. *They won't break me. They can't break me. I'm too strong. Yep, I'm too strong.*

Jeff patted me on the shoulder. "Allison? We're waiting."

"My history of abuse," I finally answered.

"And where does that abuse stem from?" Lydia asked.

"My father."

Jeff knelt beside me and looked me in the eyes. "Where else?"

"Nowhere."

His gaze darted toward his wife's, and in an instant, a jolt of electricity shot through me. My muscles tensed and convulsed. My eyes rolled into the back of my head.

I was wrong once again.

*What's the point of continuing? Until someone comes to rescue me, they're gonna keep shocking me regardless of what I say. I might as well just stay quiet.*

Lydia quickly cut the power, and my seizing came to an abrupt halt.

There was no point in trying anymore. I was better off giving up.

"And where else does that abuse stem from?" Jeff repeated, his tone much harsher now like a staff sergeant's.

I remained silent. There was no reason to respond; no reason to continue playing along in their little game. They weren't going to fix me because there was nothing to fix. They weren't going to let alone let me go either. Though I didn't precisely know what their plans were for me once they finished, I was certain setting me free was not an option. *I've seen too much. Of course, they're not gonna let me go. They only have two options: kill me or lock me away in some institution like a madman. Whichever, they better make sure I don't get to them first.*

"Allison, if you don't answer, we'll have to shock you again," Jeff said.

"Go ahead, I don't care anymore!" I exclaimed. "I'm done being your lab rat."

I didn't waste my breath pleading with them this time when Jeff motioned for Lydia to zap me again. I gritted my teeth and bore the agony like a warrior, acknowledging the grim fact that my life was going to end right here, tied to the chair, naked and afraid. And that pain continued for many minutes, excruciatingly, until everything went black.

# Chapter

# 26

When I finally came to, I didn't expect to see Brett standing before me, his finger pressed to his lips, signaling me to stay silent.

"Good, you're awake," he whispered.

"Oh, like you care."

"Shh, don't be loud. And what do you mean? I do care. That's why I'm here."

My head throbbed with immense pressure and I winced as he leaned forward and unbuckled the straps around my feet.

"What are you doing?"

"What's it look like? I'm getting you out of here."

He lifted his head and unbuckled my wrists. With my arms now free, I could loosen the strap around my torso so I could stand. Once on my feet, I thought, *I guess he isn't on his parents' side.*

"I've already packed our things and put them in the car. Now grab my hand. Let's get out of here."

"But what about my clothes?" I whispered. "I'm freezing. And I've gotta pee."

He grabbed my left wrist and guided me toward the door. "We don't have time for that, Allison. We'll stop at a gas station once we reach the highway."

We exited the room, and moved silently down the hallway, tip-toeing across the basement floor like mice. The chill of the hardwood beneath my bare feet made me shiver. I glanced toward the windows that overlooked the backyard. A black sky blanketed the world outside, a pre-dawn darkness that hinted at the arrival of morning. A glimpse of purple sat on the horizon beyond the mountaintops, signaling the sun was on the cusp of rising, ready to illuminate the lake and chase away the night.

"We need to be quick if we're going to escape," he said, sliding open the patio door. "Because once the sun's up, my parents will find us."

As soon as my bare feet touched the cold stone, a sudden light flicked on overhead, casting thin lines of light onto our bodies through the deck planks above. I froze. *Shit, we're caught!*

Before I could even catch my breath, Brett grabbed my arm and pulled me back on course. "It's just the deck light above," he whispered in my ear, his subtle tone calming my frayed nerves. "We tripped the sensor. Now c'mon, follow me."

*I must not've tripped the sensor last night.*

We left the stone patio behind and set off down the breezeway. The gentle breeze coming off the water kept me alert, the chill making me shiver every few seconds. Damn that hospital gown. Always brisk and open. And though it was summer, the early morning air was still cold enough to even chill the birds and the bees.

I gripped Brett's hand tighter as we stumbled past the garage toward his Acura. I felt his heartbeat pulsing through his hand. Thump, thump, thump. He must have been just as nervous as I. Just as frightened, knowing firsthand how dangerous his parents could be. There was no doubt in my mind I would fall asleep in my bed tonight, snuggled up next to Brett once we made it home, then wake the following morning to find him cooking me breakfast; shirtless. But then I had a moment of doubt.

*Why is he helping me, let alone lied to me in the first place? It just doesn't make any sense. Why bring me here and torture me for two days? I doubt Connor's death has something to do with it. Brett's a grown man. He's free; lives on his own and everything. Why help me escape now? Was he really hypnotized? We've been dating a year. How can someone remain under hypnosis for an extended period? Through life? Work? Meals? Sex?*

By the time we reached the car, the night sky had transformed into a breathtaking shade of crimson. With the first light of dawn coming over the horizon, I could finally see Brett's features. They were no longer obscured by the shadows of the night. With a tap of the key fob, the car's doors unlocked.

"Hurry up, get in," he said, opening the driver-side door.

I hurried around the car and slipped into the passenger seat. I buckled my seatbelt as he started the engine. Then, with a flick of a switch, the headlights came on.

"What the hell?!" I gasped.

His parents stood directly in front of us, dressed in their nightgowns. They'd been watching us all along, biding their time for the perfect moment to strike. I thought the worst. I imagined them rushing the car and jarringly pulling open the doors, then dragging us out at gunpoint as if committing grand theft auto. But that wasn't the end of it. I pictured Lydia taking a kitchen knife to the car's tires, destroying our last chance for escape. I shuddered at the gruesome vision and vowed not to let them ruin our chance to escape. We had to leave; fast.

I gripped the gear shifter and yanked on it, screaming, "DRIVE!"

Brett slammed his foot on the accelerator, and the car surged forward, sending me hurtling back into my seat like a roller coaster ride. Panic flooded me as I realized my mistake; I'd accidentally shifted the car into drive instead of reverse. It was too late to correct it now though. We were headed straight for the garage.

*Bang!*

# Chapter

# 27

WHEN I REGAINED CONSCIOUSNESS, the rising sun and cloudy sky were high above me. It was morning now, and I was freezing, despite the air around me being no longer cold. I tried to sit up, but my body was numb and unresponsive. Then I noted the dampness on my gown, and my heart sank. *Dammit, I peed myself.*

I looked back at the sky. It wobbled back and forth as if I were floating. It was a strange sensation that made me wonder if I was having an out-of-body experience. My heels scraped against the asphalt and I winced. *Ouch! Nope, this is real.*

The sharp burning sensation in my heels led me to believe I was being dragged back into the house by someone. But who? I tried to steal a glance of who it was, but couldn't. My neck was tight. In defeat, I looked forward again, where I then spotted the snaking trail of blood coming from Brett's sedan. The car's front end was crumpled, and the engine hissed in protest. We had collided with the stone pillar that separated the two doors of the garage.

*Oh my God, is that blood? Am I bleeding?* I quickly scanned my body in search of any marks or gashes but found nothing. *Brett? Is he okay? Wait, maybe he's the one pulling me right now.*

I forced a squint toward the driver's seat to verify whether he was there or not, but couldn't see anything. All I could make out was the deployed airbag. *I guess the blood came from his parents. Maybe we hit them; killed them. Good riddance.*

My back cracked against something hard. The jolt of impact sent a wave of agony through my body, shattering my focus. I craned my neck back again. This time I spotted a trail of blonde hair hanging above me. *Oh no, Lydia!*

I looked back at the car in defeat. Our last hope of escape was now a twisted mass of metal and smoke, its fluids staining the pavement like a grotesque painting. I was trapped, with no way out. *So much for not dying.*

Up the breezeway we went, my mind racing with questions of why this was happening to me. *I knew I shouldn't have come here. I should've just stayed at my apartment and watched TV all weekend. Now I'm gonna die and it's all my fault. What did I do to deserve this?*

I'd been living in a self-made prison, where the only way out was through self-acceptance and forgiveness. I couldn't keep running away from my problems, hoping that they would vanish into oblivion. Hoping that I would eventually forget the past. Forget the pain, abuse, bruises, and broken bones; how I didn't fight back; how my father and Ryan did me wrong. I was naïve; purposefully ignored how I was being mistreated, believing alcohol and drugs would help me cope.

*Perhaps that's what Lydia and Jeff were trying to get me to see.*

I closed my eyes, believing I couldn't keep living like this. I knew I couldn't keep fighting myself. I needed to take a stand, even if it meant going through more pain in the process. I hadn't been a victim for some time now. But the time had come again to take back control of my life.

When we reached the entrance to the basement, I refocused on the situation. With my eyes still closed, I listened out for the patio door. Jeff opened it and Lydia hauled me in. Once we were inside, he closed the door and locked it, which meant Brett had to have been either inside already or at the hospital. They wouldn't dare leave him in the car.

I opened my eyes slightly, my heart pounding uncontrollably. Jeff walked over me and headed for the hall where the ominous black door stood. *I need to get out of here before it's too late.*

I knew that once they locked me back inside that wretched room, strapped to that old wooden chair, I'd get shocked until I drooled like a baby. Jeff's footsteps grew faint and I drew in a breath and opened my eyes fully. *You're brave; and strong. You can fight back. You can win.*

As soon as I heard the black door open, I yanked my hands forward and slipped out of Lydia's grasp. Then I clambered to my feet as quickly as I could and sprinted toward the staircase. Though my body ached, I ignored the pain, knowing it would only be temporary.

"Get her!" Lydia yelled.

I ascended the stairs, my ragged breaths drowning out the sound of Jeff's heavy footsteps. This was my last chance to fight back, to flee to safety, to escape this living nightmare once and for all. When I reached the main floor, I had two options: bolt to the door and make a beeline for Tammy's, taking the shorter but overgrown route and pray that I didn't trip and fall, or make a beeline for the kitchen and snatch the first knife I got my hands on to use in self-defense. If I chose the former, my fate was uncertain.

Sprinting barefoot on an unkempt trail, laden with rocks and thorns, could lead to my downfall. A single stumble could cause a brutal head injury, or a broken leg, rendering me helpless. And so, I took the latter option and made my way toward the kitchen, opting for better odds.

*GO! GO! GO!*

I dashed for the sink as the thumping on the floor grew louder. I could sense Jeff's looming presence behind me as I crashed into the cabinetry and reached for the knife set. Quickly clasping the hilt of the knife, I withdrew it from its slot and spun. Almost instantly, he slammed into me like a linebacker, and I stumbled backward against the sink. I expelled a booming gasp.

After pausing to regain my composure, I discovered I'd

thrust the knife into Jeff's chest. He staggered backward as his hands searched for the hilt. Speechless and stunned, he struggled to come to terms with what had just happened to him. He looked at me, his gaze vacant. He was in shock.

*Good riddance you son of a bitch!*

With all my might, I clutched the hilt of the knife and pulled it free. Jeff let out a gasp and placed his hand over the hole in his chest as if it would help slow the bleeding enough for him to make it back downstairs to his wife. But he wouldn't. I knew that for sure.

He turned and fell against the island, trying to catch his breath. I lunged forward, stabbing him in the back. He spun in an attempt to defend himself and I stabbed him again and again. Over and over, I plunged the knife into him, then I pulled it back out and stabbed him again. At least ten times, I repeated this process until eventually he stumbled backward against the island and collapsed to the floor.

Jeff was finally dead.

His shirt was soaked in blood and a pool was quickly forming around him. His entire torso was covered in puncture wounds and deep cuts. Even though I regretted having resorted to such measures, I knew it was either going to be me or him. And I'd be damned if I was going to die by the hand of any man.

With Jeff's body lying lifeless beneath me, my reflection in the grand mirror adorning the dining room across the hall caught my attention. I was a hot mess; hair disheveled. I looked as if I'd been the first to die in a horror movie. Jeff's insides had stained my gown, creating an unsightly pattern of red across it. My face, too, was splattered with blood; remnants of my unbridled fury.

I wiped my face with the back of my hand to rid myself of the muck, but it only blended the blood with my sweat. I turned from the mirror and made my way toward the staircase, my mind already turning to what came next. I crossed the hall, looked at the front door. *I should just leave. Run away. No, I can't. It wouldn't be right. I can't leave Brett behind.*

I reached for the house phone on the nearest wall to call the police. But when I brought it to my ear, the line was dead. *So much for calling for backup. Perhaps Lydia cut the power just in case I got free. Maybe that's why she stayed downstairs. Unless—*

I gasped.

*She's torturing Brett!*

By now, I stood at the top of the staircase, dreading returning downstairs. I strained to hear any sounds from Lydia or Brett, but I couldn't hear a word. *Should I make a break for it? I could race over to Tammy's and have her call 911. I could stay with her until they arrive.*

Then I thought about Brett's safety. Was it worth risking my own life to save him, especially when I didn't even know whose side he was actually on? For all I knew, he could be downstairs, standing right beside his mother, waiting for my return with a gun in hand. I doubted it. But then again, anything was possible.

I rubbed my temples in agony, contemplating what to do. I feared if I went to Tammy's and returned with the police, it'd be too late. Brett would be dead. I also felt Lydia would soon realize just how long Jeff had been gone and come look for him. And when she found his lifeless body on the kitchen floor and me missing, she'd have no choice but to exact revenge on her son. But that was only in the event they weren't working together.

I couldn't predict what horrors she would inflict on him. The image of her strapping him to the same chair that held me captive and torturing him until he was a vegetable made me shudder. She could vanish afterward, staging the scene to implicate me, ultimately adding my name to the ever-growing list of wanted criminals. There were other scenarios far more perilous that I couldn't bear to imagine. And though I wanted so very badly to leave, some part of me felt compelled to shield Brett, to keep him safe from her madness.

Was it love?

I had no clue.

I was torn.

Abruptly, the creaking of the staircase drew my attention, and my mind snapped back to reality. My gaze darted toward the source of the noise, where I found Lydia standing on the bottom step, her fingers clenching the banister like an eagle to a fish.

"Jeff, honey? Did you catch her?" Her tone was high-pitched like a witch's.

My grip on the knife grew tighter as I refused to answer. I knew that within seconds, Lydia would become suspicious of Jeff's failure to respond. So, I withdrew from the staircase and advanced toward the dining room, pressing my back against the far wall, ensuring I was concealed from view.

"Honey?" she called again.

Again, no answer.

At long last, I'd finally freed myself from the grip of oppression and mental control. And now, I held all the cards. I was determined not to let this opportunity slip away. Sure, I could have run away, but that wasn't my plan. I was through with running. I was going to stand my ground and fight back like I had years prior because there was a score to settle.

It was time for payback. Time for them to pay for what they'd done to many others. I was back with a vengeance, ready to unleash my years of pent-up aggression on those who had brought me to my knees, who had brought nothing but pain and chaos into my life. It was time to take back that pain. Time to take back what was rightfully mine.

Chapter

# 28

THE SOUND of faint footsteps echoed up the stairs, causing me to freeze in anticipation. My heart raced, my senses on high alert, as I listened intently for Lydia's movements. She was being cautious as if she sensed that something was amiss.

I gripped the knife tighter, my fingers growing more numb as I prepared to strike. I was concealed in the shadows, my back pressed against the wall that separated the kitchen from the dining room. *Just breathe, just breathe, just breathe.*

All Lydia needed to do was turn the corner, then I'd strike her multiple times just as I'd done her husband. Suddenly, the silence was broken by a rattling sound. Lydia had reached the top of the stairs. I cautiously peeked around the corner, but she was nowhere to be found. Silence loomed for another second before a sharp gasp echoed throughout the house. She'd discovered her husband. Time was of the essence now.

Without hesitation, I slid across the dining room, my heels scraping against the polished floor as I made a break for the basement to save Brett. If I could avoid confronting Lydia before rescuing him, then I'd have more help in defeating her. The reason for my logic wasn't because I feared her. Nor was it that I needed help, but rather because I didn't want to take another life. My actions with Jeff had been solely in self-defense, simply because I feared returning to that concrete room where much of my recent torment had occurred. So I felt Brett would like to do the honors of finishing the job, knowing they had tortured him as well for many years.

With a fierce determination, I charged down the stairs, my heels thudding loudly with every step I took. But then, disaster struck. I missed one and tumbled down the remaining steps. My body crashed onto the landing below, my lungs crushing under the pressure as my chest smacked the floor. The knife cascaded across the hardwood, leaving behind a small trail of blood.

Groaning, I lifted my head just as Lydia's footsteps grew louder. She was closing in on me; fast. *I need to keep going.*

No matter how much grueling pain I felt, no matter how badly I wanted to give up, I knew I couldn't. For I knew Brett was counting on me to save him, and I wasn't going to let him down. I gritted my teeth and crawled to my feet. My body ached with every movement. I took off again, snatching up the knife before sprinting straight toward the black door. My lungs burned. They were starving for oxygen. But I knew I couldn't stop. Not now. Not when Brett's life was on the line.

I didn't dare look back as Lydia's footsteps thundered behind me like a hurricane. I refused to let her catch me; to be tortured by another deranged person. Then, with a final burst of adrenaline, I flung open the black door and spun around, my knife poised and ready for action.

"Don't move!" I barked.

Lydia stopped in her tracks. But she seemed unfazed by my threat, almost as if she had no fear. Could she tell I was bluffing? Did she believe I wouldn't harm her like I had her husband? It didn't make any sense. She'd seen Jeff's lifeless body in the kitchen, riddled with stabbed wounds, his blood saturating the floor like a wood stain. There was no way she could have believed I was bluffing.

Tremors coursed through my body. My thoughts were a mix of chaos and insanity. Then, a faint sound caught my attention, drawing me to look to my left, where I found Brett, with his mouth gagged and his clothes soaked with blood. He was tied to the same chair he'd freed me from hours earlier.

From out of the corner of my eye, I spotted Lydia, taking another step toward me. I wiggled the knife, signaling to her that I was serious. "I said, don't move!"

She raised her palms and ended her approach. However, she still carried a calm expression. "Allison... can we talk about this?" she asked, her voice calm as if trying to defuse the situation.

"No!"

She took another step forward. "I know you're upset. I know you think I'm probably upset at you for killing my husband. But to be honest... I'm not."

"You're lying! I can see the tears in your eyes. You're just trying to trick me."

She took another step. "I know that's what you may think, but—"

"But nothing!"

Tears streamed down my face as I realized the gravity of what I'd done. Brett's past torture, Lydia's twisted desire to inflict pain, and that I'd taken yet another person's life had me digging my fingers into my scalp in frustration.

"You're just sick, dear. It's okay," she said, plainly.

"No, you're sick!" I shot back.

Despite the chaos unfolding around me, I turned away again and fixated on Brett, who looked utterly powerless and in need of help. His muffled cries only intensified my urge to free him, as if doing so would somehow make up for the mess I'd made of my life.

In a split second, Lydia came at me like a bull, but I stood my ground with my knife in hand. Its sharp edge sliced through her nightgown and nicked her breast. But I didn't stop there. As soon as I pulled back, I drove the blade into her shoulder next, feeling it scrape against the bone.

She grabbed me, trying to get the upper hand. I pushed her off her feet and we tumbled to the floor with a thunderous crash. Our bodies collided on top of one another with a force that sent shockwaves rippling through the room. We gasped for air, the shock of the impact stealing our breaths away. In a swift motion, I retrieved the knife from her shoulder and climbed on top of her. Then, with the weapon poised above my head, I hesitated, uncertain of what to do next.

*Just do it and get it over with already. You've done it once, you can do it again. What are you waiting for? Just do it!*

Sweat dripped down my face and onto her nightgown, quickly absorbing into the bloody fabric. I stared into her eyes, searching for a glimmer of remorse. Yet, there was nothing of the sort. Only a cold and evil presence, much like I'd seen in Ryan's when he held me at gunpoint. Eventually, I faltered and I lowered my grip on the knife.

I pondered the best course of action. *I should leave her for Brett. He deserves to take care of her. Not me.*

I mulled over the idea of subjecting her to the same torture that Brett and I endured, administering a slow and painful demise. But before I could decide, she made a move to grab the knife from me. Without hesitation, I balled my fist and struck her in the face. Her cheekbone cracked beneath my knuckles. Then I struck her again and her lip split open like a ripe fruit. And then I once more, rendering her unconscious.

I dropped the knife to check my hand that throbbed with pain, thinking, *Shit, I hope I didn't break it.*

Blood from Lydia's busted lip was smeared across my knuckles and along my white nails. My body shook with fear, the adrenaline rush now replaced by a creeping sense of dread. I couldn't take my eyes off her. Not for one second.

I was afraid that if I turned my back for even a second, she'd try to attack me again. I was trapped between conflicting emotions, torn between the urge to defend myself and the moral imperative to spare her. The thought of taking another life made my stomach churn. I didn't want any more blood on my hands, simply because there was too much on them already.

I rose to my feet, my gaze still fixed on Lydia's still form. I nudged her with my foot to see if she'd move.

Nothing.

Stillness.

I couldn't shake the feeling of unease that settled in my gut. *I should flip her over. Yeah, that'll do the trick.*

I knelt and rolled her over onto her stomach. What better way to give her another obstacle to overcome in case she was to wake while my back was turned? I slowly backed away, my gaze still fixed on her. I had to be ready for any sudden movements. I refused to allow my decision to spare her to come back and haunt me.

Once I reached the black door, I wondered if now would be the right time to go seek help. But then I turned to Brett and the troubled look he gave me helped me decide. He was filled with dread, his eyes heavy as if he were fighting to stay awake. And his face was covered in blood that was still oozing from the gash on his forehead. *I can't leave him here alone. Lydia might wake up any second now. No, I have to get him out now.*

I rushed into the room, dropped to my knees before Brett, and worked to loosen the straps around his wrists. I intended to act fast, but for some reason, I couldn't. My mind was still a jumble of conflicting thoughts. With each passing moment, my breathing grew heavier and more uneven, reminding me of how I hadn't taken my medication.

I began to panic.

*Relax. Just breathe, just breathe, just breathe. You're almost out of harm's way.* "Are you okay?" I asked, struggling to loosen the metal buckles.

Brett answered, but I couldn't understand him through the tape that had been put over his mouth. I knew every second spent trying to loosen his binds would only give Lydia the chance to wake and stop me. So instead, with trembling hands, I used the knife to cut the leather straps on the chair. Then I tore off the duct tape on his mouth, and his words came rushing out like a raging stream.

He reached for my arms and pulled me in for a kiss.

We hugged.

"I'm so glad you're okay," I said.

"Me too. Now c'mon, let's get out of here."

With Brett's hand in mine, I scrambled to my feet and pulled him toward the door. But when we turned the corner, my heart sank to the pit of my stomach.

Lydia had vanished.

# Chapter
# 29

"She's gone!" I exclaimed, before turning to Brett and adding, "We need to leave, now!"

But just as those words left my lips, Lydia reappeared from around the corner as if summoned by a sinister force. This time, she bore a weapon. The grey metal of the pistol gleamed ominously under the sun that shone through the nearby windows. I couldn't fathom where she'd obtained such a weapon, but now, I found myself staring down its deadly barrel just as I had that fateful night with Ryan. Death stared back at me, taunting me with a sense of déjà vu. I was frozen, unable to move, my ears deaf. Everything was still; silent.

"Brett... why are you helping her?" Lydia asked, breaking the daunting silence. "I thought we had a deal."

*Thought we had a deal? What in the world...*

Before I could comment, he answered.

"I don't want to be a part of your sick game anymore, Mother. Now move! Let us go."

In a swift motion, Brett seized the pistol from his mother's hand and forcibly shoved her to the ground. I hadn't expected him to be so aggressive toward her, but his actions assured me he was on my side now. Even if, at one point, he was on theirs.

"Brett?" I called out as he almost reached the staircase.

He turned back to me in bewilderment. "What? C'mon, let's get out of here."

"I left your mother for you to kill. It'd be best to do the deed."

"Well, I don't want to kill her," he admitted. "I'd rather let her rot in prison like she did..." Brett's sentence was left unfinished as he turned and began climbing the stairs. I could sense the pain and sorrow weighing heavily on him through his sullen tone and wondered if it was because of the pain he still felt from the loss of his brother or if it was from the betrayal of his parents. Whichever, I knew the weight of those emotions could crush even the toughest of men; soldiers. It was as if he wanted to disappear and escape it all, much like me. And as he continued up the stairs, I followed.

"Connor?" Lydia called out to us.

Connor's name on Lydia's lips was a mystery to me. He was gone, much like the countless victims of her atrocities. Nothing could bring him back. He was now a person to be remembered; a memory to be thought about on occasion; a person to visit at a cemetery. So why call his name?

I collided into the back of Brett. He'd stopped in his tracks, which led me to ask, "Why'd you stop, Brett? We need to leave while we still have the chance."

"Because he's not Brett, Allison," Lydia said tersely as she crawled to her feet. "He hasn't been Brett since yesterday morning; since we discovered his brother's body in the garage."

Brett turned, and we locked eyes.

My mind reeled in disbelief. *There's no way he's Connor; no way the person I've spent the last day with, out on the water discussing our relationship, and in bed where we almost had sex, is an imposter.*

But as I delved into his un-denying demeanor, a series of recollections surfaced. The way he refused to indulge in my carnal fantasies of kissing my feet, his thunderous snore, his transparent admission about his parents' true occupation as brutal torturers, and finally, his eagerness to help me escape this perilous environment meant he couldn't have been Brett.

They had tormented not only him and his brother, but many others for decades. It was then the man I thought I knew was, in fact, none other than Connor; the man who had escaped from Central State Hospital. But what shook me even more was the realization that he'd slain his sibling. If he was capable of that, what was stopping him from ending my life now that I knew of the truth?

"Is that true? Are you Connor?" I asked dreadfully.

His silence was deafening, which confirmed my worst fears. I pressed my hand on his chest. But he gently pushed me away, and drew the pistol, aiming it directly at his mother.

"Well, I guess the cat's out of the bag now, aye," he said.

"Why did you do it, Connor?" Lydia asked as she slowly approached us. "Why did you kill your brother?"

"Stay back or I'll shoot!" he shouted, descending the few steps back onto the basement level.

"You won't shoot me, son. You haven't done wrong all your life. I don't see you changing now."

Connor's hand trembled. His apprehensiveness was palpable. He seemed unwilling to take another life. That was if he'd taken his brothers. Had the weight of killing his kin burdened him? Perhaps he'd murdered Brett on accident, out of self-defense.

"I'm surprised you're able to hold that gun right now, let alone kill your brother," Lydia continued as she crept closer and closer, slithering like a snake.

"Stop!" he shouted again, his body starting to shudder. "I didn't want to kill him. But I had no choice."

"No choice?" I repeated, unsure of what he meant.

He looked back over his shoulder. "I've been locked up for so long, I haven't lived."

"Yes, you have, dear," Lydia continued, still approaching.

Connor pulled the trigger, sending a bullet right into the floorboard beneath her feet.

"Dammit, Connor! You know better than to do that. Have I not taught you better?"

"Shut up, shut up, shut up!" he yelled, grabbing his head in agony as if experiencing an excruciating headache.

With the way he was prancing, waving the gun carelessly around the room, I feared I'd catch a stray bullet. Then, suddenly, he stopped and re-aimed the pistol at his mother.

"You're the only reason why I haven't lived," he claimed. "So when I escaped, I came here... so I could kill you. All of you."

"But you weren't expecting me to be here, huh?" I asked, descending the steps where I came up beside him.

He looked at me with a sorrowful gaze as tears welled up in his eyes. "I couldn't bring myself to kill an innocent person. You haven't done anything to me. In my eyes, you don't deserve death. Or any of this, for that matter. And I'm sorry you had to experience this."

"You don't need to apologize, Connor. It's not your fault."

"Yes, it is! If I hadn't told Brett my plan—that I was going to run away so I could finally live—we wouldn't be having this conversation."

"But he said he'd tell me, didn't he?" Lydia asked. "Which ruined your plans."

Connor aimed the firearm at his mother once more, but he remained silent. His finger rested lightly on the trigger.

"Is that what happened, dear?" she continued. "Did he threaten to tell on you?"

Connor's cheeks were awash with tears, each droplet falling to the floor in a steady rhythm. It was clear he felt betrayed, not just emotionally, but mentally as well. His family had forsaken him. Though I felt my family had done the same, it still didn't affect me as much as it had done him. But that was simply because I hadn't been locked away, unable to live a life full of freedom. I was allowed to travel, to see the world in its entirety. It was clear I had no clue what sort of mental anguish Connor had experienced while locked up in Central State Hospital. But I understood one thing for certain: he was hurting.

"I had to," he regrettably admitted. "I couldn't let him ruin my plan; ruin my life. I can't go back to that place. All I want is to live. And that's exactly what I'm going to do."

Our eyes met and there was a forlorn expression in Connor's gaze. He quickly looked away, his attention returning to his mother. It was then her hold over him waned. I looked at Lydia and witnessed fear take root in her eyes; a fear that mirrored the primal instinct of a deer frozen in the heart of the woods at the crack of a twig; those wide eyes locked onto the hunter, who stood poised to pull the trigger. It was a chilling tableau of imminent danger, the unspoken understanding of mortality hanging heavy in the air.

"Honey... you don't have to do this," she pleaded. "I can help you."

Connor took another step forward, the hardwood creaking beneath his feet. "You can't help me, Mother. All you've done is tied me up, tortured me, and thrown me out with the rest of the crazy people in the world. But the beautiful thing is... not *all* of them are crazy. In fact, some of them are quite gifted and brilliant. But you'll never know because you don't *want* to know. You just want to lock them all away."

Lydia retreated from Connor's menacing advance until her back hit the far wall near the bookshelf. Her eyes scanned the room, searching for a weapon or an escape route, but there was none. The only options were the bedroom where he and I had slept the past few nights or the torture room across from it. Neither was ideal. The living area, where the sofa and bookshelves were, offered no solace. It was clear her chances of survival were slim.

Tears welled up in her eyes as she continued pleading. "Connor, please don't do this. Let your mother help you. Let me—"

*Bang! Bang! Bang! Bang! Bang!*

## Chapter

# 30

Lydia's lifeless body dropped to the floor with a heavy thud. She and the wall that stood behind her were riddled with holes. Blood pooled around her corpse as her eyes remained fixed open in a look of terror.

Witnessing such a heinous act, where an unarmed victim was mercilessly killed, made my heart churn. The onset of nausea caused me to hunch over and vomit. I heaved and heaved until I was retching nothing but bile onto the floor.

Connor dropped the gun.

Still hunched over and spitting out the bitter taste of vomit, I glanced at him to see if he was okay. Murdering my mother surely would have sent me spiraling into a psychotic break. Surely, he was headed that way. But given the traumatic history he'd endured, I couldn't even fathom how he was holding up mentally.

"Are you all right?" I asked, coming up behind him and resting my hand on his shoulder.

No response.

He just stood there frozen in time like a mammoth trapped in a block of ice.

"Connor?"

He walked away, heading toward the bedroom.

"Connor? Please answer me. I need to know if you're okay."

He disappeared into the bedroom.

I followed him, feeling the need to keep an eye on him for my own safety. There was no telling what he might do, given the fact he'd just murdered his mother. For all I knew, he could be plotting to murder me next.

When I set foot in the room, he was rummaging through the bureau. I wondered what he was searching for. Perhaps it was the scrapbook that contained his family's dark secrets. But I knew he wouldn't find it there anymore, as he had moved it. I thought to wait behind him, hoping for an explanation on why he had, but the lingering taste of bile in my mouth had grown unbearable. So instead, I set the knife on the bureau and headed for the bathroom to rinse my mouth.

I turned on the faucet, cupped my hands under it, then brought it to my mouth. I gargled while listening intently, overhearing him sniffling through the running tap. It was as if he were crying. But I wasn't sure.

I spat out the water, then called out to him. "Connor?"

"I'm fine, Allison," he finally answered. "I'm just a little frustrated is all."

I cupped my hands under the faucet again, brought it to my mouth, then spat. "Are you frustrated because of what happened to your mother, or because you forgot where you hid the scrapbook?"

I rinsed and repeated, then checked in the mirror for any remnants of dirt in my teeth.

"What are you talking about?" he asked, poking his head into the bathroom.

With the water running, I turned to face him, leaned my back against the vanity, and said, "I assume you hid the scrapbook from me because I was going to report your family to the authorities, and you didn't want that to happen. Not yet, at least. That's why it's not there. Correct me if I'm wrong."

"You're not wrong," he regrettably admitted. His tone was dismal. "I did hide the scrapbook from you. But it was only because I feared my mother would dispose of it in some way."

I massaged my temples in aggravation. "Well, because of your plan to save me, things got blown out of proportion. What makes you think I didn't have a plan to escape?"

No response.

"Dammit, Connor. I feel like this all could have been avoided if you hadn't moved that scrapbook."

He crossed his arms and leaned against the doorjamb. "How so?"

"Because I was working with your neighbor." I turned

and cupped my hands under the faucet to get another fill; spat. "If I had that book, your parents would still be alive, serving life sentences."

"Neighbor? What could you be... You know what, they're dead now. Move on. That's what I plan to do." He turned and left the doorway.

I couldn't simply move on after experiencing such a nightmare. It took more than just a few drinks and a good night's rest. The entire weekend had been a shit show; worse than my three-year stint with Ryan. How could Connor recommend such a thing? Perhaps he was more cold-hearted than I was. I rinsed my mouth again.

"And if you can't move on, I'll help you," he continued. "But first, I need to know, are you going to turn me in?"

His question threw me askew. *Did he really just ask me that? How absurd. Why would I turn him in? For Christ's sake, we're both covered in blood. Evidence is all over the house. That should be the least of his worries right now. If anything, we need to take a minute and gather our thoughts. Yeah, we should get our stories straight. After all, we're the victims, not his parents.* But then I thought, *He did admit to killing Brett. Perhaps I should turn him in.*

"Say again," I said, running my mouth under the faucet for the last time.

"I said, are you going to turn me in, knowing who I truly am now?"

His voice was a little louder this time as if he were standing behind me.

I gargled and spat, then blindly reached for the towel on

the nearby rack to dry my mouth. "Eh... I don't know. I was thinking we discuss that after the police get here and question us about your parents."

"I was afraid you'd say that."

I winced upon hearing his voice so close to me as if he were breathing down my neck and pulled the towel away from my face to respond. And when I did, he was standing behind me in the mirror's reflection, his eyes dark and unforgiving as if I were staring into the abyss.

Connor didn't say a single word once we locked eyes. He didn't need to. The menacing look on his face was enough to convey his intentions. I looked at his hand and found him wielding the same knife I'd used to kill his father. He was going to kill me next.

I spun just as he lunged at me, but I was too slow. The knife nicked my tricep, sending blood spurting onto the mirror, like flicked paint. Amid my panic, I fell back, colliding into the glass shower enclosure. Luckily, it had held me in place, preventing me from crashing onto the cold tiles. But when Connor came at me, the surround gave way, and it collapsed.

*Crash!*

He had thrown all of his weight on top of me amid his second attempt to stab me with the knife that we broke through and crashed onto the tile floor of the shower. The entire enclosure shattered upon impact.

I shrieked.

My entire back half had been painted in an array of transparency. But that wouldn't amount to anything if the eight-inch blade Connor wielded plunged deep into my chest. Luckily, I'd used the hand towel as a blinder to prevent him from stabbing me before we fell. Was it the best maneuver? I'd like to think so. But with him now on top of me—and with what felt like thousands of needles pricking my back—I was far from out of the woods.

Suddenly, a promising thought emerged. *If I can get my hands on that gun, I can shoot him.*

But if I were going to go for the gun, first, I'd need to get him off me. I kicked and screamed but failed to escape his grasp. He had me pinned down with all his might, one arm pressing me awkwardly against the tile floor, the other hovering over my chest with the knife in hand. I was inches away from death, but that didn't stop me. I refused to become another victim at the hands of a madman. I'd been through too much already to die now.

Connor stabbed the towel and missed. Then he stabbed the towel a second time, and yet again, the same result. I could only hold him off for so much longer. I was all too aware of the term 'third time's the charm.' I wasn't going to give him the satisfaction of making a third attempt, though.

Then, suddenly, a striking third attempt caught me off guard, and I tried to dodge it. The knife nicked my breast and I let out another shriek. He'd almost punctured my lung. So, with all my might, I kneed him in the balls.

Connor yelped like a hurt dog and dropped the knife. It slid across the tile, coming to a stop beside the commode.

That was my chance to escape. If he were going to kill me, he'd need a weapon to do so. And now with the knife no longer in his possession, I had the upper hand. I scrambled to my feet and rushed to the door as he went for the piece of cutlery. The glass shards under my heels hurt like hell, but I didn't care as long as I survived.

"Come here, bitch!" he shouted, reaching for my ankles as I left the bathroom.

By the time I'd heard his words, I'd left the bedroom and was now traveling down the hall where I grabbed Lydia's gun. As soon as my hand was on the trigger, I spun and aimed the weapon toward the bedroom door and waited.

There was no point in running away, knowing he was still alive. I feared if I had, I'd encounter the same dilemma as I'd contemplated with Jeff—the option of running barefoot along the trail while on my way to Tammy's, now bleeding immensely from all the glass shards coating my back, only to be hunted and eventually caught much like a raccoon during trapping season. The image of Connor holding my corpse up by the hair as if I were some deer he'd shot flashed before my eyes, sending me shuddering at the thought.

*I'm not gonna die. Not today.*

Connor trudged out of the bedroom, winded. He leaned against the doorjamb and glared at me. He'd gotten his hands back on the knife, but that didn't matter because I had my hands on a better weapon. They say to never bring a knife to a gunfight. At that moment, that statement rang true and I felt mighty optimistic about the whole situation to the point where my anxiety diminished entirely.

"Any last words?" I said with a grin.

Connor's steely gaze didn't falter though. It was as if he knew his fate wasn't sealed. That this wasn't the end of the line for him. It was as if he wasn't aware that the same brutal end that had befallen his mother was now looming over him.

The image of my father beating my mother, the one event that had started it all, flickered in my mind's eye, fueling the inferno of anger and resentment that had been building inside me for so long. My blood boiled like molten lava, my rage reaching a fever pitch. I vowed to make Connor pay for all the pain and suffering he'd caused. Every ounce of my being was focused, my pent-up aggression from a lifetime of being beaten and mistreated finally coming to a head.

With my eyes closed, I pulled the trigger. But only only silence followed. No recoil; no deafening bang; no ear-splitting blast; nothingness. I was taken aback by the lack of action from the pistol, inciting my anxiety to come back in full force. Without my medication, I certainly felt I'd die; whether from a panic attack or a slit throat. Nonetheless, my gaze returned to the threat before me, and I found Connor smiling.

"Looks like you're out of ammo, Allison," he said drily. "You should've just fled. But it's too late now."

He stormed toward me and I spun and sprinted up the stairs in defeat. Now I had to opt for Plan B.

# Chapter
# 31

I CLIMBED THE STAIRS, mumbling the words, "Please, God, please, God, please, God."

I imagined law enforcement stationed outside with their guns drawn, poised to apprehend the deranged man chasing after me following the gunshots that had been fired off. But when I reached the top step, the house was just as empty as I'd experienced upon our arrival. But this time it was a bloody mess.

No blaring sirens echoed in the distance, no flickering lights trickled in through the windows, no sound of a doorbell ringing, and no lingering voices from a bullhorn screaming, "Come out with your hands up!"

Suddenly, Connor's grip clasped around my ankle, and he pulled. I stumbled forward and cracked my chin against the floor.

"You're not getting away that easy!" he shouted.

"Let me go!" I yelled as I clawed at the floor to escape him.

I screamed, but it was no use. No one was within earshot to hear my desperate pleas. The closest dwelling was Tammy's, but I highly doubted she'd heard me. She may have heard the gunshots. But that was it.

I rolled onto my side just as Connor made another pass at me with the knife. I narrowly dodged it. The sharp blade plunged deep into the wooden step between my legs. I drew back my foot and kicked him in the stomach, causing him to loosen his grip on me. Then, with all my strength, I scrambled to my feet and bolted toward the kitchen. I didn't dare look back to see if he'd fallen down the stairs. I was too focused on my survival.

I grabbed another knife from the set, spun, and stood my ground, mustering the courage to fight. Though the weapon I wielded was much smaller than the one I originally had, I knew it would do the job of slitting his throat just fine. I clutched the knife tightly as my heart beat with fear and uncertainty. Despite my gratitude for Connor's earlier help in freeing me, I knew that my only chance of survival now was to defend myself and, if necessary, take his life like I had his father. It pained me to even consider it, but I had no choice. After everything he'd endured as a child and now as a man, he didn't deserve to die by my hand. The realization that he was now my enemy filled me with sadness and dread.

I stood there, prepared to take his life. But the lack of his reappearance heightened my anxiety. *Where are you? Come on out you son of a bitch!*

I huddled in the corner of the kitchen, my back pressed against the sink, clutching the knife with a deadly grip. My nerves were raw, and my body trembled with the weight of what was to come. *The gun! I hope he didn't go for it.* I pressed my hand to my head in aggravation. *You idiot. He probably knows where to get more ammo. Dammit, you shouldn't have let him out of your sight.*

The thought of him knowing where to find more ammunition for the pistol shook me to the core. I imagined he was hiding in the shadows, waiting for me to come out of the kitchen so he could put a bullet between my eyes. *That'll be the day I lose it all. But that day's not today. I don't care how clever he is. Or thinks he is. Yeah, he convinced everyone in the house he was someone else. So what? No one knows who I actually am. He's not smarter than me. A little devious yeah, but not smarter. This game of cat and mouse is about to end... because I'm the cat.*

Silence filled the room. Connor had vanished from my senses. There was no trace of his crooked smile, no sound of his shallow breathing, not even a hint of the fear that had filled the room just moments before.

He was gone.

I took a step forward, wincing at the pain from the glass shards still embedded in my feet. A nagging suspicion crept over me. *He wouldn't dare run away. Not with me still alive. I know his little secret. He's a dead man walking. No, he's somewhere around here.*

I took another step forward, only to feel a sudden chill that seemed to emanate from my foot. I looked down, and the horrifying sight of Jeff's corpse lying in a pool of blood greeted me. I'd been so fixated on my survival that I'd completely forgotten about the other person I'd killed. *Shit. Now he can track me. I've gotta find something to wipe this off with.*

A loud, jarring sound of shattering glass drew me away from Jeff and I turned toward the living area. But everything appeared to be in its place. I slightly tilted my head and that's when I found it. The window that had shattered was the one that swiveled; leading to the back deck. He'd also knocked over the ceramic flower pot beside the fireplace. It now lay on its side, fresh topsoil and the fairly large cactus spread among the floor like freshly spilled paint.

Connor's presence was undeniable. The idea that he'd fled the scene was preposterous. He was waiting for me, lurking in the shadows, biding his time to strike with his knife, using the broken window and flower pot as bait to draw me out. *He's stupid if he thinks I'm gonna run. Nice try.*

I let out a faint scoff. I wasn't going to fall into his trap. I also wouldn't attempt an escape through the front door either. I needed to finish the job; needed to rid the world of the Eldridge family once and for all.

Despite the gruesome state of Jeff's shirt, I used it to wipe the blood off my foot as best I could before sneaking toward the foyer. If my bloodied footprints didn't eventually give me away, I surely felt my overbearing gasps for air would. It seemed the world was conspiring against me, leaving me with the short end of the stick. But I wouldn't let it deter me.

I tip-toed toward the front door, listening intently for Connor. The crashing waves from the nearby shoreline were a constant distraction; an indication that Connor had done an excellent job blending in with the soothing sounds of mother nature; from the rising tide to the chirping birds, and even the hum of the whistling wind.

I made my way past the plastic sheets and into the unfinished side room, where darkness descended upon me. When my vision finally adjusted, they landed on the hammer amid the pile of tools I'd seen earlier.

I'd made the mistake of coming into the room that was under renovation, considering he had everything he could need to successfully take my life. While Connor may not have been aware of the renovations before his arrival, he was undoubtedly aware of the many tools at his disposal if he'd noted the room's current state.

With a trembling hand, I knelt, set the knife aside, and picked up the hammer. Before I stood, something lunged at me from behind, knocking me onto the stacked pile of lumber.

It was him.

# Chapter 32

I CRACKED my face hard against the pressure-treated wood, the impact from the fall knocking the wind out of me. I desperately tried to get to my feet, but it was too late. Connor was on top of me. Once again, he had the upper hand.

He wrapped a plastic sheath around my face and pulled back with all his might. Death seemed inevitable at that moment. I was blinded and struggling to breathe. I gasped for air, but it was no use. Much like a cornered animal, my time was coming to an end. Slowly, Connor was robbing me of my breath and it seemed I couldn't escape it.

Connor grunted, and another sharp pain shot through my lower back.

He'd finally stabbed me.

Pain wracked my entire being, consuming me in a way I

never thought possible. *Oh God, I hope he didn't get one of my kidneys. Or worse, my lower intestine.*

To think he'd nicked an organ frightened me. Whether it was my kidneys, my intestine, or my liver, I feared either one would have ended my life shortly. Stomach acid could drain and coat my internal organs until they disintegrated, or I could bleed out internally. Regardless, I no longer felt confident about the situation.

The lack of air and the weight of the plastic suffocating me drew me from my thoughts. I felt like I was already in my grave; the darkness that consumed my vision like a heavy veil, drawing me closer to the afterlife. God was beckoning me. It was a terrifying thought, to have all that I knew and loved slip away into the great unknown. But I wasn't ready to go just yet, not when there was so much left to do. I had to finish what I started, to help those who were suffering and to right the wrongs that had been done.

Despite the pain and numbness spreading through my body, I fought to hold on, to cling to the fading light. And then, in an instant, everything went dark.

———

THEY SAY WHEN YOU DIE, your life flashes before your eyes. Well, during my last breath, I was beginning to think that statement rang true.

I pictured myself inside a luxury movie theater, sitting in a leather recliner with a bag of popcorn in hand, watching my memories play out on the screen. And during that moment, I realized just how fleeting life was. Strangely enough, many of the memories were from my childhood. Seeing everything I'd done and everything I'd ever experienced, down to even the tiniest of details, made my heart warm.

But as the movie continued, I saw my life in a new light. The moments of happiness, love, and triumph stood out more prominently than before. Things like the heavy grin I wore as I received my first paycheck from my first job, the joy in my heart as my father taught me how to ride a bicycle, and the pride I felt as I walked across the stage to receive my nursing degree. Those were the moments that truly defined my life.

As a child, I'd viewed everything as dark and depressing. Now, I understood through the fear and the pain that it was all a shroud of negativity. At a young age, I strongly believed my life was rotten, and that what I'd experienced was nothing compared to how my friends at the time lived.

Looking back now, their lives weren't much better than mine. Much, much later, after graduation when I ran into them at the mall, or the gym, or even at the state fair, I'd found out my so-called friends in high school had talked shit about me behind my back to the popular crowd so they could get in with the cool kids who were now, overweight, out of shape, illness-ridden bitches. Granted, they say not to believe everything you hear, but I highly doubt hearing said information from a sibling was not practically getting it from the source.

Kacy—who I thought was my best friend—also grew up

in a troubled household. Her father had committed infidelity. Her parents didn't divorce, simply for the sake of the children, her being the baby. But as soon as she graduated and left home, her parents went their separate ways.

Crystal—the girl I always partnered with in gym class—was sexually molested by her stepfather during all four years of high school. Her mother left him once she found out, resulting in him getting charged with rape and serving a few years in prison.

And last but not least, Brenda—the one friend who spread rumors across the entire school about me having crabs even though I was a virgin until my twentieth birthday—ended up becoming a stripper because her parents had died in a tragic car accident when she was five, leading her and her sister to be put up for adoption, only then to be mistreated and beat on by countless unfit parents. That easily explained why I never got invited over to her place for sleepovers.

It was painful to know the people I'd thought were my friends had never truly cared about me. It made me wonder how many other times I'd been wrong about the people in my life; friends, coworkers, cousins. But at that moment, as my life flashed before my eyes, I knew it didn't matter anymore. It never did.

What mattered were those who had always been there for me, who had supported me through thick and thin, who never judged me or abandoned me, and everything I did for them and others without an expectation of reciprocation.

An image of my parents emerged next. They were there for me through everything, even when they struggled with their own issues. Then another person emerged. My best friend from college who was always there to listen and offer a shoulder to cry on. And then many others. My patients, whose lives I'd helped change for the better. And most of all, Kathleen, the girl whose case drove me to continue down this dangerous path.

We all were the same, just broken people with broken families. But we weren't truly broken. Only deranged people like Lydia and Jeff thought we were. Those who had sick minds and twisted agendas. People who claimed to want to help us, but only wanted to see us squirm for their enjoyment or for science and notoriety.

I refused to allow anyone else to get hurt. I refused to allow anyone else to be a victim at the hands of the Eldridge family. Though I'd already killed everyone involved in the sadistic torture of myself and many other helpless women, I still needed to handle the last person in the family.

# Chapter
## 33

With a sudden jolt, my eyes sprang open and I let out a sharp gasp. *Thank, God I'm alive.*

Feeling grateful for the second chance at life, I knew I had to do the right thing, to rid the earth of Connor's existence. An intense pressure pulsed behind my eyes, which led me to fear I'd lost a significant amount of blood. *Geez, how long have I been unconscious?*

I rolled to my side to sit up and pressed my hand against the floor. A muddy liquid swam between my fingers. I looked and found an unsightly pool of blood around me. *Shit, that's a lot of blood.*

I scanned the room, noting how I was in the same empty room near the foyer where I'd fought Connor. *That son of a bitch left me for dead. What an asshole.*

But considering he wasn't towering over me now that I was awake, meant he must have been elsewhere in the house, or gone entirely. Because if he'd heard me wake, he surely would have returned to finish the job. With no clock in the room and no phone to check the time, I felt I'd come to hours later and Connor was now long gone.

Perhaps he'd left, taking the white pickup south toward Mexico to flee the country and start a new life where he could be free and do as he pleased. Maybe he was playing off the situation to the best of his ability, by calling the police and reporting that I'd killed his parents out of delusion and that he stopped me by killing me in self-defense—him still playing the Brett card. If that were the case, wouldn't the police have arrived by now? I glanced up at the curtains in search of any flashing lights shining through, but none were present.

I planted my palms on the hardwood and pushed, slowly rising from my burial. My body felt frail as I struggled to my feet. Eventually, I regained my balance. I pressed my hand to my head, feeling my body sway slightly as if I were about to pass out and collapse. That was when I noted my knife still on the ground beside the hammer, its splitting edge glimmering in the flicker of light that peered in through the slit of the curtains.

I knelt and reached for it, being careful not to tumble over. To create a ruckus amid the silence, not knowing whether I was alone, would only put an end to my plan before it even started. I imagined reaching for the knife, then stumbling back to regain my balance and crashing into the scaffolding behind me; all the paint supplies that rest on it tumbling to the floor in an avalanche of pinging sounds. Then I'd look toward the plastic sheet that covered the room to find Connor rushing in to find me disoriented.

I shuddered at the thought of how terrible of an ending to my mediocre life that would have been. With the knife tight in my hand, I brought it close to my chest, then hugged the wall and tip-toed toward the foyer. When I reached the hallway, I slowly pulled back the plastic sheet that kept me hidden from the rest of the home and peered out.

Connor was nowhere to be found.

I listened intently, and still, I heard nothing but the gentle stream of rain. I was certain he'd left me for dead now. There was no sign of him anywhere, no aroma of freshly cooked food, no streaks of blood leading out of the kitchen from having moved his father's body, and no sound of a frantic plea for help as if he were on the phone speaking with the police.

Nothing but silence.

I drew in a breath and crept into the foyer and down toward the kitchen. Empty. I spun to inspect the living area —a feeling of lightheadedness still apparent—and still, there was nothing. I braced myself against the sofa in fear I'd pass out, almost dropping the knife as I did. *Don't pass out, don't pass out, don't pass out. You've got this. Just take it slow.*

I maneuvered around the broken flower pot and came to the window where I looked out at the mountain. Who knew a beautiful sight could only be had in a deathtrap of a home? Suddenly, movement down on the boat dock caught my eye. Connor was relaxing in the misty rain on the sun lounger. I squinted and nudged my neck forward. *Did he change clothes? What a freak. Well, at least now I know he's still here. I guess I wasn't out for that long. But why would he stay? Shit doesn't make any sense. Someone must've heard the gunshots. The cops have gotta be on their way.*

I opened the deck door and stepped out, carefully dodging the remnants of shattered glass from the window. My fingers grazed the house's exterior as I crept toward the stairs. I refused to take my eyes off Connor for one second. If I had, there was a chance he'd disappear right out from under me, never to be seen again. I couldn't allow it to happen.

Right now I had him in check mate. And though we were more than a couple of feet apart, I still had him trapped, with nowhere to go but in the water. *But what if he does? Hmm? What are you gonna do then, huh? Jump in after him? You're too weak. You'll drown.* I groped my head and cursed myself. *Shut up, dammit! But it's true. You won't be able to chase after him. He won't do it because I'm gonna sneak up on him and slit his throat.*

I believed that was the only way to successfully end this horrid nightmare; embody their dark and twisted ways. I grabbed the banister and took one step, then another. I gritted my teeth as my pain level steadily increased. *God, I wish I had a Xanax right now.*

When I reached the bottom step, I turned to travel down the walkway toward the boat dock. But as soon as I did, he moved. I stepped to my left and hid behind a row of decorative juniper trees that lined the walkway to the garage and waited. The thought that he was headed out to the truck to leave, swirled in the back of my mind. But I knew I couldn't let him leave.

I couldn't allow him the freedom to hurt another soul; to take another life; to seek vengeance on the employees who'd held him captive at Central State Hospital. I also couldn't allow him to discover I wasn't dead if for some strange reason he went back inside to check because then, I'd no longer have the element of surprise.

Desperately controlling my breathing with my all might, I patiently waited for Connor to stroll up the boat dock. My chest rose and fell. Deep breaths. Frantic breaths, but still faint. And as my patience grew thin, I also grew lightheaded. More and more, my vision blurred. *Don't pass out, don't pass out, don't pass out. You're right there. For the love of God, stay awake!*

I poked my head out from around the tree, but it was no use. From where I stood, I had no visual of him. No clue whether he was aware of my presence or not; aware of me lingering in the shadows, waiting to strike him down like a mountain lion. Then suddenly, sirens echoed in the distance, and my heavy eyes widened.

*The police! They're finally here!*

A shadow zoomed by. Connor's back was to me. His alertness was palpable. He must have also heard the sirens, which was a good sign because now I knew I wasn't hallucinating from the blood loss. The sirens were real. My hope had been restored, and I was now going to kill Connor.

In one swift movement, I squeezed the hilt with all my might, drew in a breath, and forced my way out from behind the trees, plunging the knife deep into his shoulder as I tackled him to the ground.

I yanked the knife from his shoulder and stabbed him again. Over and over, I stabbed him. Once in the kidneys, then another in his side. By the time I'd stopped thrusting, I'd lost count. I wasn't really taking note of how many times I'd stabbed him. All I knew was that I was doing it, and now he was no longer moving. Regardless, it was finally over. I'd finally defeated the Eldridge family. Somehow, someway, I'd mustered up enough strength to take Connor down despite my wounds, and now, I could finally move on.

I tried to stand, but then everything went dark and I passed out.

# Part Four:
# Resurrection


## Sunday, April 16th, 2023
## - many hours later -


**"Our wounds are our sources of growth."**
**- Rachel Naomi Remen**

## Chapter
# 34

WHEN I REGAINED CONSCIOUSNESS, I was in the hospital; in bed, in pain.

A burly man sat in a chair at the foot of my bed, his legs crossed, and his focus drawn to the notepad in his lap. He wore a white button-up, shrouded in a black blazer with khakis and some chocolate loafers. His entire wardrobe screamed police.

A sharp jolt shot up my spine, causing my head to pulse. I went to rub my temples to ease the pressure, but couldn't. One of my hands had been cuffed to the bed frame.

"I'm glad you're awake," said the man without sparing a glance. "How're you feeling?"

"A little disoriented," I answered irritably.

His eyes met with mine. "That's to be expected. You'd lost quite a lot of blood, on top of getting surgery."

"Surgery?"

"Yes. Whoever stabbed you had nicked a kidney."

*Kidney? Shit, he hit it.*

My mind finally cleared and I recalled everything that had happened. Being in a hospital wasn't exactly what I would have preferred, but at least I was finally safe and out of harm's way. Not to mention, healed.

"So, who are you?"

"I'm Detective Barnes, the person assigned to your case. I'm here to ask you a few questions about your weekend."

"What else is there to say, sir? Those people tried to kill me."

"That may be true. However, I still need to cover all the bases since you're the only one who's alive."

I struggled to sit up in the bed, another sharp pain making me wince again. "All right then, go ahead and ask your questions. It's not like I have anywhere else to go."

Detective Barnes drew in a breath and began.

Three hours passed before I grew tired of recounting everything that had transpired. Though my exhaustion hadn't fully stemmed from the actual reciting of what treacherous acts I'd endured, but rather because Detective Barnes insisted that I was to blame for the tragic deaths of the Eldridge family; that I had done the unspeakable acts out of spite. Preposterous.

I wasn't crazy enough for that. They had brought it onto themselves. They were the ones responsible for their own deaths. Not me. I must admit, my story did sound bizarre; a young woman who had a history of abuse, claiming to have killed a family in self-defense all because they had tortured her. But their demise was bound to happen at some point. They would have eventually died at the hands of someone, if not for me. Because eventually, you reap what you sow.

"So you said there were three bodies?" Detective Barnes asked.

"Yes, sir. And I acted in self-defense, as I've said for the past three hours. I wouldn't lie to you. Now, please"—I jiggled my left wrist, the handcuff digging into my skin like claws—"can you remove these cuffs? They're quite uncomfortable."

He scribbled something onto his notepad before fixing me with a suspicious glare. "I'm sorry, but I can't do that, Ms. Sellers."

"And why's that? I've done everything you've asked of me. I've endured your grueling interrogations for the past three hours. The least you can do is free me from these cuffs."

"The reason I can't do that is because your story isn't all there."

"All there?" I repeated in disbelief. I turned toward the window and groaned. "This is just ridiculous."

Suddenly, thunder crackled overhead, leading me to peer out the window at the pouring rain.

"Be that as it may," he continued, as my eyes remained fixed on the gloomy sky. "Your story still doesn't match up with the evidence we gathered. You said there were three people. However, we only have two bodies; one riddled with stab wounds and the other with multiple gunshots."

I gasped in disbelief as a treacherous wave of anxiety

washed over me, sending me turning from the window and locking eyes with him. *There's no way Connor could've survived. I'd stabbed him multiple times.*

I started counting on my fingers, trying to recall how many exactly, but couldn't. I closed my eyes and shook my head, trying to remember.

"What's wrong?"

"There were three bodies, not two," I said, reluctant to believe what the police had found.

"I'm sorry, but we only recovered two from the scene. The one in the kitchen and the one in the basement."

"Yes." I sighed harshly, with fatigue and distress. "But there was another body where I was found, right before you reach the garage."

Detective Barnes sifted through his notes. "The police have no record of a third body, Ms. Sellers. Perhaps you are referencing—"

"I told you there was a third body!" My plea seemed to fall on deaf ears as he continued to skim over his notes while giving a noncommittal hum of acknowledgment in response to my statement.

Someone knocked on the door. It opened and a nurse poked her head into the room. "I don't mean to interrupt," she said, pushing the door wide. "I just came by to drop off dinner."

Detective Barnes gestured her in.

The woman came to my bedside and presented me with a plate of unappetizing hospital food I'd ordered. I grabbed her wrist as she turned to leave and said, "Miss, can I have some Ambien, please? I haven't gotten much sleep the past few days."

*I hope she caught the hint.*

I prayed she did, for the weariness in my eyes—a weariness that'd been brought on by three grueling hours of unrelenting interrogation from the skeptical, bearded detective across from us—might not have done it. As if the physical torture hadn't been enough, he seemed to be determined not to believe me; that I hadn't acted in self-defense against the Eldridge family's madness; that there wasn't a third body. He needed to leave so I could recoup from the previous day's nightmare and think about where Connor could have run off.

The nurse pulled the clipboard that rested in the pouch on the wall beside my bed and scanned it, presumably checking to see if any medication given would counteract another. Then she met my gaze and gave me a reassuring smile. "Okay. I'll be right back."

The nurse left. I examined the bland meal she'd placed before me; the seasonless grilled chicken as white as snow, overly cooked broccoli as soft as the pillow supporting my back, and the thick mashed potatoes that carried the consistency of porridge. It seemed too early to eat given the clock that hung on the wall across from my bed read five minutes after five. I wasn't even hungry.

"Some meal, ain't it?" Detective Barnes said drily.

I scoffed, annoyed at his failed attempt to make me laugh. "Are we done here? Because if so, I want you to leave."

He stood and approached the window, placing his hands on the sill as he looked out into the city. "Ms. Sellers, please," he said. "I know this is difficult, but you need to tell me what happened. I've got two people dead—"

"Three!" I yelled.

He sighed in resignation, shaking his head slowly. "I know, I know. A third body. But there's no record of another body."

"I don't believe you. Somehow, some way, the police missed something."

"Miss? We don't miss things, Ms. Sellers."

*He's toying with me, I just know it. First, he tries to trip me up; get me to confess. Now tell me they didn't miss anything. Connor was right there. He was dead. I didn't murder those people without reason. I only acted in self-defense, that's it.*

I shuddered as another sickening thought emerged. *If Connor somehow survived, then why didn't he kill me? The police couldn't have closed in that quick, could they have? He must not have had time to act. Maybe he wanted to torment me instead; be a chip on my shoulder. Maybe he's gonna come visit me here. No, that's bullshit. That fucker is dead. D-E-A-D.*

Frustration and fatigue filled me. "That's bullshit!"

Startled by my sudden outburst, Detective Barnes spun around and menacingly approached the bed. I pulled back, fearing what he might do. Strangely enough, he gently rested his hand on top of my thigh and said softly, "What you went through was traumatizing. I can't begin to imagine what you endured up there in the mountains. But trust me... it's all over now; you won't have to endure anymore."

My throat tightened at hearing those words—hollow promises of security when all I felt was fear coursing through my veins from years of unrelenting trauma dating back far longer than this scarring situation I'd been thrust into.

I clenched my fists tightly. "Hearing those words doesn't make me feel any better, Detective. If anything, they reassure me that you know nothing about trauma; that you have no understanding of what it's like—the inner turmoil that extends far beyond your psyche." I winced in pain as I readjusted myself in bed. "Trauma affects every aspect of your life; job prospects; relationships; everything. You have to rely heavily on managing anxiety that is simply unbearable at times. I even take medication for it."

I peered out the window, watching as the rain lashed against the glass like a whip. My time of abuse had left a permanent mark on me; an indelible scar I could never escape regardless of what I did to distance myself from it.

"But it doesn't end there," I continued, my voice steady despite the quiver in my heart. "I've had this chip on my shoulder for years now, Detective. Even after I escaped my ex in Dallas, Ryan, I still couldn't shake off that fear. So, when I first got out, I bought a gun and learned how to use it."

My gaze returned to his as he stepped back tentatively. He seemed taken aback by my admission.

"It was as if his form of *love* was etched into my

memory like a coffee stain on a white shirt," I continued. "No matter how many times you wash it, or attempt to treat it and nurture it, there's still that shadow of a scar that remains."

"And God, don't get me started on the nightmares." My voice had grown louder. "I wake up almost at the same time every night, drenched in a cold sweat because of this debilitating fear. It's like a black cloud that forever looms over me. But you wouldn't know anything about that now, would you?"

His clueless expression only fed the fire inside me until I felt so hot I could hardly breathe. I grew angrier still as he remained silent, seeming as if barely attempting to understand what had happened or how deeply it still affected me.

"No, I wouldn't expect you to. But that's just because you didn't ask. But why would you? You don't care about me." I gripped tightly onto my plate and hurled it toward him with all my might—a final display of anger and unspoken pain that seemed to fill the air around us. "All you care about is arresting me while one of the people responsible for this madness is still out there!"

I winced in pain as I retracted my arm. Pieces of mashed potato had clung to the detective's blazer—a reminder of how quickly my anger and hurt had exploded into action. I was so loud that I'd even garnered the attention of a passerby; my nurse. She'd returned with my medicine and a glass of water to wash it down.

Her face was etched with worry as she looked around

the room to find I'd dumped my dinner all over the detective. I let out a grueling sigh and lay back in the bed.

"You okay, Allison?" the nurse asked, coming up beside me.

"My back... it hurts."

The nurse set the glass and my medicine aside on the over-bed table and leaned me forward to assess my back. She lifted my gown and applied pressure to my dressing. I pulled away and gritted my teeth as she touched my wounds.

"Oh, dear, you've gone and popped your stitches." She pressed the call button to signal another nurse to come down and assist her in fixing me up. Then, to the detective, she added, "Sir, I'm sorry, but I'm going to have to ask you to leave. We need to stitch her back up, and"—she glanced at the mess on the floor—"by the looks of it, need to get her another plate too."

Though my body radiated a great deal of pain because the stab wound on my back had reopened, the joy I'd received from witnessing Detective Barnes covered in food —and his glaring expression afterward—seemed to numb it. Even his beady eyes that bore deep into my soul, didn't have an effect.

I chuckled a little as he tucked his notepad into the inner lining of his blazer and headed for the door, but not before turning around once more and saying, "I'll be back tomorrow."

# Part Five: Atonement

## Monday, April 17th, 2023

> "In violence, we forget who we are."
> — Mary McCarthy

# Chapter
# 35

I awoke the following day after my grueling incident and was met with a promising face. Tammy sat in the chair across the room, her presence bearing a sense of calm. She was dressed in gray sweatpants and a white tank top as she stared out the window, looking down at what I believed was the morning traffic. She turned to face me as I shifted in bed, making my presence known.

"Good morning," she said with a smile.

"Morning. So, what do I owe the pleasure?"

"I've just come to check up on you. You know, to make sure you're still alive."

We both giggled, my body still aching. "I guess you're to thank for the police, huh?"

"Sure am. Once I heard the gunshots, I knew you were in trouble."

I smiled. "Thank you. If it weren't for you, I'd be dead."

"Please, it seems like you handled yourself quite well if you ask me."

Her kind words brought warmth to my heart, a feeling only a genuine human connection could bring. It was as if she knew exactly how deranged the family was, and how difficult surviving their twisted ways were. Perhaps she'd experienced a similar feat; one where she had to fight to survive. Her husband maybe, if she had ever been married.

Then, the reminder that I'd failed to kill everyone caused my heart to sink within seconds. "I don't think so," I said dreadfully.

"Why?"

"Because I only managed to kill two of them, not all three."

"What? You killed them?"

"Yes. I killed them in self-defense. They were torturing me, and then Lydia tried to shoot me with a gun after I failed to escape."

"I guess that explains the gunshots."

"But the thing is, I didn't fire the weapon. Neither did she. Her son did."

Tammy tilted her head to the side, trying to comprehend what I was getting at.

"But that's not all," I continued. "Remember when I told you they had two kids?"

She nodded.

"Well, one of them was actually good and helped me escape. Or at least tried to. And he was the one who shot his mother with the pistol. But afterward, he tried to kill me when I wanted to get the police involved."

"And tell me again why you think you didn't handle yourself well enough?"

"Because I failed to kill him, the one who helped me. The police only recovered two bodies from the house. His parents."

"And how do you know this?"

"Because a detective came in asking me a shitload of questions yesterday, and he told me. He's still out there, Tammy. Connor's still free." I jerked myself up from the bed and a sudden pain shot up my back. "He's probably outside the hospital right now, patiently waiting for me to fall asleep so he can finish the job."

"I highly doubt that, Allison. But wait... You said, Connor, not Brett?"

I nodded. "Yes. He faked his death. Killed Brett and took his place."

"I don't believe that."

"Well, believe it. You don't know any of them like I do. He's just as sick in the head as they were."

"Well, if it's any consolation, there's an officer stationed outside your room. So if he is still out there somewhere, I highly doubt he'll be able to get to you."

I exhaled in relief, knowing I was being watched by the police. However, I still felt a sense of impending doom. It was as if at any moment, whether through a shift change between officers, a measly bathroom break, or even an officer falling asleep on the job, Connor would sneak into my room and off me while I slept. Or worse, I'd be arrested and charged with murder.

"Now about the case." Tammy stood from the chair and approached my bed.

"Which case?"

"Kathleen's. Her disappearance is still unresolved."

I adjusted the height of my bed as she took comfort at the foot of it.

"So... did you manage to find Kathleen's name on any of the medication?"

I gritted my teeth, hesitating to answer. Knowing I'd failed at locating the evidence after we'd spoken on the phone, I felt as if she'd get angry. Yell at me, even. All because the two years she'd spent trying to put away the Eldridge family had now gone to waste.

"About that, I..." I couldn't finish my sentence. I couldn't admit that I'd failed.

"You did look for them, right?" Her eyes were filled with eager anticipation.

"Yes, but..."

Tammy sank her head in disappointment, sending me to do the same. A cloud of uncertainty loomed overhead. If Tammy hadn't reported back to Kathleen's family, they would never find closure for the loss of their daughter.

"I'm sorry, but soon after we discussed the pills, I went looking for them. But they were gone, just like the scrapbook."

Tammy let out a sigh of frustration.

"I know you're angry, Tammy. Hell, I would be too, after

spending as much time as you did on this case. But look at the bright side. They're dead now. They won't be harming anyone else. Well, I can't speak for Connor, but I doubt he'll follow in their footsteps."

"That's not the point, Allison."

"Then what is?"

"I was paid to do a job. So, I have to prove they killed her."

Then, during our argument, I had a surge of clarity. I remembered the garage containing all the evidence the Eldridge family had on every person they'd kidnapped and tortured, categorically stored away on paper and on video. The sudden image of Kathleen's file emerged, showcasing the insignia of the company at the top of the page: Central State Hospital. I must have had a lapse in memory from all the electroshock therapy.

"Central State Hospital!" I exclaimed.

"Excuse me?"

"Kathleen's still alive! And I believe she's in Central State Hospital. I bet a majority of the recent people they've kidnapped are in there."

"And how do you know this?"

Someone knocked on the door and Detective Barnes entered.

"Morning, ladies," he said, his tone and confident demeanor overbearing.

"Right before I got caught and tortured, I discovered a collection of files on all of their patients stored in boxes in the garage, dating back at least thirty years," I continued. "I believe the evidence on the whereabouts of every woman on your list that has vanished over the past four years is there."

"You think so?" she asked.

"That's where I found Kathleen's information. I bet the family locked all of them away in Central State Hospital after they were done with them."

"I hope you're telling the truth," Detective Barnes opined.

I turned to face him. "I have no reason to lie."

"Allison, please," Tammy said, gently patting my thigh. "He's on our side."

"It sure didn't seem like that yesterday."

"Well, that was before I knew your history, *Deborah*."

"Deborah?" Tammy questioned.

My heart skipped a beat, causing me to let out a booming gasp. After everything that had happened, after all the crippling torment I'd endured, my truth had finally come to light. I looked at Tammy, then back to Barnes. In their subjective expressions, I knew I had no choice but to speak the truth.

"Go on, tell her," he urged.

Tammy's gaze fixed on mine. "Tell me what?"

I tucked my chin and regrettably admitted, "That I'm not who I say I am. My real name is Deborah Collins. I changed my identity after I left my previous relationship because I was too scared to fight back; was too afraid he'd find me."

"Again with the lies," he barked after dropping a large manilla folder in my lap.

"I'm not lying!" I yelled. "It's the truth."

Tammy picked up the folder and opened it. I had no clue what lay inside that tan folder. It could have been anything; photographs, hospital records, a warrant for my arrest. The possibilities were endless. And though I had a feeling what it could be, I refused to accept it as fact.

"Who's this?" she asked, tilting the folder to show me a photograph.

I looked at the picture. It was of our old bedroom; Ryan lying in our bed with his throat slit and the headboard and sheets covered in blood.

I gasped.

"Do you know that man, Deborah?" Detective Barnes asked.

"I don't," I lied.

"I don't see why not. He was your husband, after all, wasn't he?"

"Husband?" Tammy questioned.

I snatched the folder from Tammy's hand and attempted to return it to Detective Barnes, not wanting to accept the fact he was correct. That that picture was of Ryan, my deceased husband. "I'm sorry, Detective, but I don't know the man in this picture."

Even though I felt the detective was simply phishing, once he reached into his blazer and pulled out a small photograph of Ryan and me together on our wedding day, and tossed it at me, I knew it was game over.

"I guess we'll see about that in front of a jury of your peers. Deborah Collins, you're under arrest for the murder of Ryan Collins."

"Murder?!" Tammy took ahold of my right hand and caressed it with a mother's touch. "Tell me it isn't so."

I turned to Detective Barnes. "How'd you find out?"

He smiled and chuckled. "When you brought up your previous relationship yesterday, I thought perhaps doing a little research on your past might give me some insight on whether or not you were telling the truth. But when I checked your records and found I couldn't go back more than four years—that there was no criminal record of domestic abuse, no medical records of any broken bones or hospital visits—I knew something was off. So then I searched for every Ryan in Dallas, Texas; alive and dead to see if I could find him. And that's when I discovered a warrant. You were wanted in connection to the murder of your husband. And once I saw the picture, I knew it was you."

"You're a clever man," I admitted. Then to Tammy, I added, "I'm sorry, but... it's true. I did murder my husband."

"Why?"

I looked out the window, catching a glimmer of the beautiful glow of the morning sun that cast a shadow of rays across the room. I was reluctant to explain what treacherous act I'd done, but I knew my past had finally caught up with me, and I'd been caught. So, it didn't matter now. I was ready to accept my fate. Atone for my past mistakes.

I drew in a breath, turned to her, and began. "There's something I neglected to mention when I came over to your place, Tammy. I was married once to a guy back in Dallas, Texas. Somehow, I'd gotten myself in a bind. I blame love as an excuse. Regardless, by the time I realized it, there was nothing I could do. We were bound by the state. You know, 'til death do us part. It all started when I found some bank records in his toolbox one day. Now I know what you're thinking. Why would I be in the garage looking through his toolbox in the first place? Well, it's quite simple really. I was looking for the perfect hiding place for his birthday gift.

"I couldn't confront him about what I'd found, because the first thing he'd do is ask me why I was in the garage, snooping around. And I didn't want that. It would've only ruined the surprise. In hindsight, I should've come out and asked him about the bank records then, even if it would have created more tension in our relationship. Doing so might have prevented him from doing what he did to me. May have altered our future altogether. However, looking back now, no amount of communication between us could have saved him. He was a lost cause."

I could feel the power of my truth growing stronger with every passing moment as I explained what had happened. It was as if I was shedding an old skin like a snake, leaving behind the person I'd pretended to be for so long, and embracing the woman I truly was; the dark, twisted, manipulative woman who'd created a fake identity just to escape what she'd done.

Detective Barnes listened intently, his face a mask of professional detachment.

Tammy's eyes mimicked mine—pooling tears—which led me to believe I'd finally made a connection with her that went beyond words. "The next day, after he left for work, I took my car across town to the bank with the papers I'd found. When I approached the counter and asked the teller for the balance on the account, I was shocked by the amount the lady told me."

"How much money had he taken from you?" Tammy asked, her tone filled with intrigue.

"Not taken, but hidden from me," I corrected. "He had fifty grand in a savings account. Now I know you're probably thinking he was entitled to that money, that it was all his, and that I shouldn't have touched it, but I disagree. The reason why I deserved that money, why I took it was simply because he'd lied to me. Because he'd used me for his personal gain."

I balled my fists in anger and resentment toward the memory of what that sick bastard had done to me.

"How'd he use you for his personal gain?" Tammy asked.

"Because for the past year, I'd been the breadwinner of the household due to him getting laid off from his job. Or what I thought was his job. I was paying the mortgage, the utilities, food, and gas for both of our vehicles. There was no way in hell he'd scrummed up that amount of cash legally, considering he didn't have a paycheck. He must have been doing something illegal, using me like some dim-witted broad to pay his bills."

"So then you killed him?" Detective Barnes suggested.

"No," I answered. "That accounted for some of it, but not all. Now can I continue?"

He nodded.

"I'd made up my mind about Ryan that day. My feelings for him had evaporated entirely. Whatever lingering emotions I had for him were gone; dried up like a raisin in the sun. What drew the line for me, though, was when I confronted him about it later that night and he decided to throw a gun in my face instead of admitting he'd done wrong.

"I didn't understand why at the time. Perhaps he was afraid I'd report him to the authorities. Maybe he thought I knew more than I let on. I even entertained the thought that he didn't want me to get involved in whatever crime he'd committed in fear I might get hurt or arrested, thinking love was what led him to keep it from me.

"However, I highly doubted that was the case though because he was so quick to deflect and act like I was crazy. But whatever the reason, I refused to be a part of a lie, refused to take part in a world where I was the lessor, the used, the mistreated. I'm not some cheap hooker who you can take advantage of for a quick fuck and cheap thrill, you know. I'm a woman with morals who knows her value and won't accept less."

I peered down at my trembling hands, the scratches and scars from having survived such a feat bringing tears to roll down my cheeks. "And after all the lies and deceit, I just couldn't take it anymore. For years, I accepted the way things were—the merciless beatings, the disrespect, the blatant disregard of my emotions—believing things would get better. Yet somehow, some way, that night, something changed. The way he threatened me with a gun, the menacing look in his eyes, I just... I just... snapped. It was a wake-up call. I deserved better. It was then that I knew if I didn't escape his wrath, he'd eventually kill me. So after we went to bed, I snuck downstairs in the middle of the night, grabbed the largest knife from the kitchen set, and showed him what I was about."

Following those words, I felt a sense of liberation I'd never known before, a freedom that came from knowing my true identity had been revealed and that I'd finally come to terms with what I'd tried to run away from for so long.

For years, I'd remained distant from my family, shielding myself from my troubling past. No phone calls, no texts, no email. Nothing. Just silence. Yet somehow, despite what I thought, I knew one day it would eventually return. I just wish it were in my old age. Not now. Not while I was still young.

It was a spine-shivering moment, one that left me trembling with emotion and filled with a sense of awe at the power of honesty and self-discovery. And even though I understood my haunting past had finally caught up with me, I was prepared to accept what was to come.

*I guess what they say is true. You do reap what you sow.*

# Epilogue



FIVE HOURS LATER, Tammy and Detective Barnes arrived at Central State Hospital. They sat in his cruiser for a moment in deep discussion.

"I can't believe she lied to me," she muttered under her breath.

"Well, believe it," said Detective Barnes. "She's a killer. I'm surprised she didn't go after you. I guess you didn't provoke her."

"The thing is... I did."

Every taunt and every demand Tammy had made to Deborah circled her mind. Knowing well enough Deborah wasn't too fond of her, considering the conversations they'd had, she still pried in hopes of getting one step closer to finding Kathleen. And yet through it all, Deborah didn't fight back with a strike of a hand or stab of a knife. Instead, she did the exact opposite.

"So why wouldn't she?" she questioned.

"Perhaps she'd turned a new leaf," he said. "Maybe she wanted to scrum up some good karma so her past wouldn't come back to bite her in the ass."

"Maybe she did. She seems like a nice person. And if Kathleen is here, then she played a major part in helping save someone's life. Surely, that'll decrease her sentence, right?"

Barnes pulled the key from the ignition. "She's a killer and she fled, plain and simple. I highly doubt the courts will be lenient. Now stop worrying about it. It's not your problem. You'll never see her again. At least, unless you visit her. Now stop twiddling your thumbs and let's head inside."

They exited his cruiser and marched across the parking lot toward the entrance, her breathing heavy. "I can't imagine being locked up in here like some rabid animal."

"Neither can I. Let's just hope Kathleen hasn't been here long—that's if she's even here." They passed through the sliding glass doors. "Now how long's this girl been missing?"

"Two years."

"Hmm. Maybe she has been here for a while."

Tammy nervously scratched the back of her arm. "I just hope she isn't too far gone. I'd hate for her to become another victim of malpractice."

They approached an L-shaped bar-like counter that ran long and then cut off near a hallway leading to the elevators. Three people sat equally spread out. Two of the staff were on the phone, probably answering questions regarding health insurance or career opportunities, and the other was seemingly handling paperwork with how her eyes were locked in on something just beneath the ledge of the counter and her right hand was moving swiftly as if writing.

Barnes cleared his throat and the woman looked up.

"Good afternoon," she said. "What can I do for you?"

He held up a warrant and lowered it onto the counter. "I'm Detective Barnes and this is my associate. We've got reason to believe this establishment has participated in malpractice and, as a result, has been harboring abductees for the past few years. This is a warrant to inspect the premises. Now if you will... kindly take us Kathleen Otterman."

The woman set the warrant aside and clacked her fingers along the keyboard of the computer. Seconds later, she said, "I'm not allowed to leave my post, but I can give you her room number. It's 302 on the third floor."

"Thank you," he said to the woman. Then he marched down the hall toward the elevators, Tammy following behind him.

They entered the lift, tapped the button for the third floor. The doors closed, both of them leaning against the thin metal walls.

"I guess this is it, huh?" she said. "The moment of truth. Gosh, I can't believe I waited two years for this."

"Anxious much?"

"I just hate wasting time; wasting other people's time,

you know. Her family's been waiting tirelessly, day in and day out, burning dollar after dollar in hopes of finding out what happened."

"Well, I guess it's a good thing we're about to find it then."

"Yeah, I guess you're right."

"You don't sound pleased."

"Because I'm not," she said sharply. "I just don't get it. How could a woman be held captive here for two years without word ever getting out? It seems highly unlikely."

"Stranger things have happened."

"What's even worse is the fact it'd taken me this long to even find her."

He turned to her in bewilderment. "What do you mean?"

"I mean that I should've tried harder. I didn't exhaust every option, every avenue. I'd discovered the Eldridge family had a son who they'd locked up in here four months into tracking down Kathleen. Perhaps if I'd visited Connor to ask him about his family, then maybe I might have run into Kathleen, or possibly one of the other women on the list who'd gone missing. I might've even asked to see the patient list here."

"You wouldn't have gotten it," he said. "You have no credentials. You would've had to hang around this place for weeks before you'd even see half the people in here."

"Regardless, it would've been better than doing what I did."

The elevator dinged and they exited onto the third floor.

"Well, there's no reason to beat yourself about it now. The deed is done. This way."

Tammy counted the room numbers as they headed down the hall, getting closer and closer to their final destination. When they finally reached room 302, she knocked and a nurse opened the door seconds later. She was seemingly heading out. They backed away from the door, allowing the medical professional to wheel a blonde woman out who seemed to be completely braindead. Her hair was disheveled and her expression dull, as if she were heavily sedated.

Tammy turned to Barnes and pointed. "That's her!"

And though Kathleen didn't necessarily look the picture of health with how her eyes were glossed over and her skin was pale as if she hadn't seen the sun in months, she was still alive nonetheless.

# Love this
# book?

# Tell Markus.

### Leave a review on...

**www.amazon.com**
**www.goodreads.com**

AMAZON

GOODREADS

# Acknowledgments

To my Beta readers: Leila Connell and Will Nuessle, for trudging through the thick of it.

To Jenna Moreci, Abbie Emmons, and Alyssa Matesic for providing educational content on YouTube that helped me improve as a writer.

And last but not least, to my family for always encouraging me to express myself in every way imaginable.